"Perkins pens a chilling, fast-paced, horror-inducing story
that will have you quickly flipping through the pages
to find out what happens."
—**BuzzFeed**

"Addictive."
—**Bustle**

"Truly terrifying."
—**Hypable**

"If you're looking for a creepy book to binge . . .
look no further."
—**Brit+Co**

"Absolutely thrilling."
—***Paste***

"Perkins lulls readers into a false sense of security before
twisting the knife . . . The body count keeps rising, leaving readers
with questions of motive and where it will all end."
—***Publishers Weekly***

"A modern slasher-horror story spiced up with school romance
and mystery; it emulates some familiar thriller authors and
is sure to be attractive to genre readers and others who
enjoy horror with some romance."
—***VOYA***

ALSO BY STEPHANIE PERKINS

Anna and the French Kiss

Lola and the Boy Next Door

Isla and the Happily Ever After

THERE'S SOMEONE INSIDE YOUR HOUSE

A NOVEL

BY

STEPHANIE PERKINS

speak

SPEAK
An imprint of Penguin Random House LLC
375 Hudson Street
New York, New York 10014

First published in the United States of America by Dutton Books,
an imprint of Penguin Random House LLC, 2017
Published by Speak, an imprint of Penguin Random House LLC, 2018

LIBRARY OF CONGRESS CATALOGING-IN-PUBLICATION DATA IS AVAILABLE.
Speak ISBN 9780142424988

Printed in the United States of America

1 3 5 7 9 10 8 6 4 2

Design by Anna Booth
Text set in Minion Pro
Edited by Julie Strauss-Gabel

This is a work of fiction. Names, characters, places, and incidents either are the product of
the author's imagination or are used fictitiously, and any resemblance to actual persons,
living or dead, businesses, companies, events, or locales is entirely coincidental.

For Jarrod, best friend & true love

People live through such pain only once;
pain comes again, but it finds a tougher surface.

WILLA CATHER,
The Song of the Lark

THERE'S SOMEONE INSIDE YOUR HOUSE

CHAPTER ONE

THE EGG-SHAPED TIMER was on the welcome mat when she came home.

Haley Whitehall glanced over her shoulder, as if expecting someone behind her. Far in the distance, a red combine rolled through the sallow cornfields. Her father. Harvest time. Her mother was still at work, too, a dental technician at the only practice in town. Which one of them had left it here? The decaying porch boards sagged and splintered beneath Haley's shifting weight as she picked up the timer. It rattled in her hand. The day had been cold, but the plastic eggshell was warm. Faintly so.

Her phone rang. It was Brooke, of course.

"How's the blood?" Haley asked.

Her best friend groaned. "A nightmare."

Haley went inside, and the screen door banged closed behind her. "Any chance that means Ms. Colfax will drop it?" She marched straight to the kitchen, slinging her backpack onto its black-and-white checkerboard floor. *Sustenance.* This afternoon's rehearsal had been particularly grueling.

"Never." Brooke snorted. "She'll never drop it. Who needs common sense when you have ambition?"

Haley set the timer back on the countertop—where it belonged—and opened the refrigerator. "Normally, I'd argue for ambition. But. I'm really not looking forward to being drowned in corn syrup."

"If I had the money, I'd buy the professional-grade stuff myself. Cleaning up the auditorium will be hell, even with all the tarps and plastic sheeting."

Most theatrical productions of *Sweeney Todd* used at least some amount of fake blood—razors with hidden squeeze bulbs, gel capsules in the mouth, false clothing-fronts to conceal bloodstained doubles underneath. Additional mayhem could be implied with red curtains or red lights or a frenzied crescendo of screaming violins.

Unfortunately, their high school's musical director, Ms. Colfax, had an unquenchable zeal for drama by all its definitions. Last year's production of *Peter Pan*, for which she'd rented actual flying harnesses all the way from New York City, had resulted in the broken bones of both Wendy and Michael Darling. This year, Ms. Colfax didn't just want the demon barber to slit his customers' throats. She wanted to shower the first three rows with their blood. She referred to this section of the auditorium as the "Splatter Belt."

Brooke was the stage manager. An honor, for sure, but it came with the impossible task of trying to steer Ms. Colfax toward sanity.

It wasn't going well.

Haley held the phone to her ear with her shoulder as she loaded her arms with packages of deli-sliced turkey and provolone, a bag of prewashed lettuce, and jar of Miracle Whip. "Shayna must be flipping her shit."

"Shayna is definitely flipping her shit," Brooke said.

Shayna was their temperamental—often volatile—costume

designer. It was hard enough to find decent costumes in rural Nebraska with a budget of zero, but now she had to deal with bloodstain removal on top of it.

"Poor Shayna." Haley dumped the ingredients onto the counter. She grabbed the closest loaf of bread, wheat with some kind of herb, which her mother had baked the night before. Her mother baked to relax. She used a bread maker, but still. It was nice.

"Poor *Brooke*," Brooke said.

"Poor Brooke," Haley agreed.

"And how was Jonathan today? Any better?"

Haley hesitated. "You didn't hear him?"

"I was running splatter tests in the parking lot."

Haley was playing Mrs. Lovett, and Shayna's boyfriend, Jonathan, was playing Sweeney, the female and male leads. Still only a junior, Haley had been getting leads in drama club and solos in show choir for the last two years. Both as a performer and powerful contralto, she was simply *better* than her peers. A natural. Impossible to overlook.

Jonathan was . . . above average. And he was charismatic, which helped his stage presence. However, this particular musical was well beyond his capabilities. He'd been struggling with "Epiphany," his most challenging solo song, for weeks. His transitions held all the smoothness of someone stumbling across a bull snake in a tool shed, but even those were nothing compared to the way that he'd been massacring his duets.

Brooke seemed to sense Haley's reluctance to gossip. "Oh, come on. If you don't spill, you'll only make me feel guilty for venting about everybody else."

"It's just . . ." Haley spread a gloppy coat of Miracle Whip onto the bread and then tossed the dirty butter knife into the sink. She'd wash it off later. "We spent the *entire* rehearsal on 'A Little Priest.' And not even the whole thing! The same few bars, over and over and over. For two freaking hours."

"Yikes."

"You know that part where we sing different lines simultaneously? And our voices are supposed to be, like, tumbling over each other in excitement?"

"When Sweeney finally figured out that Mrs. Lovett wants to dispose of his victims by baking their flesh into her pies?" Brooke's voice was a wicked grin.

"It was a disaster." Haley carried her plate into the living room, but she didn't sit. She paced. "I don't think Jonathan can do it. I mean, I seriously think his brain *can't do it*. He can sing in unison, he can sing harmony—"

"Sort of."

"Sort of," Haley conceded. "But if someone else is singing different words? He keeps stopping and restarting. Like he's trying to work through an aneurysm."

Brooke laughed.

"It's why I left early. I felt like such a bitch, but God. I couldn't take it anymore."

"No one would ever call you a bitch."

Haley swallowed a huge bite of turkey. It was a balancing act—cradling the phone, holding the plate, eating the sandwich, pacing the room—but she didn't notice. She was worried. "Jonathan would."

"Jonathan shouldn't have gotten the part."

"Do you think I should call him and apologize?"

"No. *No.* Why?"

"For being short with him."

"It's not your fault he can't handle Sondheim."

This was true, but Haley still felt ashamed for getting so frustrated. For walking out of rehearsal. She plopped onto the ancient corduroy couch, one of the many relics from when the farmhouse had belonged to her grandparents, and sighed. Brooke said something else in best-friend solidarity, but Haley's phone chose that moment to do its usual thing.

"What'd you say? My connection is going in and out."

"So call me from the landline."

Haley glanced at the cordless, which was perched on an end table only a few feet away. Too much effort. "It's fine now," she lied.

Brooke circled the conversation back around to her current hardships as stage manager, and Haley allowed herself to drift away. She could only hear a third of Brooke's ranting, anyway. The rest was static.

She stared out the windows and finished her sandwich. The sun hung low on the horizon. It shone through the cornfields, making the brittle stalks appear soft and dull. Her father was still out there. Somewhere. This time of year, he didn't let a single ray go to waste. The world looked abandoned. It was the opposite of the loud, colorful, enthusiastic group of people she'd left behind at school. She should have stuck it out. She hated the quiet isolation that permeated her house. It was exhausting in its own way.

Haley made sympathetic noises into the phone—though she had no idea what she was sympathizing *with*—and stood. She walked her plate back to the kitchen, rinsed off the crumbs, and popped open the dishwasher.

The only thing inside it was a dirty butter knife.

Haley glanced at the sink, which was empty. A frown appeared between her brows. She put the plate into the dishwasher and shook her head.

"Even if we *can* get the sprayer working," Brooke was saying, their connection suddenly clear, "I'm not sure enough people will even *want* to sit in the first three rows. I mean, who goes to the theater to wear ponchos and get drenched in blood?"

Haley sensed that her friend needed vocal reassurance. "It's Halloween weekend. People will buy the tickets. They'll think it's fun." She took a step toward the stairs—toward her bedroom—and her sneaker connected with a small, hard object. It shot across the floor tiles, skidding and rattling and clattering and clanging, until it smacked into the bottom of the pantry.

It was the egg timer.

Haley's heart stopped. Just for a moment.

An uneasy prickling grew under her skin as she moved toward the pantry door, which one of her parents had left ajar. She pushed it closed with her fingertips and then picked up the timer, slowly. As if it were heavy. She could have sworn she'd set it on the countertop, but she must have dropped it to the floor along with her backpack.

". . . still listening?"

The voice barely reached her ears. "Sorry?"

"I asked if you were still listening to me."

"Sorry," Haley said again. She stared at the timer. "I must be more tired than I thought. I think I'm gonna crash until my mom gets home."

They hung up, and Haley shoved the phone into the front right pocket of her jeans. She placed the timer back on the countertop. The timer was smooth and white. Innocuous. Haley couldn't pinpoint *why*, exactly, but the damn thing unsettled her.

She trekked upstairs and went directly to bed, collapsing in a weary heap, kicking off her sneakers, too drained to unlace them. The phone jabbed at her hip. She pulled it from her pocket and slung it onto her nightstand. The setting sun pierced through her window at a perfect, irritating angle, and she winced and rolled over.

She fell asleep instantly.

● ● ●

Haley startled awake. Her heart was pounding, and the house was dark.

She exhaled—a long, unclenching, diaphragm-deep breath. And that was when her brain processed the noise. The noise that had woken her up.

Ticking.

Haley's blood chilled. She rolled over to face the nightstand. Her phone was gone, and in its place, right at eye level, was the egg timer.

It went off.

CHAPTER TWO

THE NEXT MORNING, the entire school was buzzing about two things: the brutal slaying of Haley Whitehall and Ollie Larsson's newly pinkened hair.

"You'd think they'd care less about the hair," Makani said.

"This is Osborne, Nebraska." Her friend Darby sucked up the last drops of his gas station iced coffee. "Population: twenty-six hundred. A boy with pink hair *is* as scandalous as the death of a beloved student."

They stared through Darby's windshield and across the parking lot to where Ollie was leaning against the brick wall of the front office. He was reading a paperback and pointedly ignoring the whispers— and not-whispers—of the other students.

"I heard her throat was slit in three places." Makani paused. The car's windows were down, so she lowered her voice. "Carved up to look like a smiley face."

The straw dropped from Darby's mouth. "That's *awful*. Who told you that?"

She shrugged uncomfortably. "It's just what I heard."

"Oh God. And the day hasn't even begun."

A long face with kohl-blackened eyes popped up beside the passenger-side window. "Well, *I* heard—"

Makani jumped. "Jesus, Alex."

"—that Ollie is the one who did it. And that he used her blood to dye his hair."

Makani and Darby stared at her, agape.

"I'm kidding. Obviously." She opened the back door, tossed in her trumpet case, and slid inside. The car was their morning hangout. "But someone here will say it."

There was too much truth in her joke. Makani winced.

Alex kicked the back of Makani's seat with a royal-blue combat boot. An exclamation point. "I don't believe it. You still have a thing for him, don't you?"

Unfortunately, yes.

Of course she still had a thing for Ollie.

From the moment Makani Young arrived in Nebraska, she couldn't keep her eyes off him. He was, without a doubt, the strangest-looking guy at Osborne High. But that also made him the most *interesting*. Ollie had a skinny frame with hip bones that jutted out in a way that reminded her of sex, and cheekbones so prominent they reminded her of a skull—the illusion of which was enhanced by his blond, invisible eyebrows. He always wore dark jeans and a plain, black T-shirt. A silver ring—a thin hoop in the center of his bottom lip—was his only adornment. He kind of looked like a skeleton.

Makani tilted her head. But maybe less so, now that his white-blond hair was a shocking hot pink.

"I remember when *you* had a thing for him," Darby said to Alex.

"Yeah, like, in eighth grade. Until I realized he's a full-time loner. He's not interested in going out with anyone who attends this school." With a rare and embarrassed afterthought, Alex grimaced. "Sorry, Makani."

Makani and Ollie had hooked up last summer. Sort of. Thankfully, the only people who knew about it were sitting here in Darby's car.

"It's fine," Makani said, because it was easier than saying it wasn't.

There were a lot of rumors about Ollie: that he only slept with older women; that he only slept with older men; that he sold opioids stolen from his brother's police station; that he once almost drowned in the shallow part of the river. That—when he was rescued—he was both blind drunk and buck naked.

Then again, their school was small. There were rumors about everyone.

Makani knew better than to believe any of them outright. Rumors, even the true ones, never told a complete story. She avoided most of her classmates for that very reason. Self-preservation. Recognizing a similarly dismal soul, Darby and Alex had taken her in when she'd been forced to relocate from Hawaii midway through her junior year. Her parents were embattled in an ugly divorce, so they'd shipped her off to live with her grandmother for some normalcy.

Normalcy. With her *grandmother.* In the *middle of nowhere.*

At least, that's how Makani told the story to her friends. And, much like a rumor, it did contain a kernel of truth. It was just missing the rest of the cob.

Her parents had never paid much attention to her, even in the best of times, and they'd only recently separated when the incident at the beach occurred. After that . . . they couldn't look at her at all anymore. She didn't like looking at herself, either.

She deserved this exile.

Now it was mid-October, and Makani had been in Osborne for almost a year. She was a senior, and so were Darby and Alex. Their mutual interest was counting down the days until graduation. Makani wasn't sure where she'd go next, but she certainly wasn't staying here.

"Can we return to the important subject?" Darby asked. "Haley is *dead*. And no one knows who killed her, and that freaks my shit out."

"I thought you didn't like Haley," Alex said, pulling her dyed-black hair into a complicated twist that required a large number of chunky plastic barrettes. She was the closest thing their school had to a Goth, if you didn't count Ollie.

Makani didn't.

Their exteriors were both comprised of black clothing and thin, pointy body parts, but Alex was hard and aggressive. She demanded to be noticed. While Ollie was as soft and silent as the night sky.

"I didn't *dislike* Haley." Darby tucked his thumbs under his suspenders, which he wore every day along with a plaid shirt and sensible trousers. He was short and stocky, and he dressed like a dapper old man.

Darby had been assigned female at birth, and though his legal name was still Justine Darby, he'd socially transitioned during his freshman year. If their school didn't like a boy with pink hair, Makani could only imagine how long it'd taken for them to get used to the "girl" who was actually a boy. They mostly left him alone now, though there were still side-glances. Narrowed eyes and pinched mouths.

"I didn't know her," Darby continued. "She seemed nice enough."

Alex snapped in a barrette that resembled an evil Hello Kitty. "Isn't it weird how the moment someone dies everyone becomes her *bestest* friend?"

Darby scowled. "I didn't say that. Jeez."

Makani let them bicker it out before stepping in. She always did. "Do you think one of her parents did it? I've heard in cases like this, it's usually a family member."

"Or a boyfriend," Darby said. "Was she dating anyone?"

Makani and Alex shrugged.

All three stared at their passing classmates and fell into an unusual silence. "It's sad," Darby finally said. "It's just . . . terrible."

Makani and Alex nodded. It was.

"I mean, what kind of person would do something like that?" he asked.

A sickening wave of shame rolled throughout Makani's body. *It's not the same,* she reminded herself. *I'm not that kind of person.* But when the warning bell rang—three sterile chimes—she bolted from the cramped hatchback as if there were an actual emergency. Darby and Alex groaned as they extricated themselves, too caught up in their own gloom to register her odd behavior. Makani exhaled and readjusted her clothing to make sure that she was decent. Unlike her friends, she did have curves.

"Maybe it was a serial killer," Alex said as they headed toward first period. "A long-haul trucker on his way through town! These days, serial killers are always truck drivers."

Makani felt the welcome return of skepticism. "Says who?"

"The FBI."

"My *dad* is a truck driver," Darby said.

Alex grinned.

"Stop smiling." Darby glowered at her. "Or people will think *you* did it."

By lunchtime, Alex's tasteless joke about the source of Ollie's hair dye had spread. Makani had heard more than one student whispering about his possible guilt. It infuriated her. Ollie was an anomaly, sure. But that didn't make him a killer. Furthermore, she'd never seen him talk to, or even look at, Haley Whitehall.

And Makani had studied *him* a lot.

She was upset, despite understanding that the rumors were

exactly that—fabrications created to distract them from the unknown. The unknown was too frightening. Makani had also overheard a group of academic overachievers gossiping about Zachary Loup, the school's resident burnout. She didn't think he was guilty, either, but at least he was a better suspect. Zachary was an asshole. He wasn't even nice to his friends.

Most students, however, were agreed on the real suspects: Haley's family. Maybe a boyfriend. No one *knew* of a boyfriend, but perhaps she'd had one in secret.

Girls often had secrets.

The thought churned inside Makani's stomach like a rotten apple. As Darby and Alex speculated, she pushed away her paper boat of French fries and glanced around.

Nearly all of the 342 students were here in the nucleus of the campus, completely surrounded by brown-brick buildings. The quad was plain. Dreary. There were no tables or benches, only a few stunted trees scattered about, so students sat on the concrete ground. Unwind a spool of barbed wire, and it could have been a prison yard, but even prisoners were given tables and benches. A dry fountain filled with dead leaves—no one could remember ever having seen the stone lion shoot a stream of water from its open mouth—rested in the center like a mausoleum.

This time of year, the weather was unpredictable. Some days were warm, but most were cold. Today was *almost* warm, so the quad was crowded and the cafeteria was empty. Makani zipped up her hoodie, shivering. Her school in Kailua-Kona was always warm. The air had smelled like flowers and coffee and fruit, and it had tasted as salty as the Pacific, which glistened beside the parking lots and football fields.

Osborne smelled like diesel, tasted like despair, and was surrounded by an ocean of corn. Stupid corn. So much corn.

Alex grabbed a handful of Makani's uneaten fries. "What about someone in show choir? Or drama club?"

Darby scoffed. "What, like, Haley's understudy?"

"Isn't that the person the *Masterpiece* detective would investigate?" Alex asked.

"The what-now?"

"Sherlock, Morse, Poirot. Wallander. Tennison."

"I only know one of those names." Darby dipped his pizza into a glob of ranch dressing. "Why don't you watch normal television?"

"I'm just saying, let's not rule anyone out yet."

Makani was still staring at the fountain. "I hope it's not a student."

"It's not," Darby said.

"Please," Alex said. "Angry teenagers do shit like this all the time."

"Yeah," he said, "but they show up at school with an arsenal of automatic weapons. They don't go after people in their *homes*. With *knives*."

Makani muffled her ears with her fists. "Okay, enough. Stop it."

Darby ducked his head, abashed. He didn't say anything, but he didn't need to. School shootings were real. With real murderers and real victims. Haley's death felt one step removed from reality, because it didn't seem like something that could happen to them. The crime was too specific. There must have been a reason for it. A horrible and misguided reason, but a reason nonetheless.

Makani turned to look at them, backpedaling the conversation in an attempt to downplay her reaction. "Well . . . Jessica didn't do it."

Alex raised her eyebrows. "Jessica?"

"Jessica Boyd. The understudy." Makani rolled her eyes when Alex smirked. "I only know she's the understudy because I heard somebody else say it. But can you honestly imagine her killing anyone?"

"You're right," Alex said. "That does seem unlikely." Jessica Boyd was a delicate wisp of a thing. It was difficult to imagine her even flushing a dead goldfish. "But did you guys notice that Haley's best friend didn't come to school today?"

"Because Brooke is in mourning." Darby was exasperated. "Like *I* would be if this happened to one of *you*."

Alex leaned forward conspiratorially. "Think about it. Haley was one of the most talented students here. Everybody knew that she'd leave us for someplace bigger and better—Broadway, Hollywood. Whatever. She was the kind of person who should be totally stuck up, but . . . she wasn't. People liked her. Which always means someone *didn't* like her. Resented her."

Makani's nose wrinkled. "And you think it was her best friend?"

"No one even knew Haley," Darby said, "unless they were in the drama club or Vocalmotion." Vocalmotion was, regrettably, the self-chosen name of the show choir. Osborne High only had three respectable organizations: the drama and choral departments, which had a nearly one-hundred-percent overlap, and the football team.

It was Nebraska. Of course their school took football seriously.

"But that's exactly what I'm saying," Alex said. "Nobody else knew her. So doesn't it make sense that one of her friends did it? Out of jealousy?"

"Should we be worried? Are you plotting to kill us?" Makani asked.

"Ugh," Darby said.

Alex sighed. "You guys are no fun."

"I believe I warned you this morning," Darby said, "not to appear so excited."

The wind picked up, and it shook a paper banner on the other side of the quad. An advertisement for *Sweeney Todd*. Each letter dripped with garish, hand-painted blood, and two long swaths of dark red tulle draped down from opposite corners like theater curtains. A gust heaved the tulle into the air, where it danced and writhed. Makani felt a chill touch her spine. Her name meant "wind" in Hawaiian, but she wasn't superstitious about it. Except when she was. They should stop talking about Haley.

"It's tactless," she said, unable to help herself. She nodded toward the banner. "The Splatter Belt. Do you think they'll cancel it?"

Alex swallowed the last greasy fry. "They'd better not. That was the first school function that I've ever planned on attending. Willingly," she added. She was in the marching band, which meant she was forced to attend the football games.

Darby stared her down until she made eye contact.

"What? It seemed like fun," she said. "Getting covered in fake blood."

Makani snorted. "There's that word again. *Fun.*"

Faux wistfulness spread across Darby's face. "I remember when you used to collect plastic horses and Pokémon cards, and your life goal was to work for Pixar."

"Lower your voice, dickpunch." But Alex grinned.

A back-and-forth taunting of childhood hobbies and idiosyncrasies ensued, and Makani, as it so often happened, found herself excluded. Her attention waned, and her gaze drifted across the quad. It was almost time. Any minute now, and . . .

There.

Her heart plummeted as Ollie appeared from the depths of the locker bay to throw away an empty plastic grocery bag. This was his daily routine appearance. He always ate a packed lunch in an uninhabited nook behind the old lockers, and then he always disappeared into the main building. He would finish this hour in the library.

Makani felt a familiar pang of sorrow. Ollie was so alone.

A small group of football players stood beneath the *Sweeney* banner, blocking the entrance to the building. Her muscles tensed as Matt Butler—Osborne's golden boy, its prize running back—said something as Ollie approached. Whatever it was, Ollie didn't react. Matt said something else. Ollie didn't react. Matt flicked his thumb and index finger at Ollie's hair. His friends laughed, but Ollie still didn't react. It was agonizing to watch.

A meaty guy with an absurd name, *Buddy or Bubba*, she thought, jumped up and snatched at the tulle, and the right half of the banner ripped and collapsed downward. He laughed even harder as Ollie was forced to duck, but the pleasure was short-lived.

Matt gestured angrily at the wreckage. "Hey, man! Show some respect."

The outburst carried across the quad. It took Buddy or Bubba several seconds to make the connection between the ruined banner and Haley, but as his expression transformed from confusion into humiliation, he was faced with a choice—either admit to a wrongdoing or double down. He doubled down. Shoving Matt's shoulder, he set off a furious chain reaction of even more shoving until they were no longer blocking the entrance.

The escalating action held the student body in rapt attention. Only Makani was staring elsewhere. Ollie still hadn't moved. He'd kept it together, but it was clear that the football players had unnerved him. She was on her feet.

"No," Darby said. "Makani. *No.*"

Alex shook her head, and her barrettes clicked against one another. "Ollie doesn't deserve your help. Or pity. Or whatever it is you're feeling right now."

Makani smoothed the front of her hoodie. She was already walking away.

"You never listen to us," Darby called out. "Why don't you ever listen to us?"

Alex sighed. "Good luck, gumdrop."

This *thing*—this unbearable weight and pressure—that had been boiling inside Makani for months was about to erupt. Ollie might not deserve her help, but she still felt compelled to try. Maybe it was because she wished someone at her previous school had helped her. Or maybe it was because of Haley, a horrific situation already beyond anyone's help. Makani glanced back at her friends with a shrug.

When she turned forward, Ollie was staring at her. He didn't look nervous or angry, or even curious.

He looked wary.

Makani strode toward him in a bold path. She always stood out among their peers. Their skin was several shades lighter than her brown complexion, and her surf-inspired wardrobe was several shades brighter than their Midwestern sensibility. She wore her hair big—in its natural curly coils—and she moved with a confident sway in her hips. It was a false confidence, designed so that people wouldn't ask questions.

Ollie glanced one last time at the jocks, still shouting and posturing, and pulled aside the dangling tulle. He went into the building. Makani frowned. But when she opened the door, he was waiting for her on the other side.

She startled. "Oh."

"Yes?" he said.

"I . . . I just wanted to say, they're idiots."

"Your friends?" Ollie deadpanned.

Makani realized she was still holding the door open, and he could see Darby and Alex through the tulle's transparent weave, spying on them from across the quad. She released her grip. It slammed shut. "No," she said, trying on a smile. "Everyone else."

"Yeah. I know." His face remained impassive. Guarded.

Her smile dropped. She crossed her arms, her own defenses rising as they sized each other up. They were almost eye level; he was only an inch or two taller than she was. This close, she could see the *newness* of his hair. His scalp was hot pink. The dye would need more time to wash out of his skin. There was something vulnerable about seeing him like this, and her body re-softened. She hated herself for it.

She hated herself for so many things.

Makani hated that she'd gotten carried away with Ollie, even though she'd been warned about his reputation. She hated that she'd tricked herself into believing she didn't care for him, when she'd always known that she did. And she hated the way it had ended. Abruptly. Silently. This was their first conversation since the end of summer.

Maybe if we'd talked more to begin with . . .

But that was it, wasn't it? There had never been a lot of talking. At the time, she'd even been grateful for it.

His pale eyes were still fixed on her, but they were no longer passive. They were searching. Her veins throbbed in response. Why did it suddenly feel like they were back behind the grocery store, preparing to do what they did on those hot, summer afternoons?

"Why are you here?" he asked. "You haven't spoken to me all semester."

It made her angry. Instantly. "I could say the same thing about you. And I *said* what I wanted to say. About our classmates. Being idiots and all that."

"Yeah." His posture stiffened. "You did say that."

Makani let out a singular laugh to show him that he wasn't getting to her, even though they both knew that he was. "Fine. Forget it. I was just trying to be a friend."

Ollie didn't say anything.

"Everyone needs friends, Ollie."

He frowned slightly.

"But, obviously, that's impossible." With one violent thrust, she pushed the door back open. "Great talk. See you in class."

She stormed straight into the curtain of tulle. She swore as she struggled to pull it aside, growing more and more ensnared in the dark red netting. A thunderous uproar surged across the quad—a chaotic mob of excited, agitated spectators.

The fight had finally broken out.

Makani stopped thrashing. She was trapped, imprisoned even, in this miserable town where she hated everything and everyone. Especially herself.

There was a quiet stir, and she was surprised to discover that Ollie was still behind her. His fingers carefully, gently untangled her from the tulle. It dropped back into a sheet, and they watched their classmates together, in silence, through the blood-colored haze.

CHAPTER THREE

"**DID YOU KNOW** that Haley girl?" Grandma Young called out from the sofa.

Makani waved goodbye to Darby as he drove away. He honked twice. Her grandmother's house was only a short walk from school, but he always picked her up and dropped her off anyway. Makani lived in Osborne's oldest neighborhood, and Darby lived in its newest. Alex lived on a muddy cow-calf operation near Troy, one town over. She had band practice in the afternoons and carpooled with a girl who played tenor sax. They could all drive, but Darby was the only one with full-time access to a car.

Ollie lived . . . in the country. Makani wasn't sure where. When the fight had ended, he'd gone to the library, and she'd gone back to her friends. Later in Spanish, she'd felt the faint pressure of his stare—it had thrilled her, even though she wished it hadn't—but nothing had actually changed. It felt like it never would.

Makani's heart sank as she locked the front door, further enclosing the scope of her world. "Yeah, I knew Haley. Sort of. Not really."

She kicked off her sneakers and socks and placed them at the bottom of the stairs to carry up to her bedroom later. Shoes were another thing Makani disliked about the Midwest. Apart from the summer months, it was too cold to wear slippers, but her feet always felt heavy in the necessary sneakers and boots. It had taken ages to build the callouses so that they didn't rub her heels into blisters.

Flip-flops, she corrected herself. *Not slippers.*

Regionalisms still tripped her up. *Flip-flops* weren't a big deal. But she cringed every time she heard someone order a *pop* instead of a *soda.*

Her grandmother was perched in front of the television, streaming *Scandal* on Netflix and separating out the edge pieces of a new jigsaw puzzle. Makani flopped into a well-loved easy chair. It had belonged to her granddaddy. Tucking her feet under her legs to keep them toasty, she picked up the cardboard lid. The puzzle was a folk-art design that featured a folksy pumpkin patch, a street of folksy houses, and a stream of trick-or-treaters dressed in folksy costumes. Grandma Young liked to keep things seasonal.

"I'm waiting for the local news to come on," she said.

Makani tossed the lid back onto the coffee table and glanced at her phone. "You still have another hour and a half."

"I want to hear what Creston has to say about all this." Creston Howard was the handsome, black half of the five o'clock news team, and Grandma Young believed his word to be infallible. "The whole thing is *awful.* I hope they catch whoever did it."

"They will," Makani said.

"She was so young, so talented. Just like you."

That last part wasn't true, but Makani knew better than to correct her. She could already hear the beats of their ensuing argument: Makani would deny it; her grandmother would accuse her of negative thinking; Makani would explain that she was simply being honest; her grandmother would press; and then Makani would explode with something like, "You aren't my mother! My own mother is barely my mother! We're not talking about this, okay?"

Instead, Makani scrolled through her phone. She no longer hoped for a text or message or email from Jasmine, her former best friend. And she no longer hoped that, for some miraculous and unlikely reason, everything would go back to the way it had been before. Those hopes had perished a long time ago. It was difficult to pinpoint the exact moment, though perhaps it began when she'd signed the official government document that changed her surname from Kanekalau to Young.

She hadn't taken her mother's maiden name because of the impending divorce. She'd taken it because it wasn't safe to be the easily Google-able Makani Kanekalau anymore, and she'd needed a fresh start in Nebraska.

Still . . . Makani checked her phone.

As usual, there was no word from back home. At least the messages of hate had long stopped. No one there was looking for her, and the only people who still cared about it—*the incident,* as she self-censored that night on the beach—were people like Jasmine. The only people who mattered. Makani would have never guessed that her friends' permanent silence would be infinitely more painful than those weeks when thousands of uninformed, condescending, misogynistic strangers had spewed vitriol at her. It was.

Even without the repeat of their most frequent fight, Grandma Young's voice turned disapproving. "You left the kitchen cabinets open again this morning."

Makani stared harder at her phone. "I'm not the one leaving them open."

"My memory is fine, hon. You'd already left for school when I got out of bed. It's basic manners to tidy up after yourself. I'm not asking for much."

"I didn't even *have* breakfast this morning." Makani couldn't conceal the swell of her frustration. "Have you called your doctor? Like I asked you to?"

"As you're well aware, I haven't had an episode in almost a year."

Makani looked up, and Grandma Young immediately lowered her gaze. It was hard for her grandmother to discuss her weaknesses . . . or have anyone question her version of the truth. They shared this trait. Grandma Young snapped two puzzle pieces together in a way that signaled the end of it as Makani kept staring, wishing that she could push the discussion while recognizing the depths of her own hypocrisy.

Her grandmother was taller than most women of her generation. She had short hair that she had allowed to age, gray with white speckles. It looked beautiful, like the negative of a snowy owl. Makani's paternal grandmother, back in Hawaii, still dyed her hair black. Grandma Kanekalau even used the same color and brand as Alex.

Grandma Young wasn't so harsh. She had soft dark brown skin, a soft figure, and a soft voice, but she spoke with the firmness of a commanding authority. She used to teach American history at the high school. She'd been retired for half a decade, and though Makani was thankful that she would never be subjected to a class taught by her own grandmother, she imagined she'd probably been a good teacher.

Grandma and Granddaddy Young had always been kind in a way that the rest of her family was not. They asked questions. They were attentive. Even before the divorce proceedings began, Makani's parents had been selfish. As a child, Makani had wanted a sibling to keep her company, to adore her, to *care* about her, but it was for the best that her parents had never had another child. They would have ignored him or her, too.

But Makani's banishment to Osborne wasn't just because of her own unspeakable mistake. Grandma Young had also done something bad. Last Thanksgiving, her neighbor caught her sleep-pruning his walnut tree at three in the morning, and when he'd tried to rouse her, she'd lopped off the tip of his nose. She'd been having trouble with sleepwalking since the unexpected death of Makani's grand-father the summer before. Doctors were able to reattach the fleshy nub, and the neighbor didn't sue, but the escalation had alarmed Makani's mother, who persuaded her father that the best solution—to *all* their problems—would be to dispatch their daughter to watch over Grandma Young.

Makani's parents couldn't agree on anything, but they had agreed to send her here. They probably believed the lopping had been ser-endipitous.

For the most part, Makani didn't think her grandmother needed a babysitter. Not a single hazardous episode had occurred since Makani's arrival. Only in the last few months with the return of these mundane, low-key episodes—open cabinets, misplaced tools, un-locked doors—had Makani realized that she was, indeed, needed.

Usually, it felt good to be needed.

It had backfired only once.

She'd been needed in July. The heat that afternoon had been stifling, the kind of oppressive humidity that lends itself to tank tops, short shorts, and bad decisions.

Makani already had all three covered.

It was the first anniversary of Granddaddy Young's death, and her grandmother wanted to spend the day alone. It was also Wednesday, double-coupon day, so Makani offered to do the weekly shopping in her stead. Greeley's Foods was less than two miles away, on Main Street. It was as plain and boxy as the high school, but with the added charm of lower ceilings and cramped aisles.

Makani couldn't understand why these places didn't expand their premises. There was plenty of room to do it. Unlike coastal Hawaii, rural Nebraska had an abundance of land. It had nothing *but* land. It was a completely different country.

She entered the store with a handwritten list and a recycled envelope stuffed with coupons. They noticed each other right away. He was wearing the green Greeley's apron and restocking the plum tomatoes. Only Ollie Larsson could make an apron look sexy.

Makani wanted to say something. By the way he stared back, she knew *he* wanted to say something. Neither of them said anything.

She wheeled around a rickety cart and filled it with healthy food. Her grandfather had died of a heart attack, so her grandmother had been recently consumed by the gospel of nutrition. As Makani hunted down boxes of steel-cut oats and bags of dried beans, she prickled with the knowledge of Ollie's movements throughout the store. When he switched from stocking the tomatoes to the squash. When he hustled over to aisle five to clean up a broken jar of sweet relish. When he drifted back to produce.

They had never spoken in school. They'd had several classes together, but he kept to himself. Makani wasn't even positive that he'd been aware of her existence before that afternoon. She'd hoped he might switch to working one of the store's three registers, but as she headed toward the checkout lanes, he vanished into the back room.

She couldn't help it. She felt disappointed.

Makani was piling grocery sacks into Grandma Young's early-nineties gold Taurus wagon when she heard the laugh—singular and derisive. She slammed the trunk closed angrily, already knowing that it had something to do with her.

Ollie stared at her from the alleyway beside the store. He was perched on a plastic milk crate, giving all the appearance of a smoke break, except instead of a cigarette, he was holding a book loosely between his fingers.

"You think my grandma's car is funny?" she asked.

An unorthodox smile grew on his lips. He let it sit between them for several long seconds before speaking. "I'm not sure why I'd make fun of yours when *that's* mine." He pointed at a white vehicle parked on the other side of the lot.

It was a decommissioned police cruiser. The force's crest had been scraped off, and it didn't have the light bar on top, but Makani recognized it from school. Everyone knew that Ollie drove a police car—a gift most likely bestowed upon him by his older brother, a cop—and their classmates ragged him about it mercilessly. Makani suspected he kept driving it just to prove that he didn't give a shit.

"So, why were you laughing at me?" she asked.

Ollie rubbed the back of his neck. "Not you. Me."

Makani didn't know if it was the summer swelter or the culmination of seven months of unrelenting tedium, but she sensed . . . *something*. She walked toward him, slowly. Her bare legs shone. "And why were you laughing at yourself, Ollie?"

He watched her approach, because it was clear that she wanted him to watch. He waited to reply. When she stopped before him, he tilted up his head and shielded his eyes from the sun. "Because I wanted to speak to you earlier, but I was too nervous. *Makani.*"

So, he knew who she was.

She smiled.

Ollie stood up from the milk crate, and his silver lip ring glinted in the sunlight. She wondered how it would feel between her own lips. It had been too long since she'd kissed anyone. Since anyone had wanted to kiss her. *Get a hold of yourself.* Makani took a physical step backward, because it was impossible to converse when they were standing that close. Chest to chest. And she was, above all things, intrigued by Ollie.

She nodded at his paperback. "I never see you without a book."

He held it up so that she could see its cover: a cluster of men hanging out the doors and windows of a moving train. She didn't recognize it, so he explained. "It's about an American who travels from London to Southeast Asia by train."

"Is it a true story?"

He nodded.

"Do you read a lot of true stories?"

"I read a lot of travelogues. I like reading about other places."

"I get it." Her smile returned. "I like thinking about other places."

Ollie stared at her mouth for a moment, distracted. "Any place but this one," he finally said. But it was clear that he was referring to the greater Osborne, and not this very specific place beside Greeley's Foods—this place that contained her.

"Exactly," she said.

He leaned against the brick wall and melted back into the shade. She couldn't tell if he was trying to regain his disinterested cool or if he was simply shy. "You're from Hawaii, right? Are you going back there after graduation?"

Makani's heart stuttered. She searched his eyes—such a searing blue—but it was unlikely that he knew. The Hawaiian media had withheld her name, though that hadn't stopped *social* media. It hadn't stopped her from needing to change her name.

"I'm not sure," she said cautiously. "What about you? Where do you want to go?"

Ollie shrugged. "Doesn't matter. Anywhere, so long as it's not here."

"What's keeping you from leaving now?" She was genuinely curious. A lot of their classmates never made it to graduation.

"My brother. And the money." He gestured at his apron. "I've been working here since I was fourteen. That's when they'll let you bag groceries."

She'd never heard of someone her age holding down a job for that long. "Jesus. That's . . . three years? Four?"

"I would have started earlier if they'd let me."

Makani glanced behind them at the desolate Main Street. Greeley's Foods faced a meager row of mismatched awnings—a tanning salon, a real estate office, an upholsterer, and a bridal shop that still had prom dresses in its window display. She'd never been through any of their doors. "I wish I could get a job."

"No," he said. "You don't."

His conviction irritated her. She'd wanted to apply at the Feed 'N' Seed, where Darby and Alex both worked, but she'd been firmly denied. "I do. But according to my parents, my job is to take care of my grandmother."

Ollie frowned. "Does she need help? She's always seemed fine to me."

Makani was startled . . . until she realized that he must see her grandmother here at the store. Grandma Young was notable enough; few black people lived in Osborne. His brother had probably even had her as a teacher. "She *is* fine," she said, sliding into her usual half-truth. "My parents are just using her as an excuse."

"For what?"

"For sending me four thousand miles away. Parents are the fucking worst, you know?" Her regret was instantaneous. It wasn't fair to say things like that in front of someone who didn't have any parents at all. She winced. "Sorry."

Ollie stared at the asphalt for several beats. When his gaze returned upward, his expression was detached, but she could still see a struggle underneath. It wasn't difficult for her to imagine how awful it would be to live in a town where everyone, even the new girl, knew that a drunk driver had killed your parents when you were in middle school, and that your brother had moved back home from Omaha to raise you.

He shrugged. "It's okay."

"No, I'm really sorry. It was a shitty thing to say."

"And I'm sorry that your parents are the fucking worst."

Makani wasn't sure how to respond—*Was that a joke?*—so when Ollie's mouth split into a grin, her heart skipped like a scratched vinyl record. She didn't want to ruin the moment. "All right, all right. I'd better get home." She strolled back to her car and shook her head. But as she opened the door, she called out, "See you next week, Ollie."

Ollie bit his lip. "See you next week, Makani."

There was nothing else to think about, so, for the next six days, Makani thought exclusively about Ollie. She thought about his lips and her lips and pressing them together. Pressing *more* than their lips together. She entered a fever state. She hadn't had a boyfriend since moving to Nebraska. Makani pleaded with her grandmother to let her take over the grocery shopping. She tested out words like *responsibility* and *maturity* and strung together other words like *valuable, learning,* and *experience.* She won.

When Makani pulled back into the lot, Ollie was sitting on the same milk crate. He was reading a book and eating a red Popsicle. Makani went straight toward him. He stood. His expression didn't give anything away, but she felt the truth of it in her bones: Ollie had been waiting for her.

She stepped inside his personal space.

Ollie bit his lower lip over the silver ring. It slowly slipped back out.

When he wordlessly offered her the Popsicle, she went for his mouth instead, because she'd long ago—six days ago—decided that being forward was the best way to approach a guy with his sort of rep-utation. Their first kiss was wet. Cold tongue and sugary fruit. *Cherry,* Makani thought. His piercing was warm from the summer sun. The surgical-steel hoop pushed against her lips. It felt dangerous.

The Popsicle hit the asphalt behind them in a frozen, quiet *thump.*

They made out there, in the alleyway, every Wednesday for the next three weeks. The fourth week, it rained. They moved into the backseat of her grandmother's car. This additional barrier of privacy led to the next natural stage.

"Hands," she explained later to her friends. "Not mouths."

"Could you make it sound any more disgusting?" Darby said.

"But it's an important distinction," Alex said. "They got each other off, but their clothes were still on. And their heads were still above sea level."

Makani made a face. "Never mind. I'm not even sure why I told you."

On the fifth Wednesday—the last before school began—the sky was clear, but Ollie slid into her car anyway, and she drove them someplace private.

It was a cornfield, of course.

They had sex, of course.

"Are you guys ever gonna go out? You know, for real?" Darby asked her that night. "Or is this just going . . . to end?"

It ended the next week. Before the first bell on the first day of school, their eyes locked across campus. Ollie's expression was un-readable. That purposeful, standoffish blankness. The truth hit Makani like an ugly slap. *No,* they had never discussed going out. She didn't even have his number. This summer had been a secret thing, a *dateless* thing, which meant that one of them—or both of them—was ashamed of it.

Makani wasn't ashamed. Confused, yes. But not ashamed.

So, it was Ollie, then.

Makani narrowed her eyes. Ollie narrowed his. *Did he know?* Had he somehow found out about that night on the beach? Now he'd act as if they'd never known each other. Shame returned to Makani full force.

So did humiliation. And rage. She refused to look at *him* anymore, and she never returned to Greeley's. She pleaded for her grandmother to resume grocery duty, claiming that school took up too much of her time. It didn't. Makani had been judged and put back in her place, but she was still bored as hell.

As she pointlessly rechecked her phone, battling two measly bars of pitifully weak service, Makani wondered if boredom had also contributed to her reapproaching Ollie at lunch. Had she really sunk that low?

Probably. Shit.

"Oh, shoot," Grandma Young said. A spinning circle blocked the television screen, and Olivia Pope had stopped talking mid-sentence. "I called the cable company just last week, but they said we're already getting their highest-speed package."

Makani pictured her beachside bungalow in Hawaii, where the internet only went out in the worst tropical storms. Where her phone always had full bars. Why couldn't landlocked Osborne figure this out? Why was *everything* so damned difficult here?

They turned off Netflix, and Makani grabbed her shoes and trudged upstairs to do homework. When she returned downstairs at five, Creston Howard said nothing new in a way that reassured Grandma Young but made Makani want to punch him in the jaw. It was all very unsurprising. They'd both already seen the footage online: the Whitehalls' crime-scene taped farmhouse, Haley's father stumbling, head down, into the police station for questioning, and Haley herself, flying around the stage last year as Peter Pan.

"Tonight, Osborne grieves for Haley Madison Whitehall," Creston said, ending the segment with a solemn head tilt. "It's a sad day for a sad community."

Grandma Young nodded as Makani's nose wrinkled with distaste. Neither her grandmother nor Creston seemed to realize that he'd insulted the entire town. At least he wasn't wrong. Sad *did* describe it.

But then she felt bad again, because a girl was dead, and it really was sad.

CHAPTER FOUR

MAKANI'S MIND CHURNED with restlessness as she helped her grandmother cook dinner. It was one of her daily chores. When Makani moved in, Grandma Young had posted a list of daily and weekly chores on the refrigerator under a magnet that read: YOU CAN'T SCARE ME. I TEACH HIGH SCHOOL. She claimed Makani needed structure. This was true, even Makani knew it was true, but it still sucked. Sometimes she felt like a child. Sometimes she felt like a caregiver. She didn't want to be either of those things.

Tonight, they prepared a heart-healthy meal of baked turkey meatballs and a simple salad with vinaigrette. It was beyond depressing. Makani lusted for flavor and fat. *Lime-topped papaya. Kalbi ribs. Poi with lomi salmon.* If she could, she'd spend her every cent on a plate lunch—steamed rice, mac salad, and an entrée. *Chicken katsu. Teri beef. Kalua pig.* Her mouth watered, and her soul ached.

Sometimes dinner was the hardest.

They'd only just sat down at the table when her phone dinged. Grandma Young aimed a lethal sigh at the heavens. Makani yanked the phone from her pocket to silence its ringer, and a text from an unknown number lit the screen: *I could say the same thing about you.* Her chest cavity froze into spiny shards of ice.

A second text appeared: *What did you mean when you said that?*

"How many times do I have to tell you? No phones at the dinner table."

Makani's head shot up. "Sorry," she said automatically.

But her grandmother was taken aback by her expression. "Who was that?"

"Mom," Makani lied.

Grandma Young examined the bait. She would have never okayed a dinnertime chat with Makani's father, whom she'd never particularly liked, but she remained hopeful that her daughter would make amends with her granddaughter. "Do you need to call her now or can it wait?"

"I'll be right back, sorry." Makani stumbled from the dining room into the kitchen, where her grandmother couldn't see her, and reread the texts. Her heart floundered, trapped in the narrow space between fear and hope. She couldn't imagine this was *him,* but . . . it couldn't be anyone else. Could it?

who's asking?

The reply was instantaneous: *Ollie.*

Her heartbeat exploded into a race. She stared at the screen, waiting for him to say more. Finally, she texted: *don't remember giving you my number*

Another quick reply: *Tell me what you meant.*

It figured that Ollie was the sort of exasperating person who would text in complete sentences *and* ignore her question.

what do you THINK I meant??

I think you feel slighted, which means there's been a misunderstanding.

Slighted. Seriously, nobody normal talked like this. But he had her attention. Makani texted back a single question mark. She watched the three dots appear and disappear on her phone as Ollie typed, paused, and then resumed typing.

The text arrived: *I thought you were ashamed of me. And I'm guessing you thought that I was ashamed of you.*

Makani's eyebrows shot to her forehead. Directness like this was rare. Admirable, even. The eternal question reemerged from the gloaming. *Does he know what I did?* It was impossible to tell without more information, but a disconcerting inkling crawled through her gut, prodding her forward. Maybe he knew. But maybe she'd been wrong. Maybe, out of the two of them, she was the one who had cast judgment.

Makani replied: *why did you think that?*

Well. We never exactly talked, did we?

didn't think you were the talking type

I didn't think you were, either.

Makani paused. Her grandmother cleared her throat—a little too loudly—in the next room. Makani texted: *so . . . you want to talk*

I want to talk if you want to talk.

She should be annoyed, but she wasn't. Not in the least.

"Makani," her grandmother warned.

"I'll be right there. Almost done."

"You aren't even talking!"

"We're texting."

"That's not talking. You need to *talk* to your mama."

Makani grinned as she sent another message: *texting isn't talking*

Her phone rang, and she jumped. "Shit!"

"MAKANI YOUNG."

Makani winced as she answered. "This isn't a good time. I'll call you later, okay?" She hung up before Ollie could respond and slunk back to her dining room chair.

Grandma Young tracked every movement. "That wasn't your mother."

Makani shoveled an entire dry meatball into her mouth. Like a child.

"Give me your phone."

Makani stiffened in alarm. "Why?" she asked, muffled through the ground turkey.

"You heard me. I want to see who you were texting."

"Fine, it was Alex." She swallowed. "I was texting Alex."

Her grandmother held out her hand, palm up.

"Fine! It was a guy, okay? Are you happy now?"

Her grandmother paused, considering her options. "What's his name?"

"Grandma—"

"Don't *Grandma* me. What's his name?"

"Ollie. Oliver Larsson." Makani already knew to add his last name. People in this town always wanted a last name.

Her grandmother frowned. "Larsson. Isn't he that young cop?"

"That's his brother, Chris. Ollie is in my grade."

Grandma Young considered this, and Makani prayed that she'd never heard the rumors about Ollie. Prayed that being the brother of a cop was a *good* thing in this town. At last, her grandmother relaxed. The slightest bit. "He was my student, Chris. A nice young man. It's such a shame what happened to their parents."

Makani also relaxed. The slightest bit.

"If you want to continue seeing Oliver, I'll have to meet him."

"*Grandma*. We were only texting."

"And then your phone rang." She pointed her salad fork at Makani, a statement and an accusation. "That boy is after you."

• • •

Makani sent the text after her grandmother had gone to bed: *is now a good time?*

Curiosity fed her anxiety. The prospect of talking to Ollie was the first exciting thing that had happened to her since, well, *fooling around* with Ollie. She stared at her phone as she paced the carpeted floor, willing it to make a noise. Who didn't keep their phone beside them at all times? But it stayed silent on her dresser.

The dresser and the rest of the furnishings had once belonged to her mother. Makani had moved into her mother's childhood bedroom. The matching set of bulky oaken furniture was an unappealing shade of golden orange. The bed was too tall, its bedposts too severe. They spiraled toward the ceiling like sharpened tusks. The dresser was heavy and long, and the mirror was equally large and repulsive. But the desk. The desk was a behemoth. It made Makani's laptop look avant-garde, as if the wood had been joined together so long ago that it had never before known a personal computer.

It was the opposite of how her mother lived now. Despite the laid-back beach environment, her house was streamlined and stainless steel. Makani had always felt that her mother's tastes left something warm to be desired, something *comforting,* but this wasn't any better. It was completely void of personality.

Her grandparents must have selected the furniture, and in the years since her mother had left, they'd removed any pictures or posters that might have provided insight into her mother's teenage years. In their place were framed elementary- and middle school–aged photographs of Makani and bland paintings of prairie lands. The solitary lingering trace of her mother was an old carving inside the desk's top drawer: SOS.

It wasn't often that Makani understood her mother, but she certainly understood the quiet desperation behind this lone act of vandalism.

Since moving in, Makani had taken down the photos of herself—
hideous—and shoved them under the bed. Only a few items from
her former life were on display. She kept a pretty bowl of coral pieces
and cowrie shells on the desk, her stuffed bear and stuffed whale on
the bed, and her jewelry on the dresser, neatly hung on a stand that
looked like a tree. But mainly she kept things in drawers. Hidden
away.

Makani checked her phone again, in case she'd temporarily lost
her hearing. Still nothing. It was getting late.

A sudden rustling outside disturbed the quiet night.

She moved to her window and peered down into the shadows.
The next-door neighbor's sleek tomcat—not the neighbor who'd lost
the tip of his nose, the one on the other side—often hunted in their
yard. Makani had never been allowed to have a cat or a dog. Someday, when she had her own place, she'd have both.

More rustling. Makani squinted through the darkness.

The sound was coming from the overgrown viburnum below
her window. She craned her neck, trying to see the bush, trying to
see *through* it. A burst of furious, quick agitation startled her. And
then . . . silence. The cat must have found a vole.

Makani pressed her face against the glass, cupping her eyes with
her hands like binoculars, shielding them from her bedroom light.
She waited for the cat to trot across the lawn with its prize, but the
lawn, illuminated by a triangle of orange streetlight, remained empty.
It held nothing more interesting than falling leaves.

She returned to her phone. Nothing had changed there, either.

Makani glanced back at the window. For reasons she couldn't explain, she felt an unsettling tingle of exposure. She crept toward the
glass and peeked out from the side.

The neighborhood was still deserted.

Hello, paranoia, my old friend.

She closed the curtains, grabbed her phone, and carried it to bed, where she laid it beside her on the ivory-colored eyelet comforter, another relic from her grandparents. She tried to study for a Spanish test, but she was distracted. Why did Ollie think that she'd be ashamed to be seen with him? Because of those rumors? If that were the case, then he probably *didn't* know about her own transgressions, otherwise he would have known that she wasn't in a position to point fingers.

Maybe they stood a chance. Maybe they'd even have a real date. After all, he'd been desperate enough to hunt down her phone number.

Even though he'd ignored her question about how he'd gotten it.

Her brow was still pinched as she pushed aside her textbook for the latest issue of *Rolling Stone*. Makani didn't normally bother with paper magazines, but she'd been unable to resist when she saw Amphetamine on its cover. Their scandalous song about an underage girl who'd broken the heart of the lead singer—supposedly based on someone real, according to the article—was a huge hit. Makani felt both the anger and the ecstasy of the song's catchy lyrics. She wondered if she'd broken Ollie's heart last summer. Had he broken hers? Or had it already been too broken to make a difference?

Her phone dinged. She scrambled to pick it up, dropping it twice in her haste and excitement.

It was a picture of an enormous, hairy, white male ass. Makani groaned and tossed the phone aside without replying. She didn't feel like indulging Alex in one of her favorite games. Alex liked to steal her and Darby's phones, type "hairy butts" into Google Images, and then slip their phones back to them. When they weren't at school, Alex texted the pictures at random.

Her phone dinged again at 11:31. It was him.

I was at work, but I'm home now. Are you still awake?

A primal panic flooded her system. Should she wait before

replying? *No,* that would be stupid. Silence got them into this mess in the first place.

Ollie answered after the first ring. "Hey, sorry about that call earlier. I was on my break, but I guess that was a bad time?"

Makani's voice was cool. "How did you get my number?"

"Oh." Ollie sounded startled. "Uh, yeah. Sorry. My brother. He can, you know . . . get things. Information."

It was his second apology in seconds. And he'd asked Chris for help, which meant he'd at least told his brother *something* about her. A smile grew on her lips, but she said, "That's a little creepy."

There was a long pause.

"I'm kidding." Makani laughed, pretending to be more composed than she actually was. "I mean, don't get me wrong. It's still creepy. You should have asked *me* for my number. But . . . I'm glad to be talking to you."

His voice loosened on the other end. "Me too."

"So."

"So."

Her fingers picked at the comforter's eyelets, but she spoke her next line flirtatiously. "So, you still work the Wednesday shift at Greeley's."

He laughed once. "I do. Though I can't help but notice that you don't come around anymore."

"Yeah, there's this real asshole who works there. He acts like I'm invisible whenever I see him at school."

"Interesting. Because there's an asshole at school who's been ignoring me, too."

Makani thrilled at the ease of their banter, but her laughter dwindled with an uneasy twinge of regret. "That was pretty lame of us, huh? Assuming."

Ollie agreed without elaboration. "Monumentally."

"Could we speak clearly for a moment?" she asked.

"I'd like us to speak clearly for all moments—present and future."

Makani almost smiled, but the gesture vanished before fully ar-riving. Her voice hardened. "Look, I only want to keep talking to you if you want this to happen in a real way. If you want to, like, hang out with me. If you only want to fuck me, I'm out."

"Whoa." Ollie exhaled. "No. *No.* That was never *only* what I wanted. It just happened. I have no idea how that happened."

"We're equally to blame. I think that's been established," she said wryly.

Their phones filled with another tense silence.

"So," he ventured, "speaking clearly . . . you like me?"

"Speaking clearly . . . yes."

A respectful pause. Or perhaps Ollie was catching his breath again. "Speaking clearly . . . I like you, too."

It had been so long since Makani had felt any amount of genuine, unadulterated happiness that she'd forgotten that sometimes it could hurt as much as sadness. His declaration pierced through the muscle of her heart like a skillfully thrown knife.

It was the kind of pain that made her feel alive.

CHAPTER FIVE

THEY TALKED FOR hours. Until Makani's hands were cramped from gripping her phone and even the singing crickets had gone to bed. His obliviousness to her past was a relief. They needed to speak clearly, yes. But only about the things that needed to be spoken about.

His parents had been farmers, and the family had been tight-knit. About a month after the accident, the police gave his brother, who'd just been hired, the old cruiser to replace the car that had been totaled. It was a generous gift. When Ollie turned sixteen, Chris had given him the cruiser as a birthday present. Ollie despised the Crown Vic and the loss that it represented, but he drove it out of respect for his brother. And his need for a car. He talked about his relationship with Chris—strained, parental, loving, frustrating—and she talked about her relationship with her grandmother. Which was the same.

"What happened to your grandparents?" Makani's house was dark and filled with old shadows. She curled up under her covers. "Why didn't they take you in?"

"Half of them are dead, and the other half are drunks." The timbre of Ollie's voice was lower than usual. It was quiet and gravelly with the night. "So, when a guy with a blood-alcohol concentration that was twice the legal limit killed our parents . . . you can see why Chris fought to be my guardian."

Makani didn't like her parents. But she did love them, and she could only imagine how shattering it must have been, must *continue* to be, for Ollie to have lost both of his in the same senseless act. They'd been on their way home from an errand at the Feed 'N' Seed, the same location where Darby and Alex now worked. Their car was struck in the broad daylight of a random Tuesday afternoon. Something about it being daytime heightened the tragedy in Makani's mind.

"How did your mom wind up in Hawaii?" Ollie asked.

"She left here right after graduation. She had this *grandiose plan*— that's what she always called it—to travel through all fifty states before picking a new home. She even had this foldout map that she'd stolen from a bookstore in Norfolk. She still has it. She showed it to me once, and there was just this big, black X through Nebraska."

"So, what happened?"

"She used all her savings to go to Hawaii first. She got a job at a resort, enrolled in community college, and then met my dad."

"A *grandiose plan*. Maybe that's what I need."

Makani made a sound between a huff and a snort. "Only if you can follow through. To me, it's just another story about my mom's failures."

"It's not about Hawaii being so great that she didn't need to see her other options?"

"No."

"I always follow through on my plans," he assured her.

• • •

He proved it only a few hours later. Makani was slumped inside Darby's car before school, seething with sleep-deprived irritation. She'd been excited to tell her friends about the call, but they weren't reacting in the way that she'd hoped.

"Of course he *gets* you," Alex said from the backseat. "You're both poor little orphans."

"I'm not an orphan," Makani grumped.

"I still can't believe you have to introduce him to your grandma," Darby said. "How did he react when you told him?"

"I didn't." Makani tried to ignore the squirming in her gut as she scanned the parking lot for Ollie. A trail of students was heading toward the corner by the road, where a memorial for Haley—flowers and cards and playbills and candles—had appeared overnight in front of the school's sign. In black changeable letters, its marquee read: WE LOVE YOU, HALEY. YOUR STAR STILL BURNS BRIGHT. "I wanted to make sure everything was okay first," she said. "You know, in person."

"It's every grandmother's dream." Alex raised her palms into sarcastic jazz hands. "A social outcast who screws her granddaughter, ignores her for months, and then illegally obtains her phone number!"

Makani winced. "You know it's not like that."

"It's exactly like that," Alex said.

"It *is* creepy how he got your number," Darby said.

"You don't think it's romantic?" Makani asked.

"No," Darby and Alex replied together.

"He should have asked you for it," Darby continued. "You would have given it to him."

"Well, I'm just glad I didn't wake up my grandma. You're right that she wouldn't have liked discovering me on the phone with a guy in the middle of the night." Makani paused, detecting the ideal opportunity for a subject change. "Although, a part of me wishes I actually *had* woken her up. I think she's sleepwalking again."

"Oh, man." Alex arched her back in a catlike stretch and yawned. "What'd your g-ma do this time? Use the hair dryer as a toaster?"

Darby laughed at the word *g-ma*. Alex gave him a wink in the rearview mirror.

"It was the kitchen cabinets again, all of them," Makani said. "I found them wide-open this morning. That's two days in a row and the fourth time this month. She needs to go to a sleep clinic, but I don't know how to convince her."

"Ever wonder what she's looking for at night?" Darby asked.

"A book on self-defense for her granddaughter," Alex said.

A loud rap on the window behind Darby made him shriek. They jumped in their seats. When they realized who it was, Darby and Alex goggled at Makani.

Makani's skin flushed with heat. "Let him in, let him in."

The locks weren't automatic, so Alex leaned over to open the door. Ollie popped in beside her with a blast of cold morning air.

"Sorry," he said. "I didn't mean to scare you."

Three sets of eyes blinked at him. Somehow, Makani had already forgotten that his hair was pink. She'd been picturing him last night in bed as a blond.

He glanced between Darby and Alex with visible nervousness. "I thought . . . Makani would have told you?"

"She did," Darby said, though he still sounded baffled.

Alex smiled like a witch in a fairy tale. "We know everything."

The undertone of Ollie's skin began to match his hair as Makani continued to gape. "What are you *doing* here?" she asked.

The pink bloomed until his entire head became a single color. It was the rare moment in which she could read his expression with complete certainty: Ollie wanted to rewind this video until he was out of the car and safely back on the other side of the lot. His hand crept toward the door handle. "You said you wanted . . . to hang out."

"I did." Makani shook her head before changing it to an emphatic nod. "I did."

She felt her friends staring at them with wide, soap-opera eyes as she emerged from the stupor of confusion. For the first time, Makani realized that Ollie's appearance and demeanor weren't merely acts of rebellion. They were armor for his shyness. It must have been so difficult for *him* to have approached *her*—without the protective barrier of his phone and in the company of her friends, no less.

Makani infused her next words with as much kindness as possible. "You just caught us off guard. That's all." And then she flashed him her fullest, most high-wattage smile. A long time ago, she'd been known for it. "I'm glad you're here."

"Me too," Darby said. Because he was good like that.

"Next time," Alex said sharply, "bring doughnuts."

Ollie risked a glance at her.

"I like the ones with chocolate frosting," she said.

Ollie settled back into the version of himself that he shared with the rest of the world. His eyebrows rose slightly, and his voice flattened. "Who doesn't?"

"Makani likes maple. Darby likes plain glazed."

Ollie jokingly booed his response, which made Alex kick the back of Makani's and Darby's seats. "See? I've always told you, you're crazy."

It was an olive branch, of sorts, and Makani was able to breathe again. Until Alex refocused her attention.

"So, Buscemi," Alex said. "What's the inside scoop?"

Ollie's eyebrows rose a little further.

"Steve Buscemi played Mr. Pink in *Reservoir Dogs*."

"I'm familiar with it," he said. "But the character wasn't named after his hair color."

Alex didn't care. "What's the scoop, Buscemi?"

He seemed wary by her vagueness. "About . . ."

"*Haley.*"

He shifted. Almost imperceptibly. "Why would you ask me about her?"

Alex punched his shoulder, and Ollie grimaced, unused to her intense style of questioning. "Your brother is a cop," she said. "So, what are the police saying about her case?"

Darby sighed. "Ignore her. She has no tact."

Ollie rubbed the offended shoulder. "Chris doesn't discuss his work with me."

"But he does give you the very personal and private phone number of our dear friend Makani Young?"

"*Alex,*" Makani warned. Sometimes it was difficult to be Alex's dear friend.

Alex scooted closer to Ollie, ignoring his physical discomfort. The knees of her ripped fishnets pressed against his thighs. "Just tell us this. Was your brother at the scene?"

Ollie forced his body into a wider position, which forced Alex back to her side. "Actually." His voice remained measured. "It should have been the sheriff's jurisdiction, because it happened out of city limits. But her dad's a hunting buddy of Chief Pilger, so he contacted him directly. The whole department was called out an hour later."

Makani imagined dozens of uniformed officers storming the cornfields. "The whole department?"

"The whole department is five people," Ollie said.

"Is it true about her throat?" Alex asked. "Three slashes in a smiley face?"

Makani fought the urge to scold her again.

"Worse," Ollie said. "Five deep cuts. The eyes of the smiley were Xs."

Darby shuddered. "Like . . . dead cartoon eyes?"

Ollie nodded once. "The killer probably took a lot of pleasure in the act. Her vocal cords were slashed. The police think it might have been intentional."

Miniscule hairs rose on the back of Makani's neck. *Dead cartoon eyes.*

But Alex straightened as she recalled a favorite theory. "They think the killer was angry because Haley could sing? That it was someone who was jealous of her talent?"

"Or," Ollie said, "maybe she said something that she shouldn't have said."

"Drugs." Darby bounced as he turned toward the backseat. "It's always drugs. Maybe she stumbled across someone's meth lab and was going to rat them out!" And then he immediately looked appalled with himself for encouraging the conversation.

These same opposing energies—guilt and curiosity—were also twisting inside Makani, but Ollie only shrugged. "They don't know much of anything yet. And there wasn't any evidence left behind. At least, none that they've found so far."

Curiosity won. "Was she . . . was Haley . . . violated?"

"No," Ollie said.

"Thank God." Makani and Darby said it together. Makani was relieved that Haley hadn't suffered through that, too.

"She was found in bed, but it doesn't look like the killer physically touched any part of her," Ollie said. "Or that she touched him. The police aren't even sure if the person was male. She didn't have any bruises, and there wasn't anything under her fingernails—no skin or fibers snagged from scratching or fighting."

Makani considered this. "So, Haley was taken by surprise."

"Maybe. Or maybe she knew her killer."

"Or maybe both," Alex said, and they all nodded like sages. She crossed her arms, triumphant and smug. "I *knew* you'd have insider information."

The wrinkles deepened in Ollie's brow. "That's *all* I know. Seriously. And you're aware that you can't tell anyone any of this, correct?"

"Please." Alex brushed him off. "The only people I'd tell are already in this car."

Darby reached into the backseat and squeezed Alex's chipped-black, nail-polished hands. "I love you, too."

Something else was bothering Makani. "How do you know all this if your brother doesn't discuss his work with you?"

Ollie shrugged. "Overheard conversations." But when she didn't look convinced, he added sheepishly. "And . . . I read his files when he's asleep."

Her eyebrows lifted in surprise.

Alex scooted back toward him. "Does Haley's dad have an alibi?"

"I have no idea," he said.

"Sure you do."

"I told you that's all I know."

"Okay, so find out."

Ollie finally laughed, glancing at Makani. "Yeah. Sure."

Laughter was the best response whenever Alex was this relentless. Makani dared to feel a cinder of hope. Through the windshield, two fragile-looking girls passed by carrying a bundle of white balloons. Tears streamed down their cheeks.

"Are they in the musical?" Makani asked.

"I don't think so," Darby said.

Makani's heartbeat stumbled with an uncomfortable realization. "Did any of you guys bring something?"

Ollie and Alex shook their heads as Darby removed a sheet of cardstock folded in half from his backpack. He'd drawn a heart on the front of it with a glittery red pen. "I made this last night, but I left room for your names, if you want."

Always reliable, Darby had remembered. Alex fished out a ballpoint and scribbled her name beside his. She offered the card and pen to Ollie. Taken aback—perhaps even touched—he printed his name at the bottom in small capital letters.

Ollie held out the card and pen to Makani.

As she stared at the glittery heart, guilt oozed through her brain's every fold and crevice. She'd never spoken to Haley when she was alive. Makani hated gossip, yet she'd been speculating about the girl's life and dissecting her death as if they were seated at the table of one of those murder-mystery dinner parties. She didn't deserve to sign the card, because it had never occurred to her that Haley might *need* a card.

"Makani?" Ollie sounded concerned.

Her vision swam as she accepted the card and pen. She signed because her friends were watching. The signature felt fraudulent.

They abandoned the car and joined the crowd. As Darby placed their card atop the mound of depressing tokens, Makani wondered who would collect these gifts, and when. Would Haley's parents feel pressured to bring everything home, or would it all stay here so long that the cards and posters and teddy bears became weather battered, only suitable for the landfill?

Students from every social group paid their respects: the drama and choir geeks, of course, but also the athletes and academics, the gamers and techies, the FFA and rodeo kids. Multiple youth groups prayed together as a single unit. The student-council president handed out flyers for a candlelight vigil, while the burnouts hovered along the edges, stoned and uncomfortable, but needing to mourn with the rest of their community.

Meanwhile, Makani pretended to be upset for the same reasons as her classmates. She pretended that the local news van, parked near the flag at half-mast, hadn't broken her into a sweat. She pretended that she was cold when she put up the hood of her hoodie and angled her face away from the cameras. She pretended to belong.

Despite unbelieving glances from the student body, Ollie rejoined them at lunch. Makani had invited him, but she was still astonished when he sat down, cross-legged, beside her. He was making an effort. It lifted her mood, even though the ensuing conversation was awkward. Ollie ate his sandwich in silence. Makani could only hope that her friends would be as patient with him as they'd been with her.

At least his presence released her from being the third wheel. Darby and Alex had never purposefully treated Makani like a charity case, but she was still the intruder on their decade-long best friendship. It didn't matter that this new fourth wheel was shaky. Makani felt steadier with Ollie there, because he was there for her.

He didn't stay. With ten minutes left in the period, he mumbled an excuse and took off for the library. His exit was so hasty that Makani didn't even get the chance to say goodbye. She shot an apologetic look to her friends and then chased after him.

"Hey. *Hey.*" Makani grabbed his sleeve. "Are you okay?"

Ollie searched for an excuse. "Yeah. I just . . ."

"No worries. I get it." And Makani was pretty sure that she did. Sometimes the pressure of a situation was too much, and you just had to run.

Ollie fidgeted with the zipper of his black hoodie. He glanced at the mostly male group of gamers and techies sitting nearby on the ground—staring at them, whispering—and narrowed his gaze. They stopped talking. He turned back to Makani and nodded.

She rolled her eyes.

He smiled.

Her confidence resurged. The anxious fog slipped away. She smoothed down his sleeve where she'd grabbed it and looked up at him through her dark lashes. "So, what are you doing after school today?"

His eyebrows lifted. "Giving you a ride home?"

Makani flashed another smile as she strutted away. "Good answer," she called out. It was the perfect parting line. Until the jerks beside them had to ruin it. "Good answer," one of them mimicked, and the others laughed.

Makani stopped. "Excuse me?"

Rodrigo Morales, a shortish guy with intense eyes and enormous headphones draped around his neck, seemed startled to be called out. His recovery was quick. "I'll give you a ride home, sweetheart."

"Ugh," one of his two female friends said.

"She's right." Makani crossed her arms. "Ugh."

"Oh, I can give you *both* a ride," Rodrigo said with misplaced swagger, and the other female threw a hamburger bun at his head.

"That'd be the only thing worse than walking," another friend said drily. His name was David, and he was a scrawny senior in an oversize T-shirt with a bright green Minecraft Creeper on it. The whole group burst into howls of laughter.

"Aw, shut up." But Rodrigo's embarrassed anger was directed at David, and it prompted a volley of outrageous insults between them.

Makani wasn't sure when Ollie had returned to her side. She was grateful that he'd noticed and was willing to help, but she was even more grateful that Rodrigo had already forgotten. They glanced at each other, self-consciously.

"See you later?" she said.

"Later," he agreed.

She escaped to the other side of the quad and inclined her head in the gamers' direction. "What do you see in that guy, anyway?" she asked Alex, who'd been harboring inexplicable feelings for Rodrigo since August.

Alex shrugged. "What? He's cute. And he's really smart."

"He's immature."

"He'll grow up." She grinned and added, "I'll help him."

"That requires speaking to him first," Darby said.

"We *speak*. We speak to each other all the time in physics."

Darby scoffed. "Like yesterday, when you blasted him for miscalculating that one equation? That had to be the first answer he's ever gotten wrong."

"Thus, the blasting."

"Poor Rodrigo." Makani's curls bounced as she shook her head. "It's hard being the unrequited crush of Alexandra Shimerda."

"I'm telling you, there's something between us."

Darby patted her leg condescendingly. Alex slapped his hand away, but they were laughing as the bell rang. Its shrill waves reverberated off the flat buildings, and they groaned as they collected their belongings.

Makani tossed her empty soda-fountain cup into the recycle bin. "Darby, I won't need a ride today. Ollie's taking me home."

Darby paused, mid-putting on his backpack, to exchange a look with Alex.

That was all it took. Makani's jaw clenched. She was the third wheel again, and it was clear that the first two wheels had been talking about her. "What? *What?*"

For once, Alex was reluctant to speak. Darby cleared his throat for the delicate attempt. "It's just . . . you haven't lived here as long as we have," he said. "We don't know if Ollie *really* almost drowned, or if he *really* sleeps with the lowlifes at the Red Spot, but there's definitely something . . . not right there. Not since his parents died."

Alex tugged on her skirt's frayed hem. "We don't want you to get hurt."

"Hurt again," Darby said.

Makani's hands trembled. "You don't know him."

"Neither do you," he said.

"So, what? A fucked-up thing happened to him, and then maybe he made some mistakes. But maybe he didn't. And if he did, who cares? Does that mean he doesn't deserve a second chance?"

Alex took a step back. "Whoa. Where's this coming from?"

Makani shoved her hands in her pockets and balled them into fists. "He's driving me five minutes to my front door. I'll be fine." She wasn't sure if they could hear her as she stormed away, or if she even wanted them to hear her. She rephrased it, wrapping the words around herself against the chill of the October wind. "I'm fine."

CHAPTER SIX

OLLIE HELD OPEN the passenger-side door of the Crown Vic. The gesture was sweet and old-fashioned. "I feel like I've done something bad," Makani said, patting the cruiser's frame as she climbed in.

Ollie gave her a wry smile. "Now you know how I always feel."

It was a truth land mine—the exact reason why they were drawn to each other, told in the form of an obvious joke—but since Makani was the only one who recognized it, she kept the unintentional epiphany to herself. She watched him walk in front of the hood and then around to the driver's side. The way his body moved reminded her of something else old-fashioned: *Rebel Without a Cause*. James Dean was never so pale or so pink, but Ollie walked like a cool guy who was still deeply unsure of himself.

The interior of the car was clean and empty. The upholstery in the front was cloth, but the backseat was vinyl. Probably so that officers could clean up more easily—sweat, vomit, urine, blood. The steel-mesh divider had been removed, and there were no special radios or computer equipment, only a short handle beside the driver-side mirror that controlled a spotlight. Everything else looked normal, but she felt apprehensive. Her memories of the police were not fond.

Ollie tossed his bag into the back and slid inside.

"So, have you?" she asked. "Done something bad?"

It was meant to be a flirtatious continuation of their joke, but it didn't come out sounding that way. Warnings from her friends rattled in her head. She wondered which of the rumors about Ollie might be true, at least partially, and felt guilty for snapping at Darby and Alex. She'd have to send them an apology text later. Maybe even a reconciliatory hairy ass.

Ollie paused, his hand on the ignition, to look at her square. "Have *you*?"

"Yes," she said. It was the most truth that she could admit.

"Yeah." He turned the ignition. "Me too."

They inched into the dusty herd of American-made cars and trucks headed for the exit. Bumper stickers and vinyl crosses on rear windows proclaimed their driver's devotion to Jesus Christ. Trademark Browning deer heads marked others as hunters, and more vehicles than not had something star-spangled or a faded SUPPORT OUR TROOPS magnetized ribbon. The dirt parking lot looked nothing like the parking lots back home, and it always made Makani feel as foreign and unwanted as a Toyota.

Ollie, lost in his own ruminations, didn't speak again until they were next in line to exit. "Which way?"

For a split second, Makani was surprised that he didn't know where she lived. But why would he? "Take a right. And then in two blocks, you'll take another."

The energy in the car deflated even further. "So, this won't be a *long* ride home."

His disappointment made her feel better. She gave him a coy smile. "I never told you," she said, "but I like your hair."

Ollie glanced at her as he maneuvered onto the street. "Yeah?"

"It's empowering. A big middle finger to gender stereotypes."

He glanced at her again, checking to make sure that she wasn't making fun of him. She wasn't. Makani hadn't been positive until this moment, but the pink was angry and defiant. It was sexy.

Ollie tried to shrug it off. "It's not like I'm the first straight guy to do it."

"But I'll bet you're the first guy, straight or gay, to do it in Osborne." This seemed to please him, so she continued. "Any particular reason?"

"It was just . . . something to do. Chris gave me hell for it."

She scrunched her nose. "That sucks. I'm sorry."

"Don't be." He touched the hair at the nape of his neck, and a devilish smile broke through his inscrutable expression. "Now I'm glad I did it."

Makani laughed, throwing back her head.

"There." Ollie sounded so certain. "That's how I know."

"Know what?" she asked, amused.

"That you aren't from around here."

Makani's heart pounded as she waited for him to expand on the thought. She would wait forever, if she had to.

"No one who grew up in this town has a laugh like yours."

Her bated breath exhaled as a disbelieving snort. "There's a line."

But his voice didn't change, and he didn't grow defensive. "I'm serious. You stand out."

"I stand out because I'm not white." She pointed at her street. "It's this one."

Ollie slowed, turned onto Walnut, and shrugged. "That, too."

He didn't deny it. Nor did he ask the dreaded follow-up, *So, what are you?* Only Darby—who also innately understood the concept of otherness—had successfully avoided this pitfall. Just as it was rude and invasive to ask him about his genitalia or sexual preference, it was equally rude and invasive to ask her about her ethnicity. It was the sort of information that should only be volunteered. Never asked for.

But people always asked. It was less common back in Hawaii, where the majority of the population was multiracial, but it still happened. Makani loathed their furrowed brows as they attempted to place her inside a recognizable box: Light brown skin. Hair somewhere between loose corkscrew curls and the tight coils of a 'fro. Chin, nose, and eyes . . . something vaguely Asian.

Where are you from?

No, where are you from originally?

I mean, where are your parents *from?*

Sometimes, she asked why they cared. Sometimes, she lied to confuse or annoy them. Usually, she told the truth. "I'm half African American, half Native Hawaiian. *Not* like the forty-fourth president," she'd be forced to add, sensing their eagerness. Obama was only born in Hawaii. His mama was a white girl from Kansas.

Ollie tapped an index finger against the steering wheel. "Which one is your house?"

"It's a few blocks down, just past those trees. On the right-hand side."

"All right turns."

"Hmm?" Her mind wasn't fully back to the present.

"To get to your house from school. That's satisfying."

It was true. This afternoon, at least, the short drive had been satisfying. She wanted it to continue. "Do you have to work today?"

"No. Do you?" But he quickly corrected the mistake. "I mean, do you have to take care of your grandma today?"

"Nope." She drew out the word. Hinting.

Ollie stared ahead, index finger still tapping. "Should we . . . do something?"

A thrill spiked through Makani. Only one final and unpleasant hurdle remained. She tried to keep her voice relaxed. "Well, I'd love to . . ."

"But?"

She braced herself. "But first, you'll have to meet my grandmother."

"Okay," he said.

Makani was flabbergasted. "Seriously?"

"Yeah." He took in her expression as they passed beneath the oak-lined, shadow-dappled portion of the street. "Wait. Weren't *you* serious?"

"Of course. But I didn't think you'd be this okay with it."

The corners of his mouth lifted into a smile. "You're forgetting you're in the Midwest. This is how we do things here." When she raised a skeptical eyebrow, he actually laughed. "It'll be fine."

She had a hard time believing that, but his confidence was reassuring. Somewhat.

"It figures that you live here," he said.

Once again, she was taken aback. "What's that supposed to mean?"

He craned his neck to look at the branches overhead. "Beautiful girl. Beautiful neighborhood."

She frowned. "For real, Ollie. I'm not into lines."

"I'm just saying, you live on the best street in town. When I was a kid, I always wished I lived under these trees."

"Until you discovered the rest of the world has way better streets and way better trees?" She pointed out a white two-story with a large porch. "That's mine."

Ollie pulled into the driveway and turned off the engine. Makani waited for him to expand upon her remark—to agree about preferring anywhere else to Osborne. When he didn't, she worried that she'd pushed him too far. He'd complimented her twice, and she'd dismissed him both times. And even though she had the impression that he was desperate to move away, it still sucked to hear someone talk shit about your hometown.

"You're right, though," she said. "It *is* the best street. I guess I'm lucky."

It wasn't a lie, and it felt strange to admit. It had been a while since Makani had felt lucky, or even grateful. Most of the towns around here had brick-paved streets in their oldest districts, which seemed both anachronistic and genuinely charming. Main Street and her grandmother's neighborhood contained the only brick pavers in Osborne. The houses here were more attractive, and they also had better landscaping. This time of year, the leaves turned comforting shades of yellow and gold, cornhusk scarecrows dotted the yards, and sacrificial pumpkins sat on porch steps, waiting to be carved.

In September, Grandma Young had filled her planters with sunny round mums, and last weekend Makani had raked the fallen leaves into those orange trash bags printed with jack-o'-lantern faces. They were tacky, but Makani liked them anyway.

She cocked her head. "I've never asked, I've only assumed. Do you still live on your parents' farm?"

Ollie nodded. "We're not selling the house until I'm done with school, but we've already sold most of the land to our neighbors. They've incorporated it into their giant-ass corn maze. Perhaps you've seen the billboards?"

This last sentence was sarcastic. The fluorescent advertisements for the Martin Family Fun Corn Maze were everywhere. The Martins were a sizable clan of longtime residents. Every single family member had a different shade of red hair, and three of them—two siblings and a cousin—went to Osborne High.

"Yikes," Makani said. "That must be weird for you."

Ollie shrugged. She'd noticed that he was a frequent shrugger. "It's not bad."

"MAKANI YOUNG."

They jump-flattened into the upholstery. Wincing, Makani looked out the window and found Grandma Young. She was standing on the steps that led to the back door, and her hands were positioned on her hips.

"Christ," Ollie said in a low voice. "How long has she been staring at us?"

"Probably for all eternity." Makani steeled herself as she exited the car. "Hey, Grandma—"

"I thought you'd been brought home by the police!" Grandma Young hustled down the rest of the stairs to meet her. "Nearly frightened me to death when I looked out the kitchen window and saw you sitting there."

"Oh, it's not—"

"But it's not a cop car, is it? It doesn't have any decals. Unless it's undercover!" Her panic bubbled back to a boil. "Are you okay? What happened?"

"I'm *fine*, Grandma. Everything is fine. A friend drove me home, that's all."

"That's not Darby's car."

"A new friend."

Grandma Young wrapped Makani into a constricting hug. She seemed enraged but on the verge of tears. "I thought something had happened to you. Something like what happened to that poor Haley Whitehall."

An unexpected lump rose in Makani's throat. Her grandmother's first thought was that she had been attacked—not that she'd done something wrong. Makani fought to keep her voice steady. "Well. Clearly nothing happened, because I'm standing right here."

Ollie's door opened, and his feet crunched into the gravel driveway.

Grandma Young's death grip loosened. And then her arms fell away completely. As Makani turned around, she realized with a flush of horror what her grandmother was seeing: a skeleton-like boy dressed in all black.

With hot-pink hair.

And a lip ring.

"I'm sorry, Mrs. Young," the skeleton boy said. "We didn't mean to scare you. I'm Makani's friend, Oliver Larsson. Ollie." He stepped forward to shake her hand.

Grandma Young gingerly accepted the outstretched hand as she examined every square inch of his appearance. Makani was glad when Ollie didn't flinch or look away, which her grandmother might have deemed weak. He only smiled, which helped to soften his sharper features. "You're the young man who works in the produce department at Greeley's," she said, finally letting go of him.

"Yes, ma'am. I've been working there for almost four years."

"How old are you?"

Makani's stomach warped, but Ollie replied with ease. "I just turned eighteen."

Grandma Young nodded toward his car. "That's some ride you've got there."

Ride, Makani thought. *Ohmygod no stop stop stop.*

Ollie held the smile. "It gets me where I need to go."

Grandma Young considered him for another excruciating moment. And then she scolded her granddaughter. "Don't just stand there. Show him inside."

Mortification followed Makani into her grandmother's original, unironic, midcentury-modern kitchen. At least it was clean.

"Would you like anything to drink?" Grandma Young asked Ollie.

"No, thank you," he said.

"We have water, skim milk, iced tea, Sprite—well, it's not Sprite, it's the off-brand Sprite—orange juice, cranberry juice, tomato juice—well, it's the low-sodium kind, so it doesn't taste as good, but it's healthier—"

"Water would be great, thanks," Ollie said.

"Tap water? Or we have a jug in the fridge. It keeps it cooler."

Makani dug her nails into her palms. "We all know how refrigerators work."

"Tap is fine," Ollie said.

"Ice?" Grandma Young asked.

"Yes, please."

"The square kind from a tray or the round kind from a bag?"

"Oh my God, Grandma. You are literally killing me."

"Either is fine," Ollie said. "Whichever's easier."

Grandma Young opened the freezer and reached into a clear bag of ice. "Oliver, I apologize for my granddaughter. For her rudeness, but also for her misuse of the word *literally*. I've corrected her at least a dozen times."

Makani made a choking motion with her hands. Ollie shared a secret smile with her as Grandma Young turned back around. Without breaking a beat, she placed the ice-filled glass between Makani's clenched fingers. Ollie and her grandmother laughed.

But the atmosphere remained unnaturally formal in the living room as Grandma Young inquired about Ollie, and he inquired about her. Makani sat with her grandmother on the sofa. Ollie sat in the easy chair. The grandfather clock beside the staircase ticked and ticked the agonizing seconds. After a conversation about Grandma Young's church dwindled to an end, Ollie pointed at the coffee table.

The edge of the jigsaw puzzle had been completed along with sections of the pumpkin patch.

"My mom liked those, too. Sometimes during the holidays, she'd pull one out from the back of the linen closet, and we'd work on it together. My dad and my brother couldn't stand it. They thought puzzles were boring. But I've always thought they were satisfying, you know? Each piece having its exact place."

Makani was stunned. Excluding their phone call last night and the badgering from Alex this morning, she'd never heard Ollie speak so many sentences in a row. He tended to use the minimal amount of words possible to express himself.

Grandma Young gestured at her with an ice-free glass of off-brand Sprite. "This one thinks they're boring, too."

Ollie shook his head at Makani. "You're missing out."

"Isaac, my husband, he didn't care much for them, either," Grandma Young said. "But they calm me down. Keep my mind occupied."

There was a pause as something like an acknowledgment of sorrow passed between Ollie and her grandmother. Unable to bear it any longer, Makani glanced at her phone and jumped up from the sofa. "Sorry! We need to get going."

Grandma Young set down her drink on an L.L. Bean catalog. "Oh?"

"Ollie has a late shift tonight, so we wanted to hang out a little before then."

"I was gonna take her to Sonic for slushes." As Ollie stood up from the easy chair, its springs gave a muffled squeak. "Last ones of the season, before it gets too cold."

"I like their limeade." Grandma Young's ankles cracked as she rose to her feet. "It was nice meeting you. And feel free to join me anytime." She nodded at the puzzle.

Ollie tucked his fingertips into the pockets of his jeans. "Thanks."

Makani marched him to the back door in the kitchen, leading them toward freedom and calling over her shoulder, "I'll be home before dinner!"

When they were tucked safely inside his car, they exchanged the same sly grin. "You're good at that," Makani said. "At lying."

"So are you."

"Yeah. Sorry about that." She laughed in an attempt to hide her embarrassment. "I promise I won't make you come back and do a jigsaw puzzle with my grandmother."

His grin held. "Who says I don't want to?"

Makani laughed again. "Okay, weirdo." She was relieved that he'd gotten along with her grandmother and spoken to her like a normal human being. But the companion emotion was that same inescapable shame. No matter how many times she'd stuck up for him with her friends, she couldn't stop underestimating him herself.

"Just promise me Sonic was a lie," she said.

"God, yes," Ollie said. The Sonic Drive-In was the only name-brand restaurant in town. It was where the football crowd hung out. "I'm taking you to the ocean."

They drove through Osborne—past Greeley's Foods and the Red Spot, past the bustling Sonic and the deserted shell of an old Sinclair gas station, past the gigantic Do it Best hardware store and the shed-size Dollar General—and out of town.

They didn't talk much, but their silence was companionable.

They crossed the railroad tracks and went over the river. The countryside was flat. Stiff vegetation, muddy fields, round bales of hay. Modest farmhouses and monstrous tractors. The view was uniform in every direction, broken only by the long, dinosaurian contraptions that Makani had learned were center-pivot irrigation systems.

The grass and dying corn plants were the same shade of drab golden brown. The occasional trees, dressed for autumn, added pointillistic yellow dots to the landscape. Everything was yellow and gold, except for the sky. It was gray.

It didn't seem like they were traveling anywhere specific, yet Makani felt a change, a tremulous sort of anticipation, as they approached their destination. Ollie turned off the highway and onto a nondescript dirt road surrounded by cornfields. It looked like any other nondescript dirt road surrounded by cornfields, but as they drove farther, Makani realized how secluded it actually was. There were no other people or houses in sight. Darby and Alex would be livid if they knew she was here.

Makani composed a text, apologizing for earlier, but the connection was too slow for the message to send. A pellet of discomfort lodged in her stomach as the car dead-ended in the middle of another field. Or maybe it was all one field.

"What's this road even for?" she asked.

Ollie turned off the engine. "I have no idea. *Literally.*"

Makani laughed with tension-releasing surprise. "Ollie Larsson. Was that a joke?"

He raised his eyebrows and smiled. "Never."

Her heart somersaulted. They weren't parked in the same location where they'd had sex, though it looked similar. That particular memory was tinted with loneliness and desperation. Now she only felt the nervous thrum of excitement.

"Careful stepping out," Ollie said, unlocking the car. "It's always muddier than you think."

Makani tucked away her phone, opened the door, and peered down. The ground was a thick marsh of wind-stiffened mud. She tested it with a sneaker toe. It seemed solid enough, so she climbed out—and tromped straight into it, three inches deep. "Shit!" But she laughed again. "I thought you said you were taking me to the beach."

"The ocean," he corrected.

The temperature had dropped. The brisk air smelled like decaying leaves, distant woodsmoke, and chilled terrain, a reminder that Halloween was around the bend. Makani pulled up the hood of her floral-printed hoodie and zipped it up. She should have worn a coat, but she still sucked at this cold weather thing. Most people here didn't even consider it cold yet. Just nippy.

She plodded forward to join Ollie. He was leaning against the front of the car, its engine ticking lightly as it cooled. But the metal was still warm, almost hot, and it felt good against her jeans. The leggy corn encircled them, two feet overhead. She turned pointedly to Ollie. He was staring straight ahead into the vast golden nothingness.

"It's not the Pacific," he said, "but it's the best I can do."

Ollie must have registered her confusion in his peripheral vision, because he met her gaze with another smile. "The fields. I know you miss Hawaii."

As her mind absorbed this thoughtful gesture, her eyes lingered on the curve of his lips. She wanted to kiss them again. She forced her head away and tried to focus on their surroundings—she really did try—but she felt him still watching her.

He slid back and up onto the hood of his car. "Here."

She hopped up beside him, metal thumping, her left leg touching his right.

Ollie pulled up the hood of his own hoodie. It was tight against his head—hers puffed out a bit with her hair—but a shock of hot pink flashed out from underneath the black cotton fabric. It looked like the only bright thing in the universe.

"Okay," he said. "Now look again."

The wind rustled the brittle cornstalks. It sounded like a spitting, crackling fire. The dry tassels reached for the open sky while the dead silks pointed down to the muddy earth. Slowly, ever so slowly, the wind strengthened and changed course, and the fields swayed as a single element, rippling outward in a current of mesmerizing waves.

Something hidden inside Makani lifted its head and blossomed. The sensation was sublime. Makani often complained that she was drowning in corn, but she wasn't gasping below the water. She was perched on the edge of the horizon.

She felt Ollie trying to gauge her reaction. She smiled, letting it linger on the fields before inclining her head toward his. "Thank you," she said.

And then she kissed him.

Makani was surprised at the familiarity of his mouth, the *taste* of it, how natural Ollie's lips felt when pressed against hers. She remembered how to work both around his piercing and with it. His breath caught, and she felt the thrill of having invoked the reaction. His hands slipped under her hood, on each side of her neck, and it was the first time that his fingers had touched her skin since the end of summer. She gasped. Her arms wrapped around him. Their hips slid against each other, digging into the metal of the car. It was painful, and Makani would have bruises, but it didn't matter. She didn't care.

They kissed—they made out like this—until the setting sun ripened the clouds into peaches and apricots. Until his phone interrupted them.

Ollie scooted back as he removed it from his pocket. "Shit. It's probably Chris, wondering where I am, oh—" He hopped off the car to answer it. "Hello? *Hello?*"

The connection must have been weak. Makani thought it was

odd when he went inside the cruiser for privacy, using it like an old-fashioned telephone booth. Wouldn't the connection be stronger outside? She could hear the rumble of his voice but none of his words.

Her blood still pulsed with heat, but she shivered. After they'd had sex, he'd turned into a ghost. She wanted to believe that he wouldn't disappear again.

Ollie hung up.

They stared at each other through the windshield. His eyes were heavy. Whatever it was, it wasn't good news. With an ominous knot of dread, Makani slid down the hood, trudged the few feet through the mud, and rejoined him in the car.

She left the door open.

"Work," Ollie said. His body was slumped into his seat. "One of our cashiers was just fired for stealing. I can't believe it. It doesn't sound like her at all. They want me to go in and run her register."

Relief rushed over Makani. She'd assumed that something worse had happened. Haley's school photo, plastered across the local media, flickered through her mind like a harbinger. *Enthusiastic smile. Bright eyes. Neatly parted hair.* She looked so wholesome, so undeserving. Not that anyone deserved her fate.

Ollie's slump deepened. "Sorry. This sucks."

"Don't worry about it." Makani scraped the mud from her sneakers against the bottom of his car. His boots weren't nearly as caked. "Besides, now we only half lied to my grandma. I promised her that I'd be home for dinner."

He didn't respond, so she asked before losing her nerve, "Why did you take the call in here? You didn't want me to hear you talking to your boss?"

It nudged him back into the present. "Sometimes I get a stronger signal in here. Something to do with the old police wiring, I don't know."

"I couldn't even get a text to send earlier."

He shrugged. "Maybe we need CB radios, like the jocks and ags."

She pointed an accusing finger. "Bite your tongue."

Leaning forward, he lightly took her finger between his teeth. She smiled. "I could call my manager back," he said, a few minutes later. "Make an excuse."

But Makani needed to believe that Ollie would return. She kissed him twice, one kiss on each temple, and closed the door. Haley's school photo vanished from her thoughts.

"Drive," she said. "We'll have plenty of time for that later."

CHAPTER SEVEN

THEY WERE UNDEFEATED. The best team in the state. And they were playing one of the worst tomorrow night. So why was Hooker being such a fucking dickweed?

For the last forty minutes, Matt Butler had been standing in the locker room showers with his eyes closed. Practice was over. The sun was down. Everyone was gone. He'd told the guys that he'd catch up with them at Sonic, but he wasn't even sure if that was true. He wanted to be alone, enveloped in water and quiet and steam, forever.

It had been a rough week. The pressure of the playoffs, pressure of the recruiters, pressure of his parents. Haley. That stupid fight in the quad and the disappointed lectures from Principal Stanton and Coach Hooker that followed. Lauren. She'd been ragging on him again for not texting her back fast enough. Worse, she was acting like she'd known Haley—like she'd been personally devastated by the tragic loss of a dear friend—when, as far as he knew, Lauren and Haley had never hung out. Not once. It was okay to be upset about someone's death, even if you never really knew the person. But Matt hated the way his girlfriend was making the tragedy about herself.

He couldn't stop thinking about Haley's parents. The media was placing ample suspicion on her father, but every time Matt saw him in the news, Don Whitehall looked gutted. His eyelids were so swollen that he could hardly keep them open. Only a psychopath could fake that kind of reaction. Then again, only a psychopath could commit that kind of murder. Haley's mom had issued a televised statement. She'd begged anyone in the community to step forward if they knew the perpetrator's real identity, but she could barely speak through her grief. Something about her physical appearance reminded him of his own mom. That made it worse.

He still felt the shock of when Buddy had ripped down the *Sweeney Todd* banner. His best friend hadn't known what he was doing—Matt could see that now, they were cool—but it had made the entire team look like assholes.

Both Hooker and his father grilled him constantly about the importance of appearance. And Matt was trying to keep up appearances, but the stress of everything, of everyone *relying* on him, had been getting to him all semester. It was making him pick these fights. Obsess over the Whitehalls. Misplace his belongings. Matt had been losing his essentials (phone, keys, wallet) in the strangest places (sock drawer, vegetable crisper, patio table) with no memory of having moved them there.

Unless . . . it wasn't the stress.

Matt's muscles clenched as three letters chorused in his mind: CTE.

Chronic traumatic encephalopathy was a disease caused by repetitive blows to the head. Early symptoms included memory loss, disorientation, and erratic behavior. Later symptoms included dementia, impeded speech, and suicide. Basically, it destroyed your brain, and football players everywhere were suffering and dying from it. Mostly old guys, who'd played pro. But plenty of young guys, too. Even high schoolers.

It was the disease that the NFL and universities didn't want to discuss, because it hurt their bottom line. Matt's teammates didn't want to talk about it, either. Ignoring it made it easier to pretend that it wasn't serious, made it easier to keep playing ball. No one wanted to ruin the game they all loved.

But Matt thought about CTE. He thought about it a lot.

Professional football was the only future he'd ever wanted. It was what his father, whose own dreams were shattered when he tore up his left knee on the field at Memorial Stadium, had always wanted.

His mother, on the other hand. She used to want it. Now every time a story hit ESPN, he'd find a printed-out article sitting on his place mat at the breakfast table. Her silent plea. To Matt's everlasting shame, he always made a show of crumpling up the articles in front of his dad. They'd been working so hard for this, for so long.

But, secretly, Matt had started pocketing them.

The first article he'd kept was about Tony Dorsett, a college and pro Hall of Fame running back. Matt was a running back, too. He was the best in the Midwest, with the Division I FBS recruiters serenading his front door to prove it, but every time he found his phone in the wrong place, he broke into a cold sweat.

CTE? Is that you?

Because what would he do if he couldn't play football?

On the mantelpiece in his living room, a framed photograph was prominently displayed. It was taken on the day he was born, and he was swaddled in a scarlet Huskers blanket. Now, only a few short months remained before he had to officially commit to one school. Because he *would* commit. He would keep playing.

The choice wasn't an actual choice.

Matt turned off the water. He examined his hands, which were pruned and gelatin white. The weak showerhead dripped water onto the tile floor. Somewhere during this exhausted mulling, Matt had decided to join his friends at Sonic.

Tomorrow was the last game of the regular season, and it was important to keep focused on their opponent and not look past them into the playoffs—even though everybody knew it was a win. It's why practice had been so frustrating. Hooker had drilled them harder than ever, yelling in an unparalleled, spittle-faced volume that they were getting too comfortable. Matt was confident, but he wasn't comfortable. He wouldn't feel *comfortable* until he'd made it through playoffs without injury.

Buddy liked to joke that Hooker yelled because of a deep-seated resentment of being forced to listen to them shout his own terrible name. Matt always laughed, but he knew the head coach's motivations came from a better, smarter place. Hooker cared.

Matt toweled off and then wrapped it around his waist. He grabbed his combination shampoo/body wash, stepped over his dirty practice clothes, and strode through the cloud of steam. His wet footprints trailed behind him. The lockers smelled like male sweat and old rust, and they were in alternating colors of scarlet and gold. Osborne proudly wore the same shade of scarlet red as the Huskers, but Matt's locker was gold, because a team superstition asserted that the scarlet lockers were unlucky. Seniors always claimed the gold lockers.

Matt ground to a halt. His combination lock was missing.

CTE? Is that you?

He shook his head, pissed at himself, as he swung open the metal door. His helmet and deodorant were on the top shelf. The larger bottom space, which normally held his backpack and mesh duffel bag, was empty.

"Aw, fuck." Matt muttered it. But then he slammed down the

bottle of shampoo/body wash so hard that the entire row of lockers quivered in shock.

He glanced around the room. Nothing appeared to be out of place. He jerked open the gold door closest to his. Despite keeping it permanently unlocked—Buddy could never remember the combination—their teammates rarely stole or hid things from him. The usual items were still inside of it. Nothing else.

Matt looked under the row of benches. More nothing.

"Fuck. *Fuck.*"

He stalked toward the showers, annoyed that his own absent-mindedness had led to this irritating prank, which was forcing him to re-dress in his soiled practice clothes. It meant that he'd have to stop by his house before Sonic to change. He'd also have to shower again, or Lauren would complain about the smell.

Matt rounded the corner, and his practice clothes were gone.

Perfect.

"All right, guys." His voice was loud and deep, and it resonated against the steel lockers. "You got me."

There was no reply.

"What do you want? A dick pic or something?" Matt kept the tone jocular. He was *done* with this week, but he refused to give his friends the satisfaction of knowing it. "Guess you should have taken my towel, too."

The steam evaporated. The room grew cold.

He rubbed the hair on his arms. "Hello?"

The question echoed.

Even more than the silence, Matt *felt* his aloneness. He headed for the coaches' offices. As expected, their windows were dark, and their doors were locked. Hooker and the assistants usually went home straight after practice, especially if it'd been a tough one. School rules required them to stay until the last student was gone, but they liked to give the guys an opportunity to vent and decompress without the fear of being overheard.

The entrance to the locker room was located beside the assistant coaches' shared office. Matt readjusted his towel and cracked open the door. He peered into the dusk, half expecting—and very much hoping—to find the team waiting outside, phones raised to capture him in all his humiliated glory.

Nobody was there.

In the distance, a crowd murmured. It was the candlelight vigil for Haley. Parents and students and teachers were already gathering at the front of the school. His stomach dropped as he realized that he'd have to walk past them to reach the parking lot. He couldn't do that in a towel. It would be disrespectful.

Matt closed the door and tried again. "Hello?"

Doubt crept in.

Did he see his practice clothes when he got out of the shower? The most logical explanation was that the guys had stolen them at the same time as his regular clothes, and that all his shit was currently in the back of someone's pickup.

Matt weighed his options. He could call Buddy and beg for it back. He could call his mom and ask her to bring him something else to wear. Or he could call Lauren. *No way. She'd tell her friends.* The only other option was to wait for the vigil to end, but how long would that take? Two hours? And then he'd still have to drive home in his towel.

Wait.

Drive.

His keys and phone were in his pockets.

Matt shouted a long, lethal expletive. Anger coursed through his veins as he threw open every non-locked locker. Crouched on his knees and peered below the benches. Jumped onto the benches and peeked on top of the lockers. He looked in the showers, urinals, stalls, and under the sinks, but his belongings were nowhere to be found.

This was it, then. He'd have to walk home.

Matt lived in the newer neighborhood across town. He had never walked it, but it was probably only thirty minutes away. Still, the temperature would be below forty by the time the vigil ended. And he'd be wearing a goddamn towel.

Defeated, he sank onto the bench outside Hooker's office. His body was a weary sack. Everything ached. Matt leaned against the cinder-block wall—right beside a telephone. He grabbed the receiver off its hook, scanning his brain for numbers.

It's not CTE. No one memorizes them anymore.

The only number he knew was his parents' landline, but when he called, no one picked up. He tried again. "Goddamn motherfucking answer the phone!" he said, and a cry emerged from the locker bay.

Matt froze.

Everything was silent. And then . . . someone whimpered.

Before this moment, Matt would have guessed that the sound of another human—no matter how distressed—would have launched him to his feet in fury. But something else kicked in. Instinct, perhaps. It was the only explanation for the overwhelming trepidation triggered by that single whimper. Why his internal sensors lit up on high alert.

His body was stone. He listened.

The person had gone silent again, but their presence was unmistakable. Matt gripped his towel and stood. He felt exposed and vulnerable, an animal lying belly up. He pressed forward without sound, yet his footsteps were still too loud.

He reached the lockers.

At the far end of the bay, at the far end of the bench, a slender figure sat with their back to him. Their hoodie was up, and their head was down. Their shoulders shook in a way that suggested crying. Matt couldn't tell if it was a girl or guy, but it wasn't one of his teammates. They were too small to play football.

"Hey." He didn't mean for it to come out so angrily.

The figure flinched.

Matt tried to calm his voice. "Who are you?"

The figure didn't move.

Matt retightened the towel, keenly aware of his genitals. "Hey," he said again, stepping forward. His tone was softer. "Are you okay?"

The figure sniffled, and Matt realized that it might be one of the special-needs kids. The second-string quarterback had a sister in the after-school program, so he knew they met in a classroom nearby. This might even be her. Sometimes Faith showed up near the end of practice and watched them run drills from the bleachers.

Matt approached with caution as he circled the wooden bench. Their face was still aimed at the floor. Matt kneeled before them, trying to get at eye level. "Do you need help? Can I help you?"

The figure raised their head. Slowly. Deliberately.

Matt frowned. It wasn't Faith, it—

The knife slid into his abdomen with shocking ferocity and immediately back out with equal vigor. Matt collapsed forward, knocking his head against the bench, while his mind remained a step behind. *What just happened? Was that an accident?*

The figure stared down at him in hatred.

Matt's mind scrambled to make sense of it. He was half on the bench, half on the floor. He couldn't find their name. "You. What the hell did you do to me?"

The reply was swift—a powerful downward thrust into his skull.

Matt screamed. His attacker yanked with gloved hands on the hilt until the knife tugged back out, and the rest of Matt's body fell onto the hard ceramic tile. He was still conscious as a crumpled piece of paper materialized from the pocket of his attacker's hoodie.

The figure kneeled before him. Held out the paper in front of his eyes. Smoothed it down.

It was an article that his mother had printed out several weeks ago. Matt had carried it around in his backpack for a few days before it had disappeared.

His eyes widened with a deeper fear.

The figure, content that Matt understood what he was seeing—the personal *violation* of it—returned the paper to the hoodie's pocket.

Matt wanted to speak. He couldn't. The last thing he saw was an arm, splattered with his own blood, as the sawtooth edge of a large hunting knife carved around the circumference of his head. With a squelch that signaled the release of suction, it popped open like the lid of a jack-o'-lantern. His brain was slashed into mush. And then the top was placed back on.

Nice and tidy.

CHAPTER EIGHT

THE COPS WERE removing students from the classrooms, one at a time, for questioning. It had taken twenty-four hours for Haley's memorial to appear, but the front corner of the school was already blanketed in fresh roses, poster-board collages, and footballs. Dozens of small red flags, normally affixed to cars and trucks on game day, had been planted in the ground and were flapping in the wind. Tonight's game—the final game of the regular season—had already been forfeited. It was the first forfeit in team history.

The entire campus was stunned with disbelief. Half of the students were dressed in school colors. Several openly wept. A dozen stuffed-animal lions had also appeared overnight at the memorial, because Matt's team number was twelve and their mascot was Leo the Lion. Last year, the youth groups had protested to change his name—*Leo* was too astrological—but this morning, their most vocal objector had led a prayer by the flagpole while wearing a LION PRIDE sweatshirt.

A custodian had found Matt's body. The nearly two hundred

mourners at Haley's candlelight vigil had witnessed the cops and ambulances scream onto the scene.

Makani had been home for less than an hour, the taste of Ollie still tingling on her lips, when the cavalry of lights zoomed past Grandma Young's front window. It looked like every emergency vehicle that Osborne had to offer. The news hit social media first, as it always did: *There'd been an accident at the high school.*

UPDATE: *There was a body.*

UPDATE: *It was a student.*

UPDATE: *It was Osborne's favorite student.*

The town climbed from local to statewide news, and the obligatory journalists had swarmed in, swelling their presence. *Matthew Sherman Butler. Haley Madison Whitehall.* When people died, the media turned them into three names. Makani had hardly known either of the victims. It felt wrong to have this much information.

The reporters clustered along the perimeter of the campus, nabbing strays for exclusive interviews. Makani had bolted around the feasting horde, but plenty of other students were willing. One news crew even had the nerve to duck beneath the crime-scene tape to film the trash bins where Matt's backpack and duffel bag had been discovered, presumably stashed there by his killer. Makani had heard the furious shouts of the police officers all the way from the quad.

Haley had been murdered at home, and Matt had been murdered at school.

Haley had been beloved in drama, and Matt had been beloved in football.

One victim, two victims.

These things made a difference.

A rumor circulated about canceling school, but Makani assumed it didn't happen so that the questioning could take place more easily.

It seemed probable that the cases were connected; there were too many similarities. Everyone, including the teachers and administrators, would be required to face an officer by the end of the day. Students were called out individually. The order was supposedly random, but it was clearly alphabetical.

Justine Darby, Oliver Larsson, Alexandra Shimerda, Makani Young.

She would be the last to go.

When Darby returned to their second-period physics class, he grabbed an empty seat beside Makani and Alex.

Makani pressed him for details. "What kind of questions did they ask?"

"Easy things," he said.

They didn't bother to hide their conversation. Everybody else was already talking. Phones, normally forbidden, were on full display as students grieved and searched for new information. It was difficult enough to pay attention on an average Friday, but even the teachers knew that no lessons would be taught today as they adopted the dual roles of counselors for the students and secretaries for the officers.

Mr. Merrick, the physics teacher, was engaged in a discussion with two football players whose heads were down. Breaking another school rule, he had a hand gripped on one of their shoulders. Comforting. Underneath Mr. Merrick's bushy and uncultivated eyebrows, it looked like he was trying not to cry.

"They asked if I knew the victims," Darby said. "If I'd ever heard any rumors about them, if I knew anyone who might not have liked them, where I was last night between six and seven. That sort of thing. The officer was really nice."

"Did you get Chris?" Makani had glimpsed him in the hallway

before class. With his pale skin and white-blond hair, it was easy to identify him as Ollie's brother. Chris was a bit broader, though, despite being more slender and less muscular than most cops.

"No, it was the lady. Officer Gage. Kinda hot, actually."

"And *good at her job*," Alex said, not looking up from her phone.

Darby waved a dismissive hand. He was a feminist, too. "You'll be fine," he told Makani, because her head was cowering and her elbows were burrowed against her sides. Unconsciously, she was making herself smaller.

Makani hated the idea of talking to the police. Answering their questions. What if they looked into her record and discovered her expungement in Hawaii? She'd always dreaded that someday, something would happen that would prompt a closer inspection of her files. *And this was it. Today was the day.* What would her friends think of her?

If Ollie were here, maybe his stillness would be a comfort. But they only had one class together and since the previous evening, they'd only spoken over text. Ollie had lain awake, afraid of getting a knock on the front door—the chief of police coming to say there'd been a third attack, and now his brother was dead, too. Chris hadn't come home until after four in the morning. Ollie had slept in and barely made it to school on time.

"Do you think the team will bow out?" Darby asked Alex.

Makani realized they'd been talking for several minutes.

"Of the playoffs?" Alex shook her head. "Their spot was already secure. And Matt wasn't the only one being scouted. The team *can't* stop playing—"

"Because this is Nebraska." Makani filled in the blank like a robot. Most conversations about football ended with that phrase.

Alex loved playing the trumpet, but she preferred concert season to marching band. She nodded her displeasure. "The boosters sent out a text-blast this morning. We're taking tonight off with the team, but practice resumes on Monday."

Darby glanced around to ensure their privacy. "I heard the coaches might be suspended, because they left school grounds immediately after practice. Someone was supposed to stay behind with the team. And if someone *had* stayed behind . . ."

Alex grimaced. "Twenty bucks says the only coach suspended is the lowest-ranking assistant."

"I didn't think Haley and Matt even knew each other," Darby said, returning to the most baffling question. "Do you really think they were dating?"

The tone of the rumors had shifted. Haley's father was taking a backseat while the secret lovers theory came under scrutiny. Suddenly, their classmates swore they'd spotted Haley and Matt sharing a banana shake at Sonic or groping beneath the bleachers.

"I mean," Darby said, "Matt's been with Lauren Dixon for two *years.*"

"Which is why it was a secret." Alex leaned in, wafting them with her favorite perfume. Her skin smelled floral and spicy. "Maybe Lauren found out and killed them both in a jealous rage."

"You seriously think a girl could've done that?"

"Of course a girl could've done it."

Darby scowled at her. "I meant, physically. Matt was a big guy."

"You don't think Lauren has bitch strength?" Alex asked.

When Makani moved to Osborne, Lauren had been the first to ask: *What* are *you?* Makani gave an honest answer, and Lauren had laughed. *So, you're a mutt!* She thought she was being cute, and everyone within earshot had laughed. Makani had despised her ever since. But even with their history, she was glad that Lauren had stayed home and would be spared—for a time, at least—what was being said about her.

"Maybe the killer doesn't even go here," Darby said. "Maybe it's someone from a rival team. Someone competing for the attention of the same college recruiters."

"But then why kill Haley?" Alex asked.

He contemplated it for a few seconds. "Love triangle?"

They startled as a voice in front of them laughed with condescension. It was Alex's tempestuous crush. As Rodrigo turned around to face them, Alex glared at him witheringly. But her posture perked up.

Rodrigo laced his fingers behind his head, cocky and relaxed. "Though, I suppose a love triangle is as likely as your secret lovers' scenario."

"It is so"—Alex pointed at his chest—"not."

David, who was sitting beside Rodrigo, rolled his eyes. Makani understood. Their friends needed to get over themselves and suck face.

"What about Buddy?" Darby asked. "In the love triangle?"

Rodrigo's expression grew even more skeptical. "Buddy Wheeler?"

"No, the other Buddy who plays football," Alex said.

Darby ignored them. "Remember last year when his girlfriend dumped him, and he punched her locker so hard that his skin got caught in the metal grate? Shit required stitches. Now there's someone angry enough to kill, *and* he's Matt's best friend."

"Buddy is too dumb to be the killer," Alex said.

"On that, alone, we agree," Rodrigo said.

Makani glanced at the classroom door. Would anyone notice if she left?

"Are you gonna throw up?"

Makani looked back to find David staring at her. He seemed more bored than interested, but that might have just been his face. It was long and plain with an odd swoop of sandy hair across his fore-head. "You're clutching your stomach," he said.

"I guess I'm just ready to talk about anything else."

He shrugged. "Is there anything else to talk about?"

It was a valid question, but it made her feel even more alone.

In addition to the most obvious—and outlandish—suspects, speculation about Ollie and Zachary was also on the rise. *Ollie and Zachary. The loner and the asshole. The bullied and the bully.* Plenty of people had noticed Matt messing with Ollie only two days earlier, and several others had witnessed Zachary taunting Matt last month after the announcement that Matt would be crowned Homecoming King.

Makani had spent the homecoming game watching a werewolf movie in Darby's basement. When the game ended and her duties to the band were over, Alex had joined them. None of them went to the dance the following night. They hadn't been asked. Now the Home-coming King was dead. It was impossible to believe.

"Who do you think did it?" David asked.

Makani stared at the door. She couldn't keep her eyes off the exit. "I don't know. Maybe their deaths aren't even connected."

Darby's, Alex's, and Rodrigo's attention snapped back to her.

"I m-mean," Makani said, "of course they're connected, but what if Haley and Matt were *exactly* who we thought they were? What if there's no great conspiracy, and they were chosen simply because they were both popular?"

Alex shook her head. "Haley wasn't popular."

"She was well liked and respected. It's almost the same thing."

"Okay," Rodrigo said, "so your theory is that someone *un*popular killed them? Someone jealous of their status?"

Makani bristled. "I don't have a theory. I'm just saying we don't know."

"They wouldn't have to be unpopular," Alex said. "Just *less* popular."

"At least it means we'd all be safe," Rodrigo said.

Up until then, Makani hadn't been sure if Rodrigo was aware that he wasn't universally admired. It made her like him a little more. She would prefer to go unnoticed altogether. Unfortunately, the sharp end of her anonymity seemed to be rapidly approaching.

The police came for her during the last period of the day. It was Makani's only class with Ollie, but they'd hardly spoken before Señora Washington asked her to step into the hallway. The young, decidedly not Hispanic, Spanish teacher looked despondent with a touch of relief. It was the final name that she would have to call out.

"Best for last," the officer said as the door closed behind her. He wore a stiff, dark blue uniform, and his name tag read LARSSON.

Right. Because it had to be him.

Makani lifted a hand in acknowledgment. She was afraid that her voice might betray her nervousness, if her clammy skin didn't do it first.

"Hope you don't mind that I requested your interview." The grin was uncannily familiar. "I was curious who my little brother has a crush on."

She had no idea how to respond, so she didn't. The word *crush* was an invigorating jolt. But this easily ranked as one of the worst ways to meet a potential boyfriend's family. She'd been praying for any other officer.

Chris—Makani decided to think of him as *Chris* rather than *Officer Larsson,* because it was moderately less intimidating—led her to an empty room filled with electric typewriters. It was the keyboarding classroom. Freshmen were taught on typewriters, because it was too easy to cheat on computers. Copy and paste. Chris gestured to the hard orange chair that was stationed beside the teacher's desk.

Makani sat down obediently. The buzzing fluorescent lights were so harsh and stark for a room that felt so neglected and out of time. They made her feel naked. She crossed her arms, worried that it looked disrespectful, and then sat on her hands instead.

Chris rolled the comfortable teacher's chair toward her and took a seat. He examined her appearance, not unkindly. "How're you holding up?"

Makani knew she didn't look right. She looked twitchy and disturbed. It was better to admit it and hope that he assumed it was for normal reasons. "Not great."

"Yeah, I hear you. Everyone's shaken up pretty bad. Even us," he said, and she assumed he meant the police. "We've never seen anything like this in Osborne. Have your teachers given you the information about counseling?"

Ollie had been so good with her grandmother, yet here she was, completely failing with his brother. She'd spoken two words and could barely look at him, and he already thought she needed counseling.

Still, all she could do was nod. At least it was true. *Every* teacher had given them the information. The counselors would be slammed for months.

"Good. That's good." Chris removed a flippable notepad from his breast pocket and clicked a pen to the ready. "Now I just have a few questions. They're totally standard. We're asking everyone."

Another nod. Her hands began to sweat underneath her jeans.

His voice remained friendly, though it grew a touch sterner. *Cop voice.* "I know you're new around here, but were you acquainted with either of the victims?"

It was a peculiar thing. Makani had lived here for almost a year—plenty of time to have gotten to know the victims—but in a town like this, she would always be made to feel like the new girl. "No," she said. "I've never spoken to Haley."

I've never spoken instead of *I never spoke.* As if there were still a chance that they might bump into each other buying iced mochas at the gas station.

She adjusted her verbs. "Maybe I spoke to Matt once or twice in government class, because he sat near me, but I'm not even sure. If I did, it wasn't memorable."

The interrogation continued: *Do you know anyone the victims might have had trouble with? Were they ever bullied? Did they ever bully someone else?*

Makani answered each question in the negative, wondering how many of her classmates had possessed the audacity to mention Ollie. They would have all known that they were talking to his brother— same last name, similar appearance, infamous car.

Sergeant Beemer had interviewed Ollie during lunch. Ollie hadn't told Makani much, only that it'd taken the entire hour. Everybody else's interviews had taken just a few minutes. Was Ollie questioned about the episode with Matt in the quad? And had there been other episodes before it?

"Sorry." Makani shrugged at the industrial linoleum. "I'm not much help. I don't hang out with either of their crowds."

"That's okay. Everything helps." His tone had softened, and she looked up. Having successfully nabbed her attention, he broke into a mischievous smile. "Where were you yesterday between the hours of six and seven p.m.?"

Her cheeks exploded with heat.

His grin widened.

"I was with your brother." Makani cringed and crossed her arms. "He drove me home at six thirty, and then I made dinner with my grandma."

"And where had Ollie driven you?"

She moaned somewhat dramatically.

"Might I remind you that I'm an officer of the law?"

He was flat-out teasing her, so Makani steeled herself with a wry, defeated smile. "I honestly don't know. It was some random cornfield off 275, between here and Troy. We made out. He got a call from work, and then we left."

Chris made another notation on his notepad.

Makani sat up a bit straighter. "Why? What did *he* say?"

"Same thing." He looked pleased with himself. "I just wanted to hear you say it."

She actually laughed, which made him laugh, too. "Can I go now? Is this over?"

He waved for her to remain seated. "Almost."

Makani rebraced in anticipation of the inevitably awkward next question—*What are your intentions with my brother?*—which she would *not* answer, so she was caught off guard when Chris asked, "How much hunting experience do you have?"

"None." Her brow furrowed. "My dad used to take me fishing sometimes, but I was never really into it. Does that count?"

"Did you ever help him gut the fish?"

"No."

"How much experience would you say that you have with a knife?"

The blood drained from Makani's face. "W-why would you ask me that?"

Chris looked up from scribbling. He cocked his head. "Because the person we're trying to find has a certain level of skill with a knife and knowledge of anatomy."

"No." Her voice trembled. *"No."*

Thankfully, he must have jumped to the conclusion that she was upset by the reason for the question rather than the question itself. "You're okay," he assured her, tucking away his notepad. "That's all we needed to know."

Her heart was racing as he led her back into the hallway.

"I still have to interview the administrators, but at least you get to go home soon, huh?" Chris held out his hand. "Until we meet again."

Makani shook it. She wanted to say that it was nice to meet him. Instead, she rushed into the restroom.

She was already crying as she burst into the first stall—not for a specific reason, but for all of them. She wished that she were in Hawaii having a normal senior year. She wished that she could have been the appropriate blend of charming and sad for Chris. She wished that there weren't psychopaths who killed for pleasure and made the world feel unsafe. She wished that Ollie were her boyfriend, and that she could make out with him again, preferably as soon as possible. And she wished that she weren't so selfish to wish for a boyfriend when two of her classmates were dead.

If she stayed here any longer, people might wonder. Makani swallowed her tears, dried her face with a scratchy paper towel, and exited the bathroom.

Ollie was leaning against the wall beside the drinking fountains. His eyes were dark with under-eye circles. "You got my brother." It wasn't a question.

"Officer Larsson requested me specifically."

Ollie sighed.

"It was fine. He was nice." Makani glanced around, but the hallway was empty. "Were you . . . waiting for me?" And then she noticed her backpack on the floor near his feet. "Why do you have that?"

"I asked Señora Washington if I could use the bathroom. She

didn't even notice when I grabbed our bags. I saw you go inside, so I waited."

She'd been in there for over ten minutes. Panic floated to the surface, instantly accessible. "I was sitting. Just sitting. I didn't want to go back to class."

Ollie nodded.

"You should have knocked," she said.

He raised his eyebrows. They both knew that he would never have dared to knock on the door to the women's restroom. Too many potential embarrassing outcomes.

"No, sorry." Makani was exhausted and confused. None of this was making any sense. "But . . . *why* do you have my bag?"

"Are you okay?" he asked.

"What?" She shook her head. It was like they were having two different conversations. "No, I'm not okay. Are you okay?"

Ollie smiled. "Not at all."

Makani stared back at him until she erupted with helpless laughter. Tears returned to the corners of her eyes. "I have no idea what's happening."

"There are still twenty minutes until the final bell, but I'm leaving now." Ollie picked up her backpack and held it out. "Want a ride?"

CHAPTER NINE

THE ONLY PEOPLE who noticed their early departure were the reporters. They hovered like vultures between the campus and parking lot, waiting for the students to be let out for the weekend. Waiting for carrion. As Makani and Ollie neared, Makani's spine stiffened. She lowered her head and walked faster. Ollie adjusted his speed to match.

The reporters erupted all at once: *Did you know the victims? How would you describe the atmosphere inside the school today? Will this hurt your team's chances in the playoffs?* Microphones and cameras were jammed in their direction, and Makani angled her body away from the intrusion in the clearest possible signal, but a woman with a wall of hairsprayed bangs chased behind them anyway. "How does it feel to have lost two of your classmates in only three days?"

Makani focused on Ollie's car at the far end of the lot.

"How does it feel to have lost two of your classmates in three days?"

Car, car, car, car, car, car, car—

A hand touched Makani's shoulder, and she screamed. Her eyes looked manic with fright. The reporter stumbled backward into her cameraman, and Makani screamed again. The woman exclaimed something in confused anger, and suddenly Ollie stood between them shouting, "Get away from her! Get the fuck away from her!"

The cameraman placed a hand on the reporter's arm, urging her back, but she wasn't ready to yield. "You," she said. "Pink hair. How does it feel—"

"How the fuck do you think it feels?"

The cameraman pleaded with the reporter. "They're probably minors—"

Through the haze, Ollie reached for Makani. An arm slid around her back as he hustled her toward his car. *Car, car, car,* she thought. *Car.* He opened the passenger's door, helped her inside, and ran to the driver's side. All five of her senses were overloading. Instead of trying not to cry, Makani just tried not to sob.

She expected—maybe even wanted—him to tear out of the lot, but he exited cautiously and stuck to the speed limit. He turned left, away from the direction of her house, and drove until they reached the park near the elementary school.

The cruiser pulled over to a stop. Makani felt him trying to decide whether or not to lay a comforting hand on her arm. "I'm sorry," she said. Her overreaction was blatant and humiliating. She had to lie. "I don't know why . . ."

"You don't have anything to apologize for."

She sniffled, rummaging through her backpack for tissues.

Ollie leaned over her to pop open the glove compartment. It was lined with crumpled napkins from an out-of-town KFC.

She accepted a wad and blew her nose. There was no attractive way to do it. She felt like a monster. "It's been such a shitty day."

"*Such* a shitty day." He laughed once.

They sat in silence for a full minute. Makani stared out the window. The park was empty apart from a mom and toddler on the swings. "I don't want to go home." Her voice was weak and dispirited. "She'll want me to rehash everything that happened at school today, but I don't wanna talk about it. I can't think about it anymore."

Ollie nodded. He understood that she was talking about her grandmother. "Where would you like to go?"

"Someplace quiet."

So, Ollie took her to his house.

It was a twenty-minute drive, halfway between Osborne and East Bend on Highway 79, another lonely road of cornfields and cattle ranches. Every mile, they'd pass another highlighter-yellow billboard for the Martin Family Fun Corn Maze. A smiling family of cartoon redheads beamed at them from the top corner of each advertisement.

NEBRASKA'S LARGEST CORN MAZE! 5 MILES AHEAD!

PUMPKIN PATCH! 4 MILES AHEAD!

HAYRIDES! 3 MILES AHEAD!

PETTING ZOO! 2 MILES AHEAD!

CORN PIT! 1 MILE AHEAD!

"What's a corn pit?" Makani already felt lighter, knowing that she had a few hours' respite ahead of her. She'd texted Darby that Ollie was driving her home, and she'd texted Grandma Young that Darby was taking her to his house. Neither seemed pleased, but they'd each correctly assumed that she needed a distraction from the news.

"Exactly what it sounds like," Ollie said. "A giant pit of corn kernels."

"Okay. But what does one *do* with a corn pit?"

He glanced at her with a smile. "You know those ball pits at

McDonald's? It's like that, but bigger. A lot bigger. It's pretty fun," he admitted. "Now, the petting zoo. That's what I could do without. When the wind blows just right . . ."

Makani laughed as circus-like flags appeared through the fields. They passed the sprawling maze and a massive dirt parking lot, which was mostly vacant. "Does anyone actually come here?"

"It's packed on the weekends. People drive in from Omaha and Lincoln. And it's loud. You can hear it in my house. On Saturdays, they even have a polka band. When our windows are open, I'll often find my feet tapping to the belch of their tuba."

She laughed again. "I'm still imagining you swimming in the corn pit."

Ollie kept his eyes ahead, but they twinkled. Or maybe gleamed.

He turned onto the next road. A gentle hill broke up the flatness of the surrounding earth. It was the hushed, eerie beauty of Willa Cather country, a century later. Sophomore year, she'd been assigned to read *O Pioneers!* in English class, and the familiar descriptions of the land had comforted her. They'd reminded her of visiting her favorite grandmother. Little did she know that, soon enough, she'd be living here.

The novel no longer held any appeal. It wasn't fictional anymore.

A house in the distance grew bigger, and Makani realized that the road was Ollie's driveway. His house was white, like hers, but peeling and weatherworn. It was a Victorian Gothic Revival—a style that was growing obsolete in these parts—with three dramatically arched windows under three steeply pitched roof points. Twin columns framed a modest covered porch. The expansive yard was unkempt and overgrown.

Makani was grateful that she didn't believe in ghosts; she only believed in the ghostlike quality of painful memories. And she was sure this house had plenty.

Not everything about it was gloomy, however. As she stepped out of the car, a set of wind chimes jangled in the breeze and two large ferns swayed on chains from opposite ends of the porch. They were dead from the early frosts. But proof of recent habitation.

Ollie shot her a nervous glance. "Home sweet home."

Had he ever brought home a girl before, or was this something new for him? Something potentially vulnerable? On the disintegrating coir welcome mat, a single word was barely visible: LARSSON.

The younger Larsson unlocked the front door, which opened into a large, dim, and dusty room. "I know." He sighed. "It looks like a haunted house."

Makani held up two innocent hands. "I didn't say a word."

He led her inside with a tight smile. The floors were old hardwood, and the boards groaned with each step. Makani waited in the threshold while Ollie threw open the curtains. Sparkling dust motes caught in the sudden light as the living room was revealed to be more homelike, more *normal,* than anticipated. She couldn't help feeling relieved. The rugs, lamps, and hardware seemed to be a mixture of Victorian reproductions and actual Victorian antiques, but the sectional sofa was firmly from this century.

Though . . . there *was* something about the space. It possessed an unnatural amount of stillness. Everything appeared unruffled. Unused.

"Would you like something to drink?" Ollie asked. "We have water, orange juice, Coke—well, it's not Coca-Cola, it's the off-brand Coke—"

Makani laughed, because he'd remembered. "Water's fine."

"Tap water? Ice? No ice?"

She trailed behind him through the adjoining dining room, which was also murky and untouched. Ollie moved like a creature of habit. "Whichever's more work for you," she called out, even though the temperature inside wasn't much warmer than it had been outside. She didn't want ice.

At least the kitchen was brighter. Much brighter. Curtainless windows looked out upon the sweeping fields, and the maze's flags waved merrily in the distance. Ollie's kitchen, though not as clean as Grandma Young's, was less dusty than the other rooms, and the dishes had been recently washed and were drying on a rack. And while the cabinetry and furniture didn't look exactly modern, they didn't look Victorian, either.

A shadow lurched out from the floorboards.

Makani shrieked as a small dog with a speckled, bluish-gray coat skittered and stumbled toward Ollie.

Laughing, he kneeled to greet the intruder. "Hey, Squidward."

For the second time in an hour, she'd completely lost her shit. Makani felt embarrassed, all over again. "Sorry. I didn't know you had a dog."

"Blue heeler." Ollie smiled as he rubbed its head. "Back when we adopted him, I was a big *SpongeBob* fan. Now he's deaf and almost blind. He sleeps most of the day—that's why he didn't notice when we came in." Squidward leaned against him, as if he were using Ollie to keep himself upright. "How are you, buddy?"

Makani squatted to pet him. "Is he friendly?"

"If you let him sniff your hand first, you'll be fine."

Squidward himself kind of smelled, but Makani didn't mind. His fur was coarse, almost waxy. But it felt nice to be petting a dog and even nicer to be this close to Ollie.

"Do you have a dog? Back home?" Ollie looked aside as he added this second question, aware of how infrequently she spoke of her past.

But dogs were a safe subject. Makani shook her head as Squidward rolled onto his back. "My mom claims she's allergic. Really, she just thinks they're too messy."

"We have a cat, too. She's probably outside right now."

"Sandy Cheeks?"

He grinned. "Raven."

"Ah. A *much* cooler name."

"Not necessarily. At the time, I had a massive crush on Raven-Symoné."

Makani laughed.

Ollie rubbed Squidward's belly. "I have no idea why my parents let me name our pets."

"Because, clearly, your parents were awesome." But she flinched as soon as it came out. Was it okay to mention them? Although, he was the one who brought them up.

And now he was nodding in agreement.

It occurred to her that perhaps Ollie appreciated the acknowledgment of his parents. Perhaps it was harder when people went out of their way to avoid talking about them—when they pretended like his parents had never existed in the first place.

Makani often pretended like hers didn't exist. At her grandmother's insistence, she called her mother once a week and her father every other week. They didn't even know what was happening here, because, until this moment, she hadn't thought to tell them. Her parents always spent the too-long calls complaining about each other.

Ollie washed the dog off his hands and grabbed two burritos from the freezer. He held them up for her. They were both bean and cheese. "One or two?"

Makani longed for a piping hot bowl of saimin, a noodle dish so common back home that it was on the menu at McDonald's. Osborne didn't even have a non-saimin McDonald's. But burritos were decent. Better than whatever she'd be making for dinner with her grandmother. "One, please," she said. "Thanks."

He slipped off their wrappers, hesitated, and then grabbed another burrito for himself. All three went into the microwave.

As she scratched behind Squidward's ears, Makani stared at a faded photograph on the refrigerator. Ollie's parents stood in front of Old Faithful. Their arms were around each other, and they were smiling as the geyser sprayed above their heads like a whale's blowhole. His father's smile was farmer-stiff, but his mother looked carefree.

Beside it was a photo of Ollie and his brother. Ollie looked old enough to be in high school, but he was still younger than she'd ever known him. His hair was an odd, streaky green, and he was wince-laughing as Chris pulled him into a forced hug. She wondered if their parents were already dead and who had taken the picture.

"I tried to dye it blue." Like always, Ollie had been watching her. "One of the first lessons that you learn in school—yellow and blue make green—and I forgot."

"You look like a mermaid. A sad, pubescent mermaid."

Ollie froze. And then he covered his face, shaking his head in disbelief. "That might be the actual worst thing that anyone has ever said to me."

"No!" As Makani burst into laughter, she smiled with all her teeth. "I mean, I stand by my assessment. But I swear I have pictures that are just as bad. Worse, even."

"I demand proof."

"Fair enough. The next time you're at my house, take a peek under my bed."

Ollie blinked. And then his eyebrows rose, perhaps at the mention of her bed.

"Seventh-grade swim team." Makani shuddered as she recalled her flat chest, gawky posture, and unflattering suit. "Let's leave it at that."

The microwave let out an extensive series of beeps. As Ollie removed the steaming burritos, he glanced at her. "You're a swimmer?"

Shit.

She couldn't believe it had slipped out. Since the age of seven, she'd dived competitively, but her grandmother was the only person here who knew it. Osborne didn't even have a swim team. And even if it did, those days had passed.

"I used to swim." She looked away. "A little."

Her eyes snagged on a brown file folder. It was sitting in the center of the breakfast table. She didn't have to open it to know what it contained.

Ollie followed her gaze. "See? He's practically asking me to read it."

"Why didn't he take it with him?"

"I'm sure he just forgot. Happens all the time."

The case file was thick. "Isn't a good memory kinda important for an officer?"

Luckily, Ollie didn't take offense. "That's why they write everything down. Cops do shit-tons of paperwork." He shrugged. "Memories aren't reliable, anyway."

Makani wished that she could forget. In the darkest hours of the night, her own memory was keen and cruel.

"You can look if you want." Ollie's voice tensed. "It isn't pretty."

Of course she wanted to look—sheer human curiosity demanded it—but there would be no *un*looking once she'd done it. Her fingertips crawled toward the file anyway. They recklessly flicked it open to reveal a stack of photographs and papers. A female body lay on her back, right arm hanging limp from a bed. Her neck had been carved open by five crude slices. One for the mouth, two for each eye. X and X.

Dead cartoon eyes.

In Makani's imagination, this scene, this smiley face, had been tidy and precise, but in reality . . . it was a bloodbath. The head was tilted too far back to see Haley's real eyes. The longest cut was deep and vicious, and her neck skin flapped open in a jagged, ugly gash. Her hair, clothing, and bedsheets were soaked with enough blood to curdle a butcher's stomach. Blood had dried inside her nostrils.

Makani closed the file with a shaking hand.

"Bad, right?" Ollie said.

It wasn't just bad. It was horrific.

A real dead body looked different from the ones on television or in the movies. There was nothing artful about it. Nothing positioned. Haley's body looked lifeless—but not like life had been taken away from it. Like it had never had life.

Ollie pressed his fingers to his temples. "I should have warned you."

"You did." Makani hugged herself. Was Matt in that stack of photos, too, or did he have a separate file? The brutality of the crime overwhelmed her. *Someone did this.* A real person had crept into Haley's house and murdered her in her own bed.

"Any chance the police have a lead?" she asked.

Ollie shook his head. "But they do think it's probably someone a lot smaller than Matt."

"So, not another football player."

"Right."

"Why?"

He waited for her to meet his eyes. "Are you sure you want to know?"

Makani nodded.

"Before the killer did . . . what they did, they stabbed Matt in the gut. But his abdomen had nothing to do with the final display of his brain. So, he was probably attacked by someone who physically *couldn't* go straight for his head. They had to weaken him first. Bring him down to their level."

Perhaps the killer was female, after all.

Dead cartoon eyes. Blood inside her nostrils.

Makani became aware of a dinner plate being pushed gently against her stomach.

"Hey," Ollie said. "It's nicer in my room."

She stared down at the warm plate. Was Matt stabbed once in the abdomen or had it taken multiple jabs for him to go down?

Wordlessly, she accepted the burritos. Ollie carried their water glasses. As the stairs creaked beneath their feet, Makani wondered how many gruesome pictures he'd seen since his brother became a cop. Sure, there had never been deaths in Osborne this violent before, but people died by accident all the time. People like his parents.

Did it get easier to look at the photos? Or did it get harder, knowing that so many people died so young—and in such awful ways? Did seeing the proof of this make you more paranoid or more careful? Or did it just harden you?

Old photographs were everywhere. A framed studio portrait of his whole family hung at the top of the upstairs landing. Ollie was so little that his mother held him on her lap. What was it like for him to look at this one every day?

"It's this one," he said, pulling the phrase from her mind.

Makani had assumed that his bedroom would be as black and unembellished as his wardrobe, so when he opened the door, she blinked in surprise.

The room was filled with sunlight and signs of life. Even the kitchen clung to a whiff of abandonment, but here, Ollie's ubiquitous paperbacks were spread across every surface. There were too many for his shelves, so they'd spilled onto his rug, been stacked on top of his desk and under it, and even lay in messy piles on his unmade bed. With its heap of mismatched blankets, the bed looked like the coziest spot in the entire house.

Makani set down the plate on his desk and picked up the closest book, *Jupiter's Travels*. "Four years around the world on a Triumph," she read aloud. On the cover, a man in an old-fashioned leather jacket rode an old-fashioned motorcycle. The paperback smelled old, too, like dusty shelves and faint mildew. She used it to gesture around the room. "I knew you liked to read, but . . . wow."

Ollie shrugged with his hands in his pockets. "I get them from garage sales and the used bookstore in East Bend. I haven't read them all. I just keep picking them up."

"I wasn't making fun of you. My last boyfriend read a lot, too."

Shit. Double shit.

Ollie wasn't her boyfriend. They barely knew each other. She wanted to know more about him—she *wanted* him to be her boyfriend—but they were each still standing behind a wall of unspoken history. She decided to act like she hadn't meant anything by it and casually picked up another book. Glanced at him. His pale skin was unable to hide an emotional flush. At least he didn't seem turned off by the idea.

Makani had been surprised in Darby's car yesterday morning when she'd realized that Ollie was more shy than he was rebellious, but she was even more surprised now to realize that she found his shyness attractive.

She held up a travel guide to Italy. "Mind if I go with you?"

"We'll leave tonight." Ollie stepped toward her, and her heart spasmed. But he had only come closer to remove his keys from his pocket and take the plate to his bed.

Disappointed, she flipped open the guidebook. "Positano. Hotel Intermezzo. Excellent value in this charming, family-run hotel overlooking the sea." She carried the book to his bed and plopped down beside him. "Shall I call for a reservation?"

Ollie smiled as he bit into a burrito. He held out the plate with his other hand. She accepted one. It was strange sharing a plate, but she liked it. It made her feel close to him.

"Tell me," he said.

Makani swallowed before speaking. The cheap burrito was thoroughly mediocre but immensely satisfying. "Tell you what?"

"About your last boyfriend. The reader."

She smiled. Caught. And then she nudged his leg with her knee-cap, pleased by his obvious jealousy. "I thought I'd steered us away from that conversation."

"You tried. Usually, you're good at that. At steering away."

It was the first time that it had been acknowledged out loud. She felt chastised but rose to the challenge. "Okay, here's my offer. I'll tell you about my last boyfriend if you tell me about your last girlfriend."

Ollie considered it for a few seconds. "Deal."

Makani steeled herself to remain honest. "His name was Jason Nakamura, and we dated for seven months." She tried to gauge Ollie's expression. It remained maddeningly enigmatic. "He was a swimmer, too. Freestyle."

But then he wouldn't talk to me anymore.

"But then I moved away."

"Did you try to make it work long distance?" Ollie asked.

She discarded her final bite back onto the plate, an end piece of freezer-hardened tortilla. "That would be a *very* long distance." When he waited for elaboration, she selected her next words carefully. "No. We didn't like each other enough."

Ollie nodded with understanding.

She braced herself. "Your turn. Last girlfriend."

He set the plate onto the floor with a hollow clunk. "No one."

It wasn't the answer she was expecting. She stared at him, searching for comprehension. He stared back as he repeated it. "No one."

"Explain. Use more words."

A smile tugged at his lips. "I've never had a girlfriend."

Makani had made out with him. Makani had had *sex* with him. She found this statement to be highly improbable. He knew what she was thinking, and he shrugged, but it wasn't a shrug of indifference. It was a shrug that was hiding some measure of embarrassment. "I've never had a girlfriend, but, yes, obviously I've had sex before you."

Makani couldn't let that one sit. "Obviously."

Ollie squirmed and glanced up at the ceiling. "Not *obviously* because I was *amazing. Obviously* because . . ."

"Oh, no. No, no, no." Her hair bounced as she shook her head. "I need to hear you finish that sentence."

His expression deadpanned. "Because I lasted more than thirty seconds."

She burst into raucous laughter, which made him smile. Ollie always smiled when he saw that she was happy. Makani leaned into the space between them. "So, are you gonna tell me about this non-girlfriend? Non-girlfriends?"

His smile widened into a grin. "Yes."

She moved in closer, beckoning. "But not today?"

Their lips were an inch apart.

"Not today," he said.

They went for each other at the same time. Mouths clashed. Jackets peeled off. She lowered herself onto her back, and he moved above her, pressing down. The weight of his body made her feral. Her fingers clawed under his shirt and up his back as his hands slid over her bra. Her hands moved to the bottom of her shirt, ready to strip it above her head, when suddenly . . . they were aware.

A third person was in the room.

CHAPTER TEN

CHRIS STOOD IN the doorway and swore. And then swore again. "Damn it, Ollie!"

Ollie scrambled to sit up, scrambled to make sure that Makani was covered even though they hadn't gotten that far. "What are you doing here?"

His brother rubbed his forehead. "Nice to see you again so soon, Makani."

Her skin burst into flames as she shielded herself behind Ollie, who tried again. "Why are you *home*?"

Chris dropped his hand and crossed his arms, drawing her eyes to the holster on his belt. "Chief sent me away to get some rest." He glanced warily at the empty plate beside the bed. "When did you get here? Did you ditch again?"

Ollie didn't reply.

"Shit, Ollie. You can't . . . you can't *do* that."

Makani wished that she could run. She wished that she were anywhere but here.

"We missed zero schoolwork," Ollie said. "Nothing was happening."

"If nothing was happening," Chris said, "then it shouldn't have been so hard to keep seated until the bell." When Ollie tightened his mouth, Chris groaned and collapsed into the desk chair. He followed it with a long sigh. "Listen. There's a killer on the loose, and we don't know who or where he is. Or if he's even a he. That means *your* ass needs to be where it's supposed to be at all times. I need to know where you are."

"Why?" Ollie sounded remarkably incredulous for this reasonable request.

"Because it's dangerous out there!"

"They murdered the star of the musical and the star of the football team. Tell me what I have in common with those victims."

"You know that's not the point. Shit," Chris said again. He turned his attention to Makani. "You've gotta stop hanging out with this kid. He's a bad influence."

Makani felt a wave of gratitude that he didn't view *her* as the bad influence. She ventured out from behind Ollie.

"Does your grandmother know you're here?" Chris asked.

She wanted to lie, but he was a cop. "No."

Chris shook his head. He picked up Ollie's keys from the desk and held them out, staring at the hardwood floor. "Ollie, drive her home."

"Chris—"

"*Ollie.*"

Ollie stomped over, snatched the keys in a way that made Chris wince, and then stalked out of his bedroom.

Makani followed, but she glanced back to lift a hand in goodbye. Chris raised a weary hand in return. "Sorry. But I have to."

It was a strange thing for a parental figure to say, and it reminded her of the unnatural relationship that he'd been forced to play in his brother's life. In that moment, she felt sorry for Chris. Ollie hadn't made it easy for him. Then again, nothing about Ollie's life seemed to have been easy, either.

That night—when Haley and the drama club were supposed to be in the middle of their first dress rehearsal, when Matt and the football team were supposed to be winning their final game of the season—Darby sent a text to Makani: *Can we talk?*

She'd just finished loading the dirty dinner dishes into the dishwasher. Grandma Young was watching a Marvel movie in the living room. She didn't know that Makani had been to Ollie's house, and Makani planned to keep it that way.

"Will Chris tell her?" she'd asked on the somber drive home.

Ollie tried to assure her, despite the crease in his brow. "I doubt it. His weakness is that he still wants to be my cool older brother."

To be safe, they made Saturday plans in full view of Grandma Young. He was going to come over before his shift at Greeley's.

I mean, phone-talk?

Makani frowned at the second message. It was always ominous when someone asked to talk instead of text. She told her grandmother that she'd join her in a minute and waited until she was safely enclosed in her bedroom before hitting the call button.

Darby picked up after the second ring. "Thanks."

"Yeah, what's up?"

An awkward silence followed. Another bad sign.

"Darby?"

"I—I just want you to know that as your friend, I love you, and that's why I'm telling you this."

Makani felt her body temperature drop. "Tell me what?"

"And you know I would never say this if it weren't important. If Alex and I weren't genuinely concerned."

"*What*, Darby?"

He mumbled something rapidly that contained the name Ollie.

A surge of hot anger replaced Makani's chill, but she tamped it down and asked him to repeat that last sentence.

The accusation spewed forth in a torrent. "Discounting rumors, it's still a fact that Matt and his friends have been bullying Ollie for years, and his alibi isn't strong for either murder, and we think he might be taking advantage of you, and Alex said I had to be the one to call, because you'd just tell her to screw herself, or you'd think she was joking, but I swear we're not." He took a breath. "Not that we think he's guilty! But that *was* creepy how he got your phone number. You have to admit it."

Makani didn't have to admit anything. It was misguided and insulting. "So, what? You and Alex just sat there at the Feed 'N' Seed all afternoon, selling cattle supplements and talking shit about me?"

"No!" Darby sounded miserable. "I'm sorry. We're worried about you."

"Yeah. You mentioned something along those lines yesterday, re-member?"

His voice dropped into a meek whisper. "It didn't seem like you were listening."

Fury overtook her like an explosion from a pressure cooker. "And what about Haley, huh? What did Haley ever do to Ollie? Why would he kill her?"

"In eighth grade, he asked her out, and she said no. She was a seventh grader. He was humiliated. It wasn't long after his parents had died, and it was the last time I heard of him asking out someone from school until . . . this weird thing with you."

It shocked her into speechlessness. She hadn't expected Darby to have a real answer. But it was still a colossal leap.

"Makani? Hello? Are you there?"

"That was four years ago." She forced her voice into a normal volume, despite the outrage swelling inside her again. "That's a long time to wait for a petty grudge."

"Just consider this: Ollie snubbed you for months. You guys hadn't talked since the end of summer. It's possible . . . he might want revenge on you, too."

She sucked in her breath.

"Regaining your trust could be a part of his master plan—"

"Master plan?"

"I only meant—"

"I was mad at him, too! It was mutual. A stupid misunderstanding."

"You're right, it's probably nothing." Darby backed down to plead with her. "But you have to understand that I could never live with myself if he turned out to be the bad guy, and I'd kept my mouth shut."

Makani's indignation dissipated. Flared back into raging life. And finally re-extinguished. Darby was trying to be a good friend. He was just getting it wrong. On paper, fine, Ollie looked suspicious. But he wasn't a murderer.

She couldn't prove it. She just knew it.

Ollie was shy and helpful, and he looked happy whenever she was happy. Darby's confrontation hurt, because he was supposed to be the thoughtful friend. Alex was the impulsive one. And it confirmed her fears; they really did talk about her behind her back.

Darby sounded distant through her buzzing eardrums. "Makani?"

"I appreciate your concern." It was a lie and not a lie. "But you're wrong."

And then she hung up.

•　　•　　•

All night long, Makani tossed and turned. The house creaked like it was alive.

Ollie, Haley.

Ollie, Matt.

Ollie, Me.

All morning long, she ignored the apology texts from Darby and the jokey texts that acted as apologies from Alex.

Ollie, Haley.

Ollie, Matt.

Ollie, Me.

At noon, she was surprised to discover yesterday's shoes still at the bottom of the stairs. She grabbed them before Grandma Young could scold her.

Ollie, Haley.

Ollie, Matt.

Ollie—

NO.

Makani threw the sneakers, hard, onto her bedroom floor. Yesterday's socks were already lying beside the closet door, but the strangeness of this did not register to her.

She had to believe that the mistakes of Ollie's past didn't guarantee that he would make even worse mistakes in his future. She had to believe that every mistake was still a *choice*. She had to believe that Ollie was a good person, because she had to believe it about herself.

He arrived in the early afternoon. After the cycle of beverage options, they settled into the living room, because—as Makani learned—it was against house rules to have a boy in her bedroom. As her friend,

Darby was the only exception. Back in Hawaii, she'd spent plenty of time in her bedroom with her ex-boyfriend. Her parents either hadn't noticed or didn't care.

The television was tuned to the closest physical station, which was broadcasting a basketball game. Neither Makani nor her grandmother followed the NBA, but Grandma Young was anxious to see the local news bumpers. Makani slouched beside her on the sofa while Ollie resumed his position in the easy chair.

Ollie hadn't been kidding. He really did like jigsaw puzzles. A countryside harvest festival was spread across the coffee table, and its repeating autumnal patterns held him and Grandma Young in a matching trance. Perched on their seat edges, they bonded over etiquette and strategy: start with the border. Then any sections that contain printed words. If someone is searching for one specific piece, but the other person finds it, it must be handed over, because it means more to the first person. And always save the sky—the hardest part of any puzzle—for last.

Makani tried to join in, but the tediousness made her hungry, so she brought out snacks and ate snacks and brought out more snacks. She wondered if her ex would have entertained her grandmother without complaint. Before the incident, she would have said yes. Jason was wild, but she had been wilder. And he was a decent guy.

He was also a coward who'd never bothered to ask for her side of the story. A coward who'd ignored her instead of dumping her outright. A coward who'd treated her like the highly contagious carrier of a deadly plague. Though, in a way, she was. Makani was a social plague. She hated Jason for his cowardice, but she understood it.

"You know, we've just been praying for their families, day and night."

They looked up at the sound of the young, country voice. A square-faced boy with a cross necklace and LION PRIDE sweatshirt—the de

facto spokesperson for the various local youth groups—was on television. The text at the bottom of the screen read: CALEB GREELEY,
FRIEND OF THE VICTIMS.

The bumper cut to a blandly handsome man in a navy-blue suit.
"Osborne reacts to the slayings and to a killer still at large. Details at
six." Creston Howard enunciated with the practiced air of a professional, managing to sound both solemn and upbeat.

The basketball game resumed. Grandma Young turned to Ollie.
"That was Pastor Greeley's boy, wasn't it?"

Ollie nodded. "He works with me at the grocery store."

It was a familiar conversation, Ollie and her grandmother swap-
ping information about mutual acquaintances. Makani hadn't recognized many of the names until now. "Oh. *Greeley*," she said. "Caleb is
related to the owner?"

"Caleb is the grandson of the original Mr. Greeley," Ollie explained. "His uncle runs Greeley's Foods now."

"And what does Caleb do there?" Grandma Young asked.

"Weekend supervisor."

Makani couldn't hear it in his tone, but she wondered if Ollie
was bitter that Caleb was a supervisor when Ollie was the one who
worked more hours. If it were her, she'd be bitter. "Caleb wasn't actually a *friend* of the victims, was he?"

Ollie smirked. "As friendly as I was."

Makani nudged her grandmother. "See? You have to turn off the
news. It's not even telling you the truth."

"You grieve in your way," Grandma Young said, "and I'll grieve
in mine."

Despite the outside world, their living room was at ease. Makani
wondered why discussing a tragedy—consuming every single story
about it—*was* often comforting. Was it because tragedies manifested
a sense of community? *Here we are, all going through this terrible*

thing together. Or were tragedies addictive, and the small pleasures that came from them the signal of a deeper problem?

Ollie handed over a puzzle piece to Grandma Young. She exclaimed with delight and snapped it into place. They high-fived.

No, Makani decided. It was impossible that this boy who was so kind to her grandmother could ever be a murderer.

CHAPTER ELEVEN

THERE WAS A machete wedged behind the empty watercooler. He couldn't believe that someone had hidden it here, of all places. He yanked out the large plastic bottle and threw it at the woman, gaining the precious seconds necessary to reach back and fumble for the weapon. The bottle hit her head with a satisfying *thonk*. As she staggered, his hand clasped around the wooden handle. The machete came loose with just enough time to thrust it forward between her ribs. She fell against the copy machine. Planting his boot on her chest, he tugged out the blade before lifting it over his head and swinging it back down through her neck in a single, swift motion. Her head splattered against the cubicle and then dropped into a recycle bin. He held out the machete to admire it.

Yes. This will do nicely.

But to keep it, he had to discard one of his other weapons, so he placed the tire iron behind the watercooler for someone else to find. That made him smile.

Rodrigo Morales paused the game and tossed aside the controller. He took off his headphones. Rubbed his eyes. It was midnight.

His parents were carousing in Vegas for their silver wedding anniversary, and he wasn't about to let a single minute of this glorious weekend go to waste. He'd spent Friday night and all today fighting the zombies in *Battleground Apocalypse* with only one short nap, and he'd fight them all Sunday, too.

He was the youngest of four children and the only son. His last sister had moved out in mid-August, and now with his parents out of town, this was the first time in his entire life that he'd ever been truly alone. He relished it.

Rodrigo stood, and his spine cracked from bottom to top. He rolled his neck in a methodical circle. Stretched his arms toward the ceiling. *Wake up,* he ordered himself.

He slumped out of the living room and into the kitchen for an energy drink. It was a new brand—JACKD, in aggressive all caps— and it came in a lurid green can. Despite the marketing campaign's flagrant promises, it wasn't better than any of the others. He'd been building up his tolerance for years. He chugged a full can. Half a sausage pizza had congealed on the stovetop from earlier, so he finished it off while checking his phone.

Kevin still uses Ubuntu lol

It was a text from David. He was binging classic anime with their other friends at Kevin's house. Anime sucked, and Rodrigo was glad to be missing it. Except, he didn't *totally* think it sucked. He liked *Attack on Titan* when they forced him to watch it last year, but he couldn't help it. Something inside him made him pretend that he didn't.

I wouldn't even put that distro on mi abuela's computer, Rodrigo replied.

David lol'd again. Their friends were a joke when it came to operating systems. Not that David was much better. He tried to keep up with Rodrigo, but nobody around here could. In elementary school,

Rodrigo had jailbroken iPhones and Kindles for extra cash. Now he had eight different PAYware games on all the app stores. His latest—a dumb game about popping rainbow bubbles—was raking it in.

Binge so lame you need me to keep you entertained? Rodrigo asked.

Nah we're watching cowboy bebop. It's cool.

Rodrigo had vaguely heard of it, but he researched its plot as he moved into the bathroom to take a piss. It was some space cowboy bullshit. He didn't bother replying. He checked his favorite message board, but the usual torch-and-pitchfork crowd were still up in arms over this new company of video game developers that was run entirely by women. His insides shrank with a familiar shame as he quickly left the page. Not that long ago, he'd been one of them.

He cringed as he remembered what he'd said to Makani Young. *I'll give you a ride home, sweetheart.* If his sisters had heard it, they would have kicked him in the cojones. But the line had just slipped out. A knee-jerk, base-level wisecrack. He wasn't that guy anymore. He still didn't understand how he'd ever been that guy.

He walked back into the living room and found that his gaming rocker was facing the wrong direction. Strange. He didn't remember tripping over it.

Rodrigo turned it around, plopped down, and put on his headphones. The game's death-metal pause music blasted in his ears. Had Makani told Alex what he'd said? Probably, which sucked. Alex was smart and sexy and kind of mean, but mean in the same way he was. And sometimes it seemed like she might like him back.

A powerful buzz hit his system. At first, he thought it was from imagining Alex in her torn fishnets, until he realized it must be the energy drink. His bloodstream glowed electric.

Rodrigo unpaused the game. A zombie shot out from the closest cubicle, but he was ready, and he hacked off its emaciated head. He ran through the dilapidated office with his machete aimed high. He was invincible.

An hour later, Rodrigo was asleep.

Somehow, he'd managed to pause the game before he crashed. But he didn't get up. He fell asleep with his headphones still on, the music still pulsing and thrashing.

The sunlight streamed in through the glass back doors. It was so bright that it was painful. Rodrigo squinted, blocking the assault with his hand, and knocked over a full can of JACKD. The chartreuse liquid spilled across his mother's immaculate Mexican rug.

"Shit!" Rodrigo uprighted the aluminum can, but the liquid had already stopped beading. It was seeping into the threads. He lurched to his feet, but the headphones cord yanked him back down, and he fumbled to throw off the whole contraption.

His ears rang in the emptiness of the house. Death metal pumped quietly from the headphones on the floor. He didn't even remember grabbing another energy drink. He only remembered the one that he'd chugged in the kitchen.

A headache ruptured his brain. Was it possible to get a hangover from energy drinks? He turned off the music, and the silence was a cathedral. Rodrigo rubbed his eyeballs through his lids with the palms of his hands. When he opened them, the pinpricks disappeared but . . . something wasn't right.

He was in his living room. Except he wasn't. Or was he turned around? Instead of facing the television, his gaming rocker was facing the couch. Rodrigo looked behind himself. The television was sitting on its stand in the middle of the room. Dead center.

There was a pause of incomprehension.

And then his mind snowballed with panic.

All at once, his gaze absorbed the rest of the room. The two chairs that flanked the couch had been switched. The coffee table was blocking the sliding doors. The fiddle-leaf fig had been moved from beside the doors to the opposite wall, and the floor lamp, usually nestled beside the couch, had been placed beside the fiddle-leaf fig.

His rocker was the only piece of furniture in the correct place.

Rodrigo's heartbeat pounded inside his ears as he tried to piece everything together. Tried to make *sense* of it.

David. It seemed like the sort of prank he'd pull. He had a weird, unpredictable side that Rodrigo didn't always like. Or maybe Sofía, his youngest and most irritating sister. The one who'd finally moved into an apartment at the end of summer.

"Sofía?" He rose to his feet. "David? Are you still here?"

The house didn't answer.

"Ha-ha. Very funny. You got me."

The house still didn't answer.

"What the *shit*," Rodrigo mumbled as he stepped straight into a puddle. In his shock, he'd forgotten about the spilled drink. He jogged to the kitchen for paper towels, but they weren't in the holder underneath the high cabinets.

They were sitting on the center of the island.

Rodrigo knew that he should laugh—whoever this was, they'd gotten him again—but he couldn't. Not yet. Maybe because no one had jumped out to yell gotcha and point their finger.

Had *he* moved everything last night?

It was possible. Maybe.

He checked all the doors, just in case. They were locked. He jogged a little faster as he checked the windows. The one in the guest bathroom was open. His blood turned cold.

Not Sofía, then. She still had a key.

David? Or Kevin? Rodrigo released a foul stream of expletives, realizing it was probably *all* his friends, those fucking assholes, getting revenge on him for turning down their stupid animefest. That's why David had texted him at midnight. They were checking to see if he was still awake. Rodrigo circled the interior of his house, waiting for them to appear. But the rooms were empty.

Rationally, Rodrigo knew that this prank was genius. Breaking into someone's house in the dead of night to rearrange their furniture while they slept? He wished he'd thought of it. It would have scared the hell out of Sofía.

But the reality of it wasn't funny. There were no silly notes, no *Are you awake?* texts, no red-lipsticked warnings on his bathroom mirror. The whole situation felt off.

Instinct told him to call the police, but . . . that was dumb. Wasn't it? He checked his phone for the hundredth time, and when there weren't any messages, he sent a text to the whole group. *LOL you got me. Who did it?*

There was an electronic *ding*, and Rodrigo spun around, yelling and tripping over his feet as he stumbled backward in fear. A slender figure stood motionless in his kitchen. Their slouched back was facing him, and they were wearing a hoodie with the hood up.

"H-hey." Rodrigo's voice came out as a croak.

The figure didn't move.

Rodrigo hated that he felt so terrified. Whoever this was, he was about to be *pissed* at them. The person was too skinny to be one of his sisters.

He crept forward. "David? Is that you?"

The figure didn't move.

"Emily?" She was the smallest in his group of friends. He felt ashamed to think about her hearing the tremor in his speech, but the figure . . . it was so unnaturally still.

What if it *wasn't* someone he knew?

His white socks touched the edge of the kitchen floor. His T-shirt was damp with sweat. He reached out to touch the figure's shoulder—

The killer spun around and lunged. The knife went straight into Rodrigo's heart and back out, a *shuck-shuck* that sunk him to his knees, and then the blade stabbed him in the back again and again and again. Rodrigo gasped. And then gurgled.

And then nothing.

The body lay on the floor like a slaughtered calf. Blood pooled beneath it. The white cabinets were sprayed with a gory red, and the thickest drops trickled down the doors like tears. The killer lifted the deflated carcass under its arms and dragged it to the living room. Propped it in the rocker. Sawed off its ears. The ears were stuffed into the headphones, and then the headphones were placed onto the head.

The killer sat on the rug—crisscross applesauce—picked up the abandoned controller, and unpaused the game. There was no hurry.

No one would be home for hours.

CHAPTER TWELVE

RODRIGO MORALES CHANGED everything. In the early hours of Monday morning, the students of Osborne High were instructed not to come to school. Classes were canceled until further notice. Students were urged to stay home or, if their parents would be at work, stay in the home of a trusted friend. It wasn't safe to be alone.

In the wake of this developing tragedy . . .

The official texts, emails, and voicemails all repeated this same illogical and clunky phrase. No information was provided regarding the third victim, but the town's collective mind was many tentacled and far-reaching. The Morales family had neighbors, several of whom had been startled awake by flashing police lights shortly after 2:00 a.m.

At breakfast, everybody followed the story on two screens—phone and television. Makani jumped as a plate was set down in front of her. She'd only been tangentially aware of Grandma Young, still in her pajamas and plush robe, mixing ingredients and cooking on the stovetop. Makani blinked at the short stack of pancakes.

"Oatmeal pumpkin," her grandmother said.

Their usual breakfast was whole-wheat toast or a bowl of fiber cereal. Makani didn't need to ask why the change. Pancakes kept her grandmother occupied while they waited for information. Pancakes gave her a task to do with her hands in a world that seemed more and more out of her control. And pancakes showed Makani that, even though the world was frightening, she was loved.

If only Makani had an appetite. The cloying sweetness of the maple syrup made her nose ache and her stomach turn.

Rodrigo.

That was the rumor. The guy who'd insulted her five days ago on the quad. The guy she'd spoken to three days ago in physics class. Alex's weird crush.

Rodrigo.

He couldn't be dead, because he was still so alive in her mind.

Makani had already texted Alex. It was her first attempt to contact her since Darby's confrontation, and she had yet to receive a reply. Now she felt guilty for ignoring their texts over the weekend.

"Well?" Grandma Young asked.

"Thank you," Makani said automatically. She'd forgotten about the pancakes.

"I meant, is there anything new?"

"—just in, we *can* confirm a third victim in the Osborne slayings . . ." Creston Howard said from the living room, and they lunged toward him. ". . . a seventeen-year-old senior, Rodrigo Ramón Morales Ontiveros."

His full name. Makani's knees buckled.

He would never be just *Rodrigo* again.

"Oh Lord." Grandma Young covered her mouth with both hands.

The news showed live footage from the crime scene. Two officers in heavy coats stood outside of a one-story rancher with a frosted lawn, discussing something with crossed arms. Neighbors huddled in the foggy street behind a banner of yellow tape.

Creston spoke over the feed. "The boy's parents discovered his body in the early hours of the morning after returning home from a weekend trip to Las Vegas. Police say it appears that he died from knife-related trauma, which has led them to believe the case is connected, though they have yet to disclose if his body faced similar mutilation."

Makani lowered herself, stunned, into the easy chair.

Her grandmother placed a hand on her shoulder.

"Hang on," Dianne Platte said, and the screen cut back to Creston's coanchor in the studio. "We've just received word that *all* Osborne schools are now closed for the day. Parents of middle and elementary school students are being asked to pick up their children immediately, and the police have issued a warning for them to not be left unsupervised until whoever is responsible has been taken into custody."

Grandma Young's willowy hand clenched into a hard grip.

Makani stared at the television in despair, but she could no longer see it. Her vision swam. *His family. His friends. Alex.*

Oh my God, Alex.

"I taught his sisters." Her grandmother's voice cracked. "I can't—"

Makani stood to embrace her, choking back tears as Grandma Young collapsed into her arms. Creston and Dianne repeated their updates. Makani peered over her grandmother's shoulder and out the large window that looked across their front lawn. She scanned the yards for the boogeyman, the Babadook, Ted Bundy.

The street was empty.

A misty chill radiated from the windowpane. Had it been this cold when the killer slipped away from Rodrigo's house? Had the killer finally left behind some evidence in the frost? Makani's bare feet were almost numb. Her hope felt even colder.

The ice crystals melted from the vegetation, but the morning remained bleak. Businesses switched their open signs to closed. Parents stayed at home and locked their doors. Fear clouded the air as panic threatened to storm.

Everyone had known Matt, and plenty had known Haley, but few had known Rodrigo. He wasn't popular. Most people remembered him as a smart-ass who actually happened to be smart. He'd never had a girlfriend, and his small group of friends rarely socialized with other groups.

Overnight, every student had become a potential target.

The story went national. Three murders had given Osborne a serial killer. And not just any serial killer, but the media's favorite kind—someone who committed heinous acts on attractive teenagers. The news spread like wildfire. Makani heard Chief Pilger's official statement during a rundown on CNN: *The Osborne PD is pursuing several leads. The killer will be apprehended, and he or she will face the full punishment of the law. If anyone has any information regarding these crimes, please call this number . . .*

Ollie called around noon. Grandma Young was in her bedroom on the phone with a church friend, and Makani was still parked in front of the television. Ollie was at the police station, performing menial tasks for his brother. Chris didn't want him to be alone, but it was also a punishment for ditching school on Friday. Ollie was stuck there until his afternoon shift at Greeley's. Assuming the grocery store stayed open.

Makani pressed him for details. "Is it true that they have some leads?"

"Sort of," Ollie said. "The police don't want to reveal too much to the public, but the killer left behind two imprints in the blood on the Moraleses' living room rug—a partial of a boot and a partial of the seat of his jeans, which included fibers."

He paused. Makani could tell he was holding something back.

"It's sick," he said, lowering his voice, "but after the murder, he stayed to play *Battleground Apocalypse* on Rodrigo's PlayStation."

Makani's heart picked up speed. "He?"

"Sorry. That's still speculation. It's just the most likely possibility."

Backtracking, her mind finally absorbed his previous statement. "The killer stayed at the crime scene . . . to play a video game?"

"Yep. They sat in Rodrigo's blood—right beside his dead body— and played Rodrigo's game for five hours."

"Five *hours?*"

"Five hours."

"Oh my God. Oh my *God.*" It was impossible to imagine. "That might be the most fucked-up thing I've ever heard."

"At least it means the killer was finally careless and left something behind."

"There weren't any fingerprints on the controller?"

"No. And most of Rodrigo's were smudged off. The killer probably wears gloves, but the police had already guessed that."

Makani was still thinking about the type of person who could sit beside a hacked and slashed body for five hours. "If the killer stayed there for so long, they must not have been concerned with getting caught. They must've known that Rodrigo's parents were out of town. They must've—"

"Known Rodrigo before the attack." Yeah. All three murders have been so personal—not to mention that killing someone with a knife is significantly more intimate than using a gun," he added, sounding like his cop brother, "so it doesn't seem probable that the killer is some random, crazy drifter. It's probably someone they all knew."

"Someone *we* know."

An unintelligible voice in the background interrupted their conversation. "Okay, okay," Ollie said with his phone pulled away from his mouth. "Sorry." He was back on the line. "Chris wants me to get back to organizing his files."

"Oh. Yeah."

Neither of them said goodbye.

"Hey." Her stomach tore open like a buzzing wasp nest. "I miss you."

His response was silence. The wasps dropped dead. But then he spoke, and she could hear him smiling. "I miss you, too."

When they hung up, she clutched her phone against her chest. It vibrated, and the sensation startled her. A long, garbled text had arrived from Darby: The Feed 'N' Seed was open, he was meeting Alex there for work, and he'd update her again after seeing Alex in person. All morning, they'd been pretending like their fight had never happened. It was more important to make sure that Alex was okay. She still hadn't texted Makani, but she'd made contact with Darby. Makani tried not to feel hurt by this.

A crocheted throw materialized over her legs. "You looked cold," Grandma Young said. She sat down on the sofa, on the side nearest to Makani's chair.

Makani pulled up the blanket with a shiver. "Thank you."

"Have you spoken with your parents yet?"

"No." She shook her head. "But I will."

Grandma Young had given strict instructions to call them both when they were awake, to let them know that she was safe. Makani dreaded it. She wanted sympathy and crocheted throws. Not her parents. With the five-hour difference, it was 7:30 a.m. on the Kona Coast. People were out of bed and checking their phones. Would her old friends notice Osborne in the news? Even if they did, they wouldn't make the connection. No one would recognize the name of the town. No one except for Jasmine.

Makani and Jasmine had once been as close as Darby and Alex, but now Makani knew that even the strongest of friendships cracked under pressure. And her bedrock with Darby and Alex wasn't nearly so thick. She had to see Alex. She had to make the effort, because, otherwise, Alex might stop making the effort in return.

"Can I borrow the car this afternoon?" Makani's question seemed loud and abrupt. "I'd only be gone for an hour."

"*May* you borrow." Despite her alarm, Grandma Young still had to correct Makani's grammar. "And what, in heaven's name, is so important?"

Her best chance of succeeding was to tell the truth. She did.

The heavy *tick* of the grandfather clock permeated the house as Grandma Young weighed her decision. "I can't let you take the car and go alone." She held up a hand to stop Makani's protests. "But I will drive you there myself."

Ollie went to work at Greeley's Foods, and Darby and Alex went to the Feed 'N' Seed. Even in times of crisis, humans and animals needed to eat, and teenagers earning minimum wage needed to be there to ring up the sales.

The sky was dim and overcast. The Feed 'N' Seed was located on the outskirts of town, and Makani arrived shortly after her friends had begun their shift. The store smelled grainy with a fetid, tangy undertone of livestock, though it contained no animals.

Alex's eyes were smeared and wholly rimmed with charcoal eye-shadow and black mascara. Evidence of crying. Darby sat beside her on a stool behind the long sales counter, as somber as a grave.

It was less embarrassing to be in public with her grandmother than Makani had expected. Grandma Young made her feel safer. The Osborne Slayer, as the media had dubbed the killer, wasn't stalking Makani—apart from Ollie, her only local connections were here, surrounded by enormous bags of food pellets—but her nerve endings were frayed, all the same. The musty scent of foreboding clung to the town like mold on a decaying house. It was impossible not to breathe its stench into her lungs.

Near a display of pasture pumps, two middle-aged men wearing Carhartt overalls and matching frowns spoke in low, tense voices. They were the store's only customers. Normally, the Feed 'N' Seed would be bustling, and the ranchers and farmers would be booming jovially as they swapped stories. Makani didn't need to hear what the two men were whispering to know that they weren't talking about football or the weather.

Darby's posture lifted when he noticed Makani and her grandmother.

"Hey," she said awkwardly. She wasn't sure where else to start.

"What're you doing here?" And then, remembering his manners, he added, "Hi, Mrs. Young."

Grandma Young nodded hello.

"We came to see how you're doing," Makani said to Alex. She corrected herself. "How you're *both* doing."

"Pretty. Shitty." Alex drew out the rhyme.

Makani glanced at her grandmother, but Grandma Young didn't blink. It was neither the time nor place to criticize. Sometimes, swearing was acceptable.

"I'm sorry." Makani reached across the counter to squeeze Alex's limp hand, injecting as much compassion into it as she could. They conversed with their eyes. Alex didn't say anything, but Makani could tell that the gesture was meaningful to her.

Grandma Young had engaged Darby in a series of questions. "Yeah, my parents are freaking out," he said. "They didn't want me to come here today."

"Oh!" Grandma Young's posture changed like she'd remembered something important. She pivoted back toward Makani. "Your parents called while you were in the shower. Both of them."

Her tone was accusatory, but Makani's avoidance had turned into genuine forgetfulness. Momentarily, she was surprised that her parents had seen the news, though she wasn't surprised that they'd called her grandmother—asking *about* her, instead of asking her directly. They'd met humanity's minimum requirement.

"Sorry, Grandma," she said.

Grandma Young cocked an eyebrow. "What about Oliver? I'm sure you didn't forget to call him. Is he all right?"

Alex's hand grew rigid.

Makani released it and stuffed her fists into her coat pockets. "He's fine," she mumbled. *I shouldn't have let go. I should have pretended like this wasn't a thing.*

But Grandma Young wouldn't stop talking. "I'm glad he came over this weekend. I don't know why he'd put that thing in his lip, but he's a nice boy."

It was the worst possible moment for her to defend Ollie's character. Makani cringed, holding her breath, as Darby and Alex exchanged a dark look. They hadn't known that she'd seen him again. She neutralized her expression and prayed that they wouldn't use this opportunity to report their insane suspicions to her grandmother.

They didn't. After another silent communication and a warning glance at Makani, Darby changed the subject. "Do you think school will be canceled again tomorrow?"

Her legs weakened in relief. "They should cancel it for the rest of the week."

"Matt was killed on school grounds." Alex kicked her toe against the counter, pointedly avoiding Makani's gaze. "They should cancel it until someone is arrested. Assuming the police are looking at *every* suspect."

Before Makani could respond, or even decide how to respond— anger, guilt, and defensiveness warring with her knowledge that Alex was truly suffering—an old man with a cowboy hat and sun-worn wrinkles appeared in the doorway of the manager's office. He was checking to make sure that his employees weren't gossiping instead of helping customers.

Grandma Young gave him a nod. "Good afternoon, Cyril."

He nodded back. "Sabrina."

"We'll let you get back to work," she said, as pointedly to Makani as it was to Makani's friends. "Please don't hesitate to call us if you need anything. Anything at all." This, she directed toward Alex with tenderness.

Alex wilted. Darby placed an arm around her shoulders. Makani and her grandmother left. And as the door's decorative cowbell gave its plaintive *clang* goodbye, the first snowflakes of the year began to fall.

Evening crept into town. Patches of white snow gathered in the blue shadows, but the flakes were still melting on the roads and sidewalks. Makani imagined the soft powder drifting onto the memorial at school, dusting the flowers and cards and stuffed lions. Because of classes being canceled, no one had been able to place any tokens on the mound for Rodrigo. It was almost unbearable.

The official texts, emails, and voicemails arrived after dusk. All Osborne schools would be closed the following day. Classes would resume on Wednesday, and deputies outsourced from the Sloane County sheriff's office would be stationed on each campus.

The sky blackened. The snow began to stick.

Grandma Young stared out the front window at the quiet street. "Maybe the killer won't strike tonight. They'd leave behind tracks in the snow."

Makani tasted fear in the wind. "Maybe."

They closed the curtains and double-checked the locks.

CHAPTER THIRTEEN

SCHOOL WAS BACK in session, but the classrooms were half empty. Even Grandma Young had debated whether or not to send Makani, and, as a former teacher, she never let her stay home. Makani had to have a fever or be vomiting, neither of which had happened since moving here. Her attendance record was perfect. Her grandmother had only decided in favor of school because of a last-minute call from a sleep specialist in Omaha. They'd had a cancellation and could get her in that afternoon. Apparently, she was more concerned about her sleepwalking than she'd been letting on.

"My appointment wasn't for three more months," Grandma Young had said. "It's impossible to get in. I should go."

Makani had agreed. And when her flustered grandmother had rushed her off to school, Makani didn't mention that she could have gone with her. She'd wanted to go to school. Something about *not* going felt cowardly, like they were letting the killer win. But as she sat in her deserted first-period class, she wondered if she'd lobbied for the wrong choice. Neither Darby nor Alex was here. Darby's parents hadn't let him, and Alex had asked to stay home. A morose spell had been cast over the campus. It felt otherworldly in its emptiness and melancholia.

After three minutes of silence during the morning announcements, one minute for each loss, Principal Stanton—who *never* did the morning announcements—broke the news that *Sweeney Todd* had been canceled. He claimed that the decision had been made out of respect for the victims with special regards to Haley and her family. This was true enough, although everyone understood that a musical about a barber who kills his customers with a straight razor was far too grisly for their grieving community.

Makani felt bad for the drama kids who'd been working so hard and looked so crestfallen. Two desks ahead of her, Haley's best friend, Brooke, lamented. "Haley would have wanted the show to go on."

Everywhere. They were everywhere.

Those who had left them and those who had been left behind.

In second-period physics, Makani stared at Rodrigo's empty seat as if it contained a phantom. David sat beside the physical vacancy in hollow silence.

The rest of their group—Rodrigo's other friends who'd decided to brave school—kept her focus at lunchtime. Through the strange osmosis of tragedy, she suddenly knew their names: Kevin, Emily, and Jesse. They shared David's anguish, though their body language expressed it in different ways from his numbness.

Kevin, *fear*.

Emily, *devastation*.

Jesse, *helplessness*.

Everyone's reaction was unique, including the football players. On game days, they always dressed in button-downs, khakis, and ties, and that's what they'd chosen to wear today. Still a team. But their pressed clothing couldn't disguise their emotional upheaval, or how similar their mourning was to the gamers. Hulking Buddy even clapped gangly Kevin on the shoulder as he waited behind him in the pizza line. They'd never been on equal terms before, but now they would forever have this terrible October in common.

Social boundaries were being crossed everywhere. Students still ate with their own kind, but each group sat a little closer to the other groups, and they weaved in and out of one another's conversations. They were all talking about the same thing, anyway.

It was sad that people only got along when everybody was unhappy.

Makani and Ollie sat beside each other in the back corner of the cafeteria. Last night's snow had almost completely melted, but no one wanted to be outdoors. It didn't matter that the murders had all taken place indoors. Walking through the open quad felt like wearing a bull's-eye. It seemed safer to remain in the thick of the crowd, although *thick* was still relative. They were the only two people at their table.

Makani hoped this was because of the low attendance as opposed to a general distrust of Ollie. It was growing in all the students, not just Darby and Alex. Ollie hadn't revealed any outward signs of acknowledgment, but it was impossible for Makani to believe that he hadn't noticed the darted glances and heated murmurs. It had never been so clear that he didn't fit in—and how much that rankled them.

Zachary Loup, asshole burnout and the other frequently rumored suspect, had been smart. He'd stayed at home.

"I spent the afternoon watching the news with my grandma," Makani said. She slid her fries toward Ollie and hoped that he'd take some. His apple, Ziploc of Cheetos, and peanut-butter sandwich seemed especially sad today. "It was depressing. All of those parents and siblings and grandparents and aunts and uncles and cousins. All of them being shouted at. 'How does it feel to know that your son's killer is still at large?'" She shook her head. "And yet, there we were. Waiting to judge and analyze their responses."

Ollie dipped a French fry in ketchup. "Thanks."

She felt an urgent need to engage him in conversation, aware of the eyes that judged *them*. They needed to look normal. Or, at least as normal as was possible today. Ollie's usual demeanor might appear suspiciously calm. Though, if he seemed happy, that would look inappropriate, too. Makani hated that she had to worry about what other people thought of him.

"What about you?" she asked. "Were you at the station again?"

"Yeah, but Chris didn't make me work. He wasn't even there. He had to drive to Tecumseh, so I hung out with Ken."

"Ken?"

"The dispatcher."

"Oh. Is he . . . cool?" The question felt dumb, but Makani wanted to know more about Ollie's life. Truthfully, she wanted to know *everything*. They'd exchanged a few texts yesterday, enough for her to know that he'd be coming to school today. Perhaps, if she were still being honest, it was the main reason why she'd wanted to come, too.

Ollie's mouth twitched with a smile. "He's a fifty-something, thrice-married divorcé who owns two ATVs. His favorite show is infomercials."

Makani laughed.

His smile turned into a grin.

"So, what's in Tecumseh? Was Chris interviewing a suspect?" She paused. "And *where's* Tecumseh?"

"About two and a half hours away, past Lincoln. It's the site of the state's only maximum-security prison. He was called out for something unrelated. Unexciting."

"Your whole day sounds—"

"Unexciting," Ollie repeated.

She laughed again. "You know, the next time we have a day off, you're welcome to stay at my house instead." It was both a practical suggestion and a flirtatious offer, but Makani quickly realized what else she'd implied. *Why* they would have another day off. Her expression collapsed. "I didn't mean . . . I hope another person doesn't . . ."

Ollie nodded. He understood.

"Ugh." Makani thumped her head dramatically against the table. "Everything is the worst." She turned her head, cheek against tabletop, to look at him.

And then he did the best thing.

He laid his head against the tabletop, too.

They stared at each other—cheeks squashed, noses inhaling the funk of an old cleaning sponge. She wished that she could reach under the table and take his hand, but they'd never shown a public display of affection. That was for boyfriends and girlfriends. She still wasn't sure what this was, she only hoped it would continue. It would feel good to be close to someone again. It would feel good to be close to *him*.

Her phone dinged. Makani swore as they lifted their heads, and she checked the screen. "Grandma. Just making sure everything's okay."

An odd look appeared on Ollie's face.

"What is it?"

He shook his head. "Something my brother said."

She waited for him to elaborate, and he glanced around before lowering his voice. "Chris told me that they worked in silence at Rodrigo's house, because they were still in shock. The only sound was

Rodrigo's phone. It was blowing up with friends who'd heard the rumors and were trying to check in." Ollie shuddered. "Chris said that was the worst part, the part that kept them all on edge. The sound of those unanswered calls and texts."

"Oh, man," Makani said softly. "That's bleak."

"If we could have your attention . . ."

Caleb Greeley and someone else from the religious crowd, a tall, mousy girl that Makani recognized as a junior, were standing on the cafeteria's modest platform stage. Caleb spoke into a microphone. Makani knew what was coming next.

". . . we'd like to lead you in a short prayer for Haley, Matt, and Rodrigo."

Yep. Makani couldn't think of a single instance of prayer during school back in Hawaii, but it happened all the time here. And *everyone* was expected to participate. That was the part that bothered her. Makani genuinely hoped that others, including her grandmother, found peace and strength through prayer. But she wasn't religious herself, and it made her uncomfortable whenever it was forced upon her.

She bowed her head and listened to Caleb and the girl not so much *pray* as *preach*. They recited many, many Bible verses. Her annoyance at Caleb rose. First, there was the prayer at the flagpole. Then, the interview on television. Now this. Was he getting something out of the attention? Was he enjoying the spotlight a little too—

Makani stopped herself. She was doing to him what everyone else was doing to Ollie. Anyone could look sinister when viewed through the lens of fear—even an overly zealous, deeply sincere boy like Caleb. She pushed her suspicions aside. But as another minute dragged by, Makani realized that she could appreciate his goodwill while simultaneously wishing that he would also suggest something they could actually *do* to help support the victims' families or catch the killer. Prayer alone wasn't action.

Underneath the table, someone took her right hand from her lap. Her eyes jolted open.

Ollie stared back. She glanced around, but everyone else, even the cafeteria ladies, had their eyes closed. Ollie laced his fingers through hers. She tightened the grip and leaned in.

They kissed.

Heat and electricity and life spread throughout her body. They opened their mouths and kissed deeper, without sound, surrounded by the prayers of the frightened. When Caleb said, "Amen," their lips pulled away, and they smiled quietly. No one any wiser to their indiscretion.

Near the end of the last period, Principal Stanton returned to the loudspeakers to thank everyone for coming today, to remind them that the school would still be open tomorrow, and to announce a small piece of good news: Rosemarie Holt won the barrel race last weekend at the Sloane County Championship Rodeo.

Makani didn't give a damn about the rodeo, and Rosemarie was a junior in none of her classes, but she cheered along with the rest of her Spanish class. Their universal joy was significantly overheightened. They felt grateful for any good news.

"Watch out, Rosemarie," Ollie said darkly.

The joke rang too true, and the happiness died in Makani's throat.

"The killer likes them talented," he said.

"*Don't.*"

She hadn't meant for it to come out so sharply. Ollie looked startled, and the space between them grew awkward. "Sorry," he said. "I only meant—"

"I know. It's okay." Makani shook her head, trying to smile. She'd understood his meaning instantly; she was upset because someone might have overheard him. She attempted to mend the delicate breach. "Is that something the police are looking into?"

He nodded as her phone vibrated, rattling the top of her desk.

The noise rattled her, too. *Rodrigo's phone. Blowing up.* Thankfully, it was more good news, this time from her grandmother: *Still in Omaha. Doc kept me waiting for over an hour just to tell me that I'll have to come back for more tests. I won't be home when school gets out. Would you please ask Darby to stay with you until I get there?*

Makani texted back: *sure! no worries.*

This time, her grin at Ollie was genuine. "Wanna come over to my place?"

CHAPTER FOURTEEN

THEY LEFT BEHIND Ollie's car at school and walked to her house, in case Grandma Young came home early and he needed to make a sneaky getaway. The irony was not lost on them that this behavior made them look suspicious, but the sun was shining, and the air was crisp with the magic of autumn.

Leaves pinwheeled from the sky and swirled across the sidewalk. Mums brightened the dull landscape with vibrant pops of yellow, lavender, and russet. Cheesecloth ghosts hung from invisible string on tree branches. Tombstones with joke names created temporary graveyards. And pumpkins—orange, white, tall, round, flat, and miniature—decorated every porch and door. Halloween was only three days away.

The afternoon felt like a gift. A respite from the ongoing stress.

Their plan was simple: Makani would encourage her grand-mother to text updates regarding her arrival time, and, when she grew close, Ollie would duck out. Makani would say that Darby had *just* left, because they knew Grandma Young was around the corner, and Darby's parents were anxious to have him home. And then Grandma Young would get mad, but it wouldn't be anything an evening couldn't fix.

Puddles of melted snow still rested beneath the oak-lined portion of Walnut Street. The north-south roads in Osborne's oldest neighborhood were all named after trees: Cedar, Elm, Hickory, Oak, Pine, Spruce, Walnut, and Willow. They'd been christened in alphabetical order, so that the townspeople could always find their way home. Lately, Makani felt irrationally relieved that she didn't live on Elm Street.

"What'd you tell your brother?" she asked.

"That I'm going into work early," Ollie said. A moment of tension arose as they rounded the side of her house, and—

Yep. All clear.

Her grandmother's gold Taurus wasn't in the driveway.

They entered through the back door. The house was quiet. The only sound was its heartbeat, the hefty pendulum of the immense grandfather clock.

"It's such an old-people house," she whispered.

"I like it," Ollie whispered back.

They didn't have to lower their voices, but they did anyway. Energy crackled between them, intense and irrepressible. "I'm pretty sure the only items made in this century are the ones that moved here with me," she said.

He laughed quietly. She led him out of the kitchen and up the stairs.

"She hasn't finished it yet?" he asked.

Makani stopped, halfway up.

"The puzzle," he said.

She followed his gaze over the banister and into the living room, where most of the sky pieces—the blues and whites and grays—were still scattered around the coffee table. She shook her head and smiled. "I think she's been waiting for you."

"Next time, I'll visit when she's home."

Makani raised an eyebrow. "Sure you don't want to work on it now?"

Ollie bit his lip. Let the ring slip back out. "Positive."

As Makani led him into her bedroom, she sensed his eyes on the curves of her body. She felt his hunger, because it was the same hunger that she felt inside herself.

She locked the door behind them. Just in case.

It reminded her to check her phone, and a new text had arrived from Grandma Young. *Accident on Route 6. Stuck in West Omaha traffic.*

"Traffic sucks. We're in luck." Makani sing-songed it as she plugged her phone into a speaker and turned up the volume. The loud music was also just in case, but Ollie hardly seemed to register it. He seemed taken aback by his surroundings.

Uneasy, she crossed her arms over her chest. "What?"

Ollie took a moment to collect his thoughts. "It looks like the rest of the house. Not like you. This looks like . . . you're a visitor."

The shrewd observation stung more than expected. "I suppose I am."

Ollie nodded, and she was surprised that the gesture contained disappointment. Her arms uncrossed as she stepped automatically toward him, but he turned away from her. The emotional barrier slammed back into place. He kneeled beside her bed.

"What are you—"

"You once told me that I'd find something under here." At her baffled expression, he added, "A picture?"

Her eyes widened as she recalled the old swim team photo.

His smile gleamed with mischief.

"No, no, no, no, no, no, *no*." Makani threw her body between him and the bed, pinning down his arms as he struggled for something just out of reach. She couldn't let him see the picture now. Not while she was trying to seduce him. "Next time," she said, laughing. "I promise I'll show you next time."

Their chests touched. They breathed heavily.

Ollie stopped wriggling to give her another tempting smile. "And what good are the promises of someone who lies to her own grandmother?"

She kissed his lips—briefly—and pulled away. "Another day. I mean it." She kissed him again. "Just not today."

Ollie leaned forward and kissed her. Makani squirmed to shed her coat and got tangled in its sleeves. They both laughed as he helped her out of it.

"I'm curious—"

"Why I'm wearing a heavy coat? Because it *snowed,* and I grew up on the *beach*."

"I'm *curious*," he said, "why you're a winter Goth."

She was about to kiss him again, but this made her stop. "What?"

"Your summer clothes are colorful, and your winter clothes are black." He motioned at her coat and sweater to prove his point and then inclined his head for more kissing, as if he hadn't just initiated a weird conversation.

Makani pulled back so that he couldn't reach her mouth.

The summer clothes were her old clothes. In Hawaii, the warmest items she'd needed were jeans and a hoodie. Here, she'd had to ask her grandmother to buy her a coat, hat, scarf, gloves, and sweaters. They'd made a special trip to a mall in Omaha, and she'd selected everything in black. She couldn't explain *why* except that when she wore it, she felt a bit more protected. A bit more hardened. But that sounded dumb, and she didn't want Ollie to think she was copying him or Alex.

She teased him instead. "I like that you pay so much attention to what I'm wearing."

"I always pay attention to you. I always see you."

Her skin flushed as she held his gaze. "I see you, too."

Their bodies connected in a frantic crush. His hoodie disappeared, and then her sweater. And then his shirt. They were on her bed, and her jeans were off, and she was only in her underwear. She reached for his zipper.

Ollie placed a hand over hers. "Is this okay? Are you sure?"

These were the questions that required honesty. "Yes," she said. "Are you?"

"Yes."

She kissed him again, gently pushing aside his hand. "Yes," she repeated.

"Yes," he repeated.

The boy with the pink hair was asleep, and her grandmother had texted thirty minutes earlier that traffic was moving, but it was still slow. They had at least another hour.

Makani replied: *no prob! keep me updated.*

Her favorite song blasted through the speaker as she contemplated the rise and fall of Ollie's bare chest. His stomach was flat, much flatter than hers, and he looked more content in slumber than he did when he was awake. He looked soothed. The sex had been surprising, and not only because it had been quiet. (Just in case.) It had been different from their first time. It had been better. It had been *more*.

Makani watched Ollie until thirst overpowered her. She re-dressed, tugged a blanket over him, and went downstairs into the kitchen. The flatware drawer was open.

Her pulse spiked. "Grandma?"

Apart from the *tick* of the grandfather clock, the house was silent. Makani closed the drawer with a shaking hand. *She can't be home yet.* She rewound an hour to their arrival, trying to remember if the drawer had been open when they'd passed through the room. She didn't think so, but, admittedly, she'd been distracted.

It *must* have been open.

Her grandmother must have opened it before leaving for her ap-pointment. It was good that she'd gone to the specialist. Maybe they would finally get some answers.

Makani filled a plastic cup with tap water and chugged it. She refilled it for Ollie but then decided to use the downstairs bathroom, her grandmother's bathroom, before returning. With the loud music, she didn't *think* he'd be able to hear her peeing in the upstairs bath-room, but she was still self-conscious about it.

When she returned to the kitchen, the flatware drawer was open. Her body lurched to a halt. She gaped at it from the threshold.

The tracks must be loose. It's been rolling itself open this whole time.

But a lump thickened inside her throat.

Makani wasn't sure why she felt afraid. She glanced at the back door, but it was locked. She glanced behind her, but she was alone. Of course she was alone.

She crept into the kitchen and pushed in the drawer, just a few inches. Testing it. Waiting for it to roll back out.

It didn't.

She pushed in the drawer, all the way.

Waited.

Still nothing. *Maybe Grandma is right. Maybe I really am the one losing my mind.* The thought was unsettling, because it could be true. A period of time did exist that was difficult for Makani to remember. Perhaps these recent forgetful occurrences were remnants of her past trauma. Or perhaps, even worse, evidence of a new progression.

Shame poured through her as she stared at the drawer, willing it to open. She pressed her ear against its veneer and listened.

Nothing. The drawer held firm.

"Shit," she whispered.

Makani shook her head. She went to grab the water, but the cup was empty.

"Shit," she said again, spinning around. She didn't know if she was searching for her grandmother or Ollie, but there was still nobody there. With trembling hands, she refilled the plastic cup and carried it toward the stairs, the water threatening to slosh over the sides. And that's when she noticed the jigsaw puzzle.

The sky was filled in.

The puzzle had been completed.

Makani dropped the cup. Water splashed onto her jeans as the cup bounced and spilled across the carpet. She scrambled to pick it up.

"Grandma?" she called out. "Grandma, where are you?"

Why had she sent those texts? Was this a test to see if Makani would lie to her? Did she know that Ollie was here? *Oh God.* She'd probably heard them upstairs, and now she was waiting for him to sneak out so that she could confront Makani. It was something her mother would do. She loved to set up Makani and then punish her for taking the bait. Was her grandmother more like her mom than Makani had realized?

Makani rushed back into the kitchen. "Grandma? Are you home?"

There was still no reply.

She slammed the cup onto the counter, grabbed a dish towel, and returned to dry the carpet around the base of the stairs. Her cheeks burned. Her heart felt as if it would burst from her chest. If Ollie had heard her yelling, he was being smart and remaining hidden. Clutching the wet towel, she headed back to the kitchen and stopped dead.

The cup was gone.

Her mind spun. Unable to process it.

"Grandma?" Makani sprinted toward her grandmother's bedroom at the back of the house. "Are you in there?" She pounded on the closed door, and when no one answered, she barged into the room. The bed was made. Everything was in its usual place. She even checked the closet—she didn't know why—but it was empty.

She hurried back to peer out the kitchen window toward the driveway and staggered backward. The cup was sitting in the center of the countertop. And every single drawer and cabinet was wide-open.

Makani felt paralyzed. The driveway was visible from here, but it held no cars.

"*Ollie?*" she whispered. She forced herself to turn around, half expecting, half hoping for him to be standing behind her.

He wasn't.

In a daze, she stumbled toward the stairs. Her eyes snagged on the completed jigsaw puzzle, and her body temperature chilled as a new horror settled in.

The killer had rearranged Rodrigo's living room furniture.

Makani remembered the drawers and cabinets—how many times they'd been left open in the last two months. What if the victims were toyed with before they were murdered? The acts against them could have been almost invisible. Gaslighting. Things that an officer would never notice while inspecting a crime scene.

The police had assumed that Rodrigo's furniture had been rearranged after his death as a part of the elaborate staging that the killer seemed to enjoy. But what if the killer had rearranged Rodrigo's furniture *before* his death?

A hooded figure stepped out from beside the grandfather clock.

CHAPTER FIFTEEN

MAKANI'S SCREAM REVERBERATED throughout the house. It rattled the pictures on the walls.

The figure jumped, startled by the volume of her terror, and dropped something. A knife thudded onto the carpet between them.

For a surreal moment, they were both frozen. A beige camouflage hoodie hung low over the killer's face, but Makani could see that he was male and white. He was also young, a teenager, judging from the slightness of his frame.

Makani glanced at his knife. It was large. The fixed blade was at least seven inches of steel, and it had two cutting edges—one regular and one sawtooth.

Its pointed tip was razor sharp.

She lunged.

Unfortunately, the killer was closer and faster, and as soon as his hand wrapped around the knife's black rubbery hilt, he thrust upward and sliced into her forearm.

She screamed again, stumbling backward. Suddenly, a yell arose from the landing. Ollie was barreling down to them, naked and at full speed.

Once more, the killer was caught by surprise, and Makani realized—in this millisecond—he had thought she'd been alone. Using his shock to her advantage, she slammed her body into his and knocked him to the floor. The hunting knife fell from his hand a second time as his hood flew back and exposed his face.

Makani blinked.

Recognizing him yet unable to place him.

He thrashed and kicked, and as she struggled to keep him pinned, a flailing limb rammed into her wound. She gasped. He clambered out from under her, snatched up the knife, and swiveled to attack. Ollie grabbed him from behind and hurled him aside.

A new battle cry rang out as a fourth person tore into the room.

Grandma Young launched herself at the killer. They hit the carpet together, and the knife plunged into her lower right abdomen. She cried out. The killer shoved the blade in deeper, wriggling it around. He kicked up his boots and pushed her off.

Makani threw herself over her grandmother's body.

Ollie chased after the killer, who was already running. The killer sidestepped and smashed into the grandfather clock. It crashed to the floor in a violent explosion of brass and tinder and glass. The carpet absorbed the cacophony into a swallowed silence.

Makani was perched on her hands and knees, panting. Blood coated the skin of her palms. It seeped through the legs of her jeans. Beneath her, Grandma Young's breathing was shallow and strained. Makani lifted her head cautiously.

Ollie and the killer were both still standing.

With a glance from Makani's narrowing eyes to Ollie's tensing muscles, the killer reassessed the situation. And then bolted out the front door.

Ollie shot off—straight through the shards and splinters—to lock it behind him as Makani leaped up and flew to the front window. "He's running left," she said.

"Where's your phone?" Ollie asked.

"Upstairs!"

"Mine too." He sprinted away. "Watch him!"

The hooded figure vanished behind a neighbor's detached garage. Makani moaned as she scoured the landscape for movement, any hint of movement. Her legs jiggled. Her arms trembled. There was a landline in the kitchen, but she didn't remember it until Ollie was already thumping downstairs with a phone at his ear.

"Ken," Ollie said to the dispatcher. He was still naked. "I'm at Makani Young's house on Walnut Street. The killer was just here."

Makani motioned for him to take the window. "He went that way! Around the corner of the garage."

"We need an ambulance. Her grandmother is seriously injured. She was stabbed in the stomach, and she's losing a lot of blood."

"Grandma? Grandma, stay with me!" Makani grabbed the nearest throw pillow and propped it beneath her grandmother's head. Her eyelids lifted open weakly.

"I'm fine," Ollie assured the dispatcher. "Makani is, too, but her arm was cut pretty badly. She'll need stitches."

Grandma Young's eyes grew worried.

"I'm okay. You're okay." Makani unbuttoned the bottom of her grandmother's blouse to get a better look at the wound. The shirt was heavy and wet.

"It's David Ware," Ollie said into the phone. "The killer is David Ware, and he's running in the direction of the school right now."

Makani peeled back the fabric, which shucked against her grandmother's stomach. Grandma Young inhaled sharply. Petrified,

THERE'S SOMEONE INSIDE YOUR HOUSE

Makani lowered it back into place as Ollie raced past her and up the stairs.

"Where are you going?" Makani shouted.

His voice carried down from her bedroom, and she realized he was standing at her window. "No, I can't see him anymore. . . ."

Ollie's phone call morphed into an unintelligible buzz. Makani's heart pounded with fear and adrenaline as she grasped her grandmother's hand, their skin slick with blood. She didn't know what to do. She didn't know how to help. The front window taunted her. At any moment, the killer might jump out from behind the bushes.

A gray shadow fell over her.

She shrieked.

"It's okay," Ollie said. But his eyes widened when he saw her arm.

She glanced down to discover that her left sweater sleeve was also soaked with blood. A diagonal slash had ripped open her flesh from elbow to wrist and exposed a throbbing gash of muscle. Her arm didn't seem like her arm. She barely felt the cut.

Getting on his knees, Ollie pressed a clean hand towel from the upstairs linen closet against her grandmother's wound. He nodded toward a second towel beside Makani. "Can you wrap that around your arm?"

He'd thrown on his clothes, but his feet were still bare. They were shredded from the glass. Frenzied trails of crimson footprints revealed his path across the carpet.

Blood. From his feet, her arm, her grandmother's stomach. It was everywhere.

"Here." Ollie gestured for Makani to take his place and to keep applying pressure.

Grandma Young's eyes were closed again. The instant Makani had instructions, the instant her grandmother's life was in her hands, her mind sharpened into focus. She held the towel in place as Ollie wrapped the other one around her forearm. She hissed with unexpected pain. A terrifying flash, a vision, accompanied it—a plain face with a dead expression.

Grandma Young tried to speak. "What did you say . . . his name?"

In the distance, the emergency sirens wailed their approach.

"David," Makani said. "That was Rodrigo's best friend."

David. David *Ware*. Had she even known his last name?

He'd never been mentioned in the speculation. Not once. He was someone who she and her friends—and Rodrigo—had even speculated *with*.

Who do you think did it?

He'd asked her that in physics class.

His pleasure must have been so perverse, asking when he already knew that he was going to kill her. Already knowing that he was going to kill his best friend.

The serial killers in her imagination, the fictional centerpieces of innumerable movies and television shows, were colorful and fascinating and impossible to keep her eyes off of. But her eyes had always glossed over David.

Who do you think did it?

She'd looked past him, even when he'd asked her.

She'd looked past him, even when he'd been sitting right in front of her.

Blazing lights. A rush of uniforms. Sense-memory panic swelled inside Makani as her house exploded into chaos. Paramedics in white shirts rushed toward her grandmother. The police swarmed Ollie, and Chris embraced him fiercely. Another officer rapid-fired questions at her. Makani's responses were a blur as Grandma Young was lifted onto a stretcher. A bearded paramedic peeked beneath Makani's towel, and she was hustled inside the same ambulance. Neighbors poured from their homes. News vans squealed onto the street. The last she saw of Ollie was a flicker of pink in the front window as the ambulance doors slammed closed.

You're in shock, they told her. As the nurses and doctor numbed, cleaned, and stitched her arm, the same police officer that had questioned her at home continued the interview.

Officer Beverly Gage. You can call me Bev.

She looked young for a Beverly, only a few years older than Ollie's brother. She had a large oval face, friendly eyes, and long hair pulled back into a ponytail. Was this the same officer that Darby had found attractive? It seemed so long ago.

Her grandmother had been rushed into an operating room, but the hospital wouldn't tell her if she was okay, and Officer Bev wouldn't tell her if David had been captured. Bev's timeline-related questions were mortifying. At least she saved the most prying inquiries until after the stitching was done, and they were alone.

Makani answered as truthfully as she could remember:

Yes, we had sex.

Um, ten minutes?

Then we talked for a while.

Maybe fifteen minutes?

I don't know. About music. And some guy who wrote a lot about Morocco . . . Paul something? I don't know.

Yes, and then Ollie dozed off.

I checked my phone, and then I watched him sleep.

I don't know. Fifteen minutes? Twenty?

It was humiliating. And now it would go on file, typed up on some kind of awful official document or digital record or both. As Bev made another notation, Makani's mind boomeranged back to her grandmother. She felt sick with guilt and helplessness. *Grandma might die because David wants* me *dead*.

Her thoughts spun again, and she imagined trying to explain herself when—*when* not *if*—her grandmother woke up. Makani had lied. Ollie had been naked. Illogically, these two facts felt so much worse than confronting the idea that someone had attempted to kill her.

I barely know him, she kept telling Bev. *No, I don't know why he'd target me.*

The first half was true. The second half was a lie.

Makani thought that she had suffered enough—she'd lost everything that mattered to her in Hawaii—but the karmic cycle of life had circled back around. This, at last, was her final punishment.

CHAPTER SIXTEEN

OFFICER BEV WAS gone, and Makani had been abandoned in the single-occupancy patient room to wait for news about her grandmother. She moved to an uncomfortable chair, not wanting to remain on the bed. The air smelled stale but sterile.

Makani didn't have her phone, so she couldn't contact Ollie or her friends. Or even her parents. The police and the hospital had been trying to contact her mom and dad with no luck. But a kind-hearted nurse with coppery hair kept checking in on Makani and brought her ginger ale and blueberry yogurt. She assured Makani that the surgical staff was brilliant, and their small hospital was fortunate to have them.

Every minute alone increased Makani's anxiety. She'd been in the hospital for nearly four hours. She turned on the television to pass the time.

This was a mistake.

Standing on her grandmother's lawn was the same hairsprayed reporter who'd chased her through the school's parking lot last

Friday. The graphic on the bottom of the screen read: FOURTH TEEN ATTACKED IN OSBORNE SLAYINGS.

"Did you hear any screams or unusual noises?" she asked an older man. He had a droopy but upturned mouth like a bulldog. It was the neighbor from two doors down.

"No, nothing at all. I was fixing my gutter when a boy tore across my yard in that direction." He pointed with a gnarled finger and then pressed the whole hand flat against his face in disbelief. "I shouted after him from my ladder, but he didn't look at me. He just shot around my carport and ran toward Spruce."

Back in the studio, the live footage was superimposed above Creston Howard's shoulder. Creston looked stiff and appropriately serious, though he couldn't resist a toothpaste-commercial smile as he led them into the break.

No one should ever have to see their own house on the news. Makani wanted to crawl into her bed and hibernate for the rest of autumn. But then it struck her that she might not even be able to go home. Her house was a crime scene.

"The suspect is eighteen-year-old David Thurston Ware," Creston said when the news returned, and goose bumps prickled her skin.

Thurston.

Now he had a middle name, too. It didn't seem right that a murderer should be allowed to have anything in common with his victims. Makani supposed it was for the sake of the world's non-homicidal David Wares, those few people unfortunate enough to share his namesake. It was like being a Katrina after 2005; it only brought one thing to mind. But at least no one could mistake a woman for a hurricane. Hopefully, the release of his middle name narrowed the inevitable misunderstandings of *which* David Ware.

Makani's name wasn't being reported, most likely because she was a minor. And a survivor. But Ollie wasn't named, either. Creston kept referring to him as a *male friend of the victim*. The police must be protecting him.

The news cut to a senior photo, and David's image leached through the screen like an odious stench. His smile was dopey and innocent, and his hair was brushed to one side as if he were a little boy. He had a faint mustache. There was nothing intimidating about his appearance, but Makani's stomach filled with caustic acid.

"The suspect was last seen wearing jeans and a camouflage hoodie," Creston said. "He's considered armed and highly dangerous. If you see him, do *not* approach him. . . ."

More footage of her house. More interviews with neighbors.

The man whose nose had been lopped off crossed his flannel-shirted arms. "Osborne, all of us, we're scared for our lives."

Makani wanted to change the channel, but fear held her hostage.

"It's like searching for a needle in the cornstalks," Creston said, and she loathed his inane glibness more than ever. But his coanchor nodded. Dianne's makeup was so unnatural and extreme that it looked airbrushed by a T-shirt vendor on a beach. "And a reminder that all Sloane County schools have been closed for the rest of the week. . . ."

Did she only report on school closings?

"Good news," a voice said beside her.

Makani startled at the jarring declaration. The coppery-haired nurse hugged her clipboard and said, "Your grandmother's out of surgery."

"Your grandma's a real trouper." The surgeon was a thickset man with dark, feminine eyelashes. "She's lucky. The knife nicked her vena cava, but it missed the aorta. If it had nicked that, well, we'd be having a very different conversation right now."

Through the room's windows, nighttime lights illuminated the buildings below—the squat brick library and a lofty brick church. Everything in Osborne was made out of brick. St. Francis Memorial Hospital was on the opposite side of Main Street, not quite a mile from her grandmother's house. It wasn't big, but it was the county's only hospital, and Makani was grateful that it was so close. Grandma Young had gone into surgery within emergency medicine's golden hour. The rapid intervention had saved her life.

"There was an injury to her intestines, which requires a long antibiotic therapy, and there was a cut to her right ureter," the surgeon said. "I've placed temporary drains, but when she's more stable, the ureter will need reconstructive surgery."

His words were a fog. Her grandmother was still in another part of the hospital, and Makani wasn't allowed to see her yet. She touched her bandaged arm for self-support. It was wrapped from elbow to wrist. "When can she come home?"

"She'll need significant rehabilitation here in the hospital. Three weeks, at least."

"Three *weeks*?"

"After that, we'll transfer her to a rehabilitation center . . ."

He was still talking as Makani, stupefied, lowered herself back onto the bed where she'd received the stitches. Three weeks . . . and then *more* rehabilitation . . .

The surgeon removed a pen from the shirt pocket of his green scrubs. He clicked it, and the finality of the sound made her look up. "Do you have any other family that you can stay with while she recovers?"

Her parents flitted in, and then straight back out of, Makani's mind as she shook her head. "It's just the two of us."

"That's okay." The nurse placed a steady hand on Makani's

uninjured arm. "Your grandmother will be awake soon, and we'll ask her where she'd like you to stay. I'm sure she has some friends who'd be happy to take you in for a while."

Makani's chest constricted. Grandma Young's church friends were *nosy*. They would ask so many questions. Maybe she could stay with Darby or Alex instead.

As the surgeon detailed the recovery process, he spoke with a brisk authority that Makani found difficult to follow. When he left, the nurse outlined it in simpler terms and reminded her where the call button was to ring for help. Makani glanced at her laminated ID badge—DONNA KURTZMAN, RN—and thanked her by name.

For the second time in a year, almost to the day, Makani was trapped inside a waking nightmare. Grandma Young had thrown herself at a serial killer to save her. The selflessness of this act was almost too big to comprehend. But equally astounding was that she'd made it home in time to do it. Makani should be the one in the operating room, not her grandmother. Her grandmother had done nothing to deserve this.

Two more excruciating hours passed alone with her thoughts.

At last, Donna led her to the ICU where Grandma Young was coming around from the anesthesia. Her enfeebled body was strung up with wire monitors and IVs and catheter tubes, and Makani had no idea what else. A reclining chair sat beside the bed. Makani perched on its cushioned edge and took her grandmother's hand. Her skin felt thin, her bones fragile. "Hi, Grandma."

Grandma Young's eyelids fluttered open. She tried to speak, but her voice came out as a whispered croak. *"What time is it?"*

"It's almost eleven. Do you know where you are?"

Her eyes closed again, groggily. She nodded.

"You had emergency surgery, but you're okay. Do you remember what happened?" There was a twenty-second pause. "Grandma?"

"What time is it?"

"It's eleven at night," Makani said. Donna had explained that the anesthesia would make her grandmother disoriented for a while.

Grandma Young gave another frail nod. "Are you all right?"

Makani had held it in since the attack. But this question, coming from this person, unlocked the dam. Warm tears spilled over, no longer containable. "I'm fine."

"Oliver?"

"Ollie's fine, too." Makani used her right sleeve to dry her cheeks. The left sleeve had been cut off. The rest of her sweater was encrusted with dried blood, and her jeans were stained with rust-colored pools. "We're all okay."

There was a knock on the door, which had been left ajar. Chris nudged it open. He was in his blue uniform and holding a small bundle of Mylar balloons. And beside him, as if summoned by their thoughts, stood Ollie.

Makani's heart cracked down the middle. But it was a good feeling.

Ollie looked pale—his skin tone even paler than its natural state—and weary. *No,* she corrected herself. *Bleary.* As if he'd been answering the same questions, over and over, for the last six hours. He glanced at her, skittish and apprehensive.

"I hope you don't mind, Mrs. Young," Chris said. "May we come in?"

If her grandmother had been anyone else, Makani guessed that he would have called her *ma'am.* This was the habitual *Mrs. Young* of a former student.

Grandma Young's eyes reopened, and her posture straightened the teensiest bit. She gained a modicum of strength as she regained the role of the adult. "Christopher. Officer Larsson," she corrected hoarsely. "Come in."

He grinned. "Christopher is still fine."

The brothers entered, and Chris presented Makani's grandmother with three balloons—a Get Well Soon, a blushing emoji, and an emoji wearing sunglasses. "There weren't many options at the hospital's gift shop," he said apologetically. "We bought flowers, but then they told us we couldn't bring them into the ICU." He turned to Makani. "They're in my car. One of the bouquets is for you, of course."

Grandma Young thanked Chris as he tied the balloons in a place where she could see them. Apart from the occasional lei and an orchid corsage at her ex-boyfriend's junior prom, Makani had never been given flowers. She smiled at Ollie, perhaps even glowed, but he wouldn't meet her eyes. Her expression faltered.

He knows. The police had opened her record, and now Chris and Ollie knew. Her heart withered. The muscle blackened into soot.

"I owe *you* the thank-you." Chris walked to her grandmother's bedside. "If you hadn't come home when you did . . ." He couldn't finish the thought out loud.

Grandma Young shook her head, barely. "They saved themselves. I only got in the way."

He smiled with a gentle laugh. "That's not what my brother said."

Ollie was staring at the floor, so Makani spared him the embarrassment of responding. "Have you caught him yet?" She didn't have to specify the *him.*

Chris's blond eyebrows pinched together, which darkened his appearance. "Not yet. There are a lot of places to hide around here, but he couldn't have gotten far. He's probably tucked up in someone's barn or grain bin." Chris sounded frustrated, and he paused to regain a measured control. "Everyone's looking for him, and everyone knows what he looks like. We'll get him soon. I promise."

He asked her grandmother how she was feeling.

Ollie knows. Chris knows. Everybody will know.

"How many stitches?" Chris asked.

It took a moment for Makani to realize that this question was for her. "Twenty-six." She was unaware that she was cradling her wounded arm. "It's nothing."

"Your nothing and my nothing are two very different things."

His tone was light, but her lungs tightened.

A nurse rolled something bulky past their door. The noise reopened Grandma Young's eyes. Her gaze locked on to Ollie, and she ushered him to her side.

Reluctantly, he complied. Each step seemed gingerly taken, evoking Makani's memories of his cut-up feet. He bit his lip ring, and the gesture revealed the truth: Her *grandmother* was making him nervous. Not her. He looked troubled because her grandmother had discovered him naked inside her house.

Makani felt a rush of temporary relief as Grandma Young reached for his hands. Ollie accepted them. "*Thank you.*" She said it as emphatically as she could, meant with every cell in her body. "I'm so glad you were there."

Chris's eyes grew misty, betraying his professional stoicism.

Ollie nodded, but he lifted his chin. It quivered.

Grandma Young, still gripping his hands, shook them up and down. She inhaled deeply. "All right, then. That's that." And then she turned to Makani and asked, befuddled, "What time is it?"

• • •

In the hospital's unremarkable and unadorned waiting room, Ollie produced Makani's phone. It had been hidden in the pocket of his hoodie. "I grabbed it before the police could confiscate it. They'll pull your records and call logs, anyway."

Chris had to ask her grandmother a few questions, so they'd been banished. Makani's eyes widened as the precious object returned to her grasp. "Thank you."

"I think you have a few messages," he said wryly.

Entering her password revealed dozens of texts from Darby and Alex: *Are you okay? Where are you?! We are SO SORRY for suspecting Ollie!!!* Scrolling through their frantic apologies was comforting, until she remembered Rodrigo's phone. Had David texted him that morning to maintain the pretense of innocence? What kind of person could murder their best friend? Perhaps they'd never been friends at all.

Makani texted Darby and Alex to let them know that she was safe and that she'd call them later. She couldn't handle talking about it now. Not tonight. Not again. Even though she was staring at the call button beside her mother's name.

Ollie acknowledged her hesitating finger. "You should."

She moved near the elevators for privacy. There were three other people in the waiting room—a conservatively dressed elderly couple and a scruffy-faced man in an orange construction vest—and she didn't want them to overhear her, either. They were caught up in their own emergencies, and none of them had realized that they were sitting with the latest victims of the Osborne Slayer. Soon enough, the town would think of her and Ollie as nothing else. Makani wanted to hold on to this normalcy for as long as possible.

Her mother's voicemail picked up. "Hey, Mom. It's me. I don't know why you and Dad aren't answering your phones. The hospital and the police have been trying to call you for hours. Grandma and I are all right, but . . . just call me back, okay?"

The same thing happened when she tried her father. She left a similar message.

"No luck?" Ollie asked on her approach. He sounded numb.

She shook her head, slumping back into the chair beside his. They zoned out and watched the television mounted on the opposite wall. Blissfully, it wasn't the news. It was a rerun of *Friends*, and Chandler was in a box. Some kind of punishment for hurting Joey.

"They're using our names," Ollie said in a low voice.

Makani tilted her head as she turned to him. "Huh?"

"Snaps, tweets. The whole town knows that you and I were attacked."

He wasn't looking at his phone, so he must have seen it earlier. Outwardly, she remained blank and unsurprised. Darby and Alex had known, either from hearing it online or seeing her house on the news. But internally, the confirmation nauseated her. People Googled. People talked.

"At least they won't know that I was naked," Ollie said.

Sweat collected along her hairline. Behind her knees.

I should tell him.

"There are certain details that we, at the station, believe are best kept private," he said, in an accurate imitation of his brother. "Believe me, no one will know . . . the nature of your visit." Ollie switched back to his own voice. "Believe me, no one will know . . . until someone writes a book."

The image hurled her into the future and slackened her jaw. He was right. Someday, their story would be a chapter in one of those sleazy, mass-market, true-crime paperbacks that were shelved in the cobwebbed corners of used bookstores—the types of paperbacks that boasted about the number of crime-scene photographs inside.

Ollie winced at her expression. "So, we're not joking about it yet."

"Just tell me something good." She put her head in her hands. "I need to hear something positive."

He considered the assigned task, taking it seriously. "They've called in a team of dogs to help with the search. They think he went into the fields near the school. There's a huge manhunt happening right now—at least half of Osborne is out there searching for him." When she didn't respond, he added quietly, "It's almost over."

Her brain swayed inside her skull. "I won't feel better until it's *actually* over."

Ollie sank deeper into his chair. His long legs splayed out, and his hands folded over his stomach. "Yeah." He sighed.

"It's weird," he said, several minutes later. "I've known him my whole life. Our families went to the same church. We were on the wrestling team together in middle school. He didn't seem like a killer. He didn't seem like . . ."

". . . anything," Makani finished. Briefly thinking about Ollie as a wrestler.

"Yeah."

"Do you think that's why?" Ollie asked. "Because he feels invisible?"

She buried her head back into her hands and shrugged.

"I just don't understand why he would target *you*."

Her breath hitched.

I should tell him. I have to tell him. I can't hide anymore.

"Hey." A hand on her back.

She startled up with a gasp. Chris was stooped beside her chair. His and Ollie's faces were creased with worry. Behind them, the construction worker and the elderly couple were staring at her tattered clothing. The woman whispered to her husband.

Chris threatened them with a police officer's glare as he helped Makani to her feet. "Your grandma said it was okay to come home with us," he said. "Why don't you say goodbye, and we'll get the hell out of here."

CHAPTER SEVENTEEN

THE BROTHERS SWITCHED on the Victorian-style lamps throughout their house to maintain the illusion of safety. It had been less than a week since her previous visit, but the creaky loneliness of the old structure had already diminished in Makani's memories. Now, it felt intensified under the black coat of night. The crumbling plaster walls contained a crawling sort of dread. They were alive with hidden ghouls—ghostly and human.

Makani lay awake in Ollie's bed, underneath his cold window. The cloud-covered moon concealed the cornfields below. The floral bouquets had been brought in from the car and were bunched together inside the same glass vase on Ollie's desk. The yellow sunflowers, golden chrysanthemums, red gerbera daisies, and brown corkscrewed twigs were cheerfully autumnal, but the shadows they cast were inky and menacing.

Her attacker—it was intolerable for her to think his name right now—had reduced her to a child afraid of the dark. She wanted her stuffed animals. Perhaps they could have kept her tethered to these more simple fears as opposed to her current reality.

She wasn't at home, because she couldn't go home.

A serial killer wanted her dead.

The drugs for her arm were also supposed to help her sleep. Instead, she was paranoid and woozy. In the darkness, Makani became aware of her cut. It *hurt*. The tightly wrapped bandage was stiff, and it made her feel clumsy. Ollie had lent her a T-shirt and plaid pajama pants. The clothing and bedsheets smelled like his skin, musky and clean and arousing. But they were a constant reminder of where she was and why.

Chris had given his brother the choice of sleeping downstairs on the couch or upstairs on the floor of Chris's bedroom. Ollie had picked a third option, a sleeping bag in the upstairs hallway. The master bedroom remained empty. It belonged to the spirits.

Ollie's sleeping bag rustled outside her door as Makani's ears strained for sounds of the uninvited: Drawers opening. Puzzle pieces snapping. She tried to listen for the *tick, tick, tick* of the grandfather clock, but then she inhaled Ollie's scent and remembered, all over again, that she wasn't at home. Remembered that the clock had been broken.

A hooded figure lurched out at her.

She curled into a fetal position to protect herself from the blade. Everything was spinning. She screamed into the pillow.

"Makani," a voice said.

She scuttled into the corner in fright.

"It's okay," the voice said. In the moonlight, Ollie was crouched beside the bed. "You were having a nightmare." He climbed onto the mattress and coaxed her out from against the wall. Held her as she trembled in his arms.

Her heart was pounding in her throat, but as she stared at Ollie's thickly socked feet, her confusion reshaped into consciousness. "Do they hurt?" she asked.

"No," he said softly, and she knew it was a lie. "How's your arm?"

"Fine," she said.

They were silent for a long time. When he made a motion to leave, her night terrors surged back like an electrical storm. *"Don't."*

He didn't.

She lay down on the narrow bed and pressed her body against the wall. He slipped into the open space. He took out his phone, and his face illuminated in aqua blue. Makani was about to protest that she didn't want to see the news, when she realized he was setting an alarm. "So you can get back into the hallway before morning?" she asked.

Ollie smiled faintly as the light vanished.

With a muted thud, his phone was placed onto the hardwood floor. They pulled up the blankets. There was a gap between their bodies, slender enough for a shadow or a whisper. Makani heard it first. And then she felt it. His breath was warm and vital.

She closed the gap, and they nestled together against the darkness.

It took hours to fall asleep. Whenever her eyes closed, a hooded figure lurched out—an endless loop of the same harrowing second. Ollie shifted and rolled and twisted the sheets, but she was grateful for his presence. She was grateful not to be alone.

When her mind finally succumbed, the sleep was restless and sweaty. And then the alarm went off.

Makani gasped, jackknifing into a sitting position.

Ollie switched off the alarm and flattened the phone across his racing heart. Through the panes of the arched, church-like window, a rosy-orange dawn was breaking over the fields. The first birds of the morning sang to one another.

Makani dissolved into the blankets as Ollie's legs swung over the side of the bed. Her hand shot out. It clutched his upper arm—that sensitive place, where bare skin met shirtsleeve. He craned his neck to look at her. Her hand crawled up, grasped the cotton sleeve, and pulled him back down. They kissed.

Quiet. Hungry. Desperate.

Ollie broke away first, a few minutes later. She stared at him. Begging him to stay. He shook his head. *I can't,* he mouthed.

Please, she said.

"I'll be on the other side of the door," he whispered. *"I'm not going anywhere."*

Less than an hour later, they gave up on pretending. The air was dewy and cold, and Ollie lent Makani his hoodie for warmth. It comforted her to remain embraced by his scent. When they shuffled into the kitchen, Chris was already in uniform and making coffee. Neither party was surprised to find the other awake. Chris looked as unrested and shell-shocked as Makani felt. Her eyes darted to the cabinets and drawers. They were closed.

How many times had David broken into her house? Her sluggish thoughts tried to recall each separate invasion. It usually happened when they were asleep. Had it ever happened when they were awake? Which was worse?

Squidward looked up from licking his bowl. His tags jangled as he moseyed up beside Ollie and followed them to the sunshine-yellow breakfast table. The seat cushions were upholstered in matching yellow vinyl. Thankfully, Chris hadn't left behind any folders. Makani wasn't ready to see the blood spatter inside her own house.

"So," Chris said. "I got up in the middle of the night to pee."

Makani and Ollie stiffened.

Chris thunked down an empty mug in front of Ollie. "You're sleeping in my room tonight, bro." More gently, he placed a second mug in front of Makani. It was a similar shade of bright yellow, and it contained SpongeBob's goofy, bucktoothed face. "I refuse to ignite your grandma's wrath when she gets out of the hospital."

Their eyes affixed on the Formica tabletop. They nodded.

Chris opened his mouth to say something. He hesitated. "You guys *are* using protection of some kind, right?"

Ollie buried his fingers in his pink hair. "Jesusfuckingchrist."

"Answer the question, and we'll never speak of it again." Chris paused. "Unless, you need me to buy—"

"*Yes.*"

Chris held up his hands. "Good. We're done here."

Makani's cheeks burned. She was already thinking about the similar conversation that she'd be forced to have with her grandmother. Somehow, she doubted Grandma Young would keep it so brief.

The coffee finished brewing, and Chris filled their mugs. No one mentioned food, because no one had an appetite. They stared at the rising vapors.

"So," Makani said. "He's still out there."

Because Chris would have told them, otherwise. The table only had two chairs, so he was slumped against the counter. "Last night, a K-9 unit tracked him to the fields surrounding the school, but they lost the trail when it hit the river. Maybe if we were a bigger town—if we hadn't needed to call up the unit from Lincoln—we would have found him before he reached water." His head hung as if it weighed heavily upon his shoulders. "The team's still searching, though. They're trying to pick up his trail again somewhere along the banks."

Makani imagined the predator slinking through the fields in his cornstalk-colored camouflage. A lion in wait.

Chris's voice firmed. "We'll get him soon. He can't hide for much longer."

Outside the windows, the fields were hushed and still.

"I know you answered a million of our questions last night," he said, "and I know you don't really know the guy, but what did you think about him, before all this? What was your general impression?"

Makani was surprised when she couldn't think of a reply.

"Anything," Chris said. "It might be useful."

"I guess . . . nothing. He was just a *nothing* guy, you know? Kind of a redneck. Scrawny. I've never really noticed any defining or distinguishing features." Makani tried to picture David at school. She tried to picture the version of David that wasn't inside her house. "It's like . . . he's all one color. Sandy-blond hair, tannish skin. They blend together. I don't remember his eyes. Maybe he has a weak chin?"

"Okay. But appearance aside, what kind of person was he?"

"Quiet?" She shrugged and then glanced at Ollie with a laugh. "Not as quiet as him, though."

Ollie gave her a small but knowing smile.

His brother also cracked a smile. "What else?"

"We sat near each other in a few classes. Alphabetical order. Ware, Young. I never took much notice of him, but he seemed smart enough."

"Can you explain why he gave you that impression?"

It was another hard question. "I guess because he always had a quick response—to jokes or whatever. And he listened and watched. Paid attention. He had a large group of friends, and I figured Rodrigo was his *best* friend, but maybe that's only because they sat near me in physics, so sometimes I overheard their conversations."

"What'd they talk about?"

"Tech stuff. Boring. I didn't understand most of it." Her arms folded over her stomach. "I still can't believe that he killed his own friend. You guys are sure he's working alone?"

"An imprint of a boot was left behind at the Moraleses' house," Chris said, and she nodded as if Ollie hadn't already told her. "It's David's size, and his parents confirmed that he wears the brand. They're missing from his closet. Combined with everything else we know, it seems unlikely that he's working with a partner."

Ollie traced his finger along the handle of his mug. "How did Rodrigo's parents react when they learned that it was David?"

"Bev gave them the news last night." Chris shook his head. "Said they appeared to be genuinely shocked. They told her that David had always been polite and respectful—more so than some of Rodrigo's other friends—and that he seemed like a normal teenage boy. Hell, they've known him since Montessori preschool."

"What about David's parents?" Makani asked.

"Chief questioned them all night, and the sheriff's guys are helping us search their property just outside of town. But they seem decent. Hard working, churchgoing. Their families go way back in Sloane County on both sides, and all the grandparents and aunts and uncles and cousins still live here. Dad had a disorderly conduct charge for public urination, but that was almost twenty years ago. And, apparently, he took David deer hunting every November, which explains a few things. But it's not unusual."

Not unusual for here, Makani thought.

"From what I heard," he continued, "David's parents were blindsided."

Ollie's brows knitted together in doubt. He was still fiddling with the mug.

"I'm sure it's hard for you to believe," Chris said, a familiar wryness to his voice, "but parents don't always know what their kids are up to."

"Then they should ask," Ollie said.

"They should. But sometimes kids lie."

Ollie's index finger stopped.

"But . . . you're right." Chris looked away. It was an attempt to defuse the old tension of him being a stand-in parent. Makani had only heard hints about the fights that had occurred since Chris had moved back home, but she did know it had taken them a few years to adjust to their circumstances. "Sometimes, parents are just shitty."

"If they're hiding anything," Ollie said, lifting his head to extend his own peace offering, "you'll find it."

Arduous days required scrupulous planning. Chris announced that he would escort them to Makani's house so she could grab some clothes and toiletries. After that, he'd go to work, and Ollie would drive her to the hospital. In the afternoon, Ollie would go to work, and she'd remain behind with her grandmother. And then when Ollie's shift ended, he'd pick her up, and they would all converge again at the Larsson house.

The brothers offered her the first shower. She'd rinsed off her skin in the sink last night, so she declined with a secret shudder. There was no way these white boys had the right hair products. She could wait another hour until she was home.

While Ollie showered, Makani faced the reality of her phone. In addition to a slew of new texts from Darby and Alex, unexpected messages had arrived from the student-council president and from Haley's best friend. Being president had given Katie access to her number, and Brooke had gotten it through Darby. Their texts were supportive and kind, but Makani couldn't deal with trying to form any polite responses right now.

She listened to her voicemail instead. Her father said that he'd heard what had happened from her mother, and to give him a call sometime. There was no urgency to this request.

There was also no missed call from her mother.

Principal Stanton had left a voicemail, which was awkward, and there was another from Tamara Schuyler at the *Omaha World-Herald*, which was unsettling. Despite their claims, Makani knew the type of journalist who hounded a minor post-trauma wasn't interested in that minor's well-being.

They were only interested in the salacious story.

Chris flashed his lights—*whoop whoop*—so that their cars could maneuver through the crowd. Grandma Young's yard had become a staging area for the media. The local truck, Omaha trucks, and cable news trucks were parked side by side with *Dateline* and *48 Hours*. There'd been a mass shooting at a university in Florida with eleven dead and six injured. There'd been a suicide bomber at a shopping mall in Istanbul with thirteen dead and twenty-seven injured. Yesterday's headlines were terrifying, but they were also so terrifyingly commonplace that the eyes of the country had turned to Osborne.

Tendons knotted inside Makani's shoulders. It was bizarre to see all the lights on in the windows when neither she nor her grandmother were home. How many strangers had prowled through their house in the hours since the attack?

How many hours had *he* prowled through it?

Makani wondered if an element of sexual perversion coexisted with David's breaking and entering. Did he watch her—through the slats of her closet door, from underneath her bed—while she changed? Did it get him off?

They parked in the congested driveway behind three other police vehicles. It felt as if a spotlight were following them as they exited and jostled through the shouting mob. Makani was still wearing Ollie's hoodie, shrouded under its black hood. Thinking about the hood hurtled her mind back to David.

Where was he hiding *now?*

Makani stared at her house, and her legs suddenly grew rigid.

Ollie's fingers clasped through hers. It was the first time that they'd held hands for anyone to see. Tethered to his grip, she felt safe. They ran together.

Inside, the situation was quiet and grim. Hideous bloodstains soiled the living room carpet. Smeary red handprints glazed the front window and door. It felt chillingly empty without the tick of the grandfather clock. The heart of the house was dead.

Makani listened in as Sergeant Beemer, a stout man with a bulbous nose, updated Chris with the latest. Splinters of painted wood from where David had been jimmying open the downstairs bathroom window had been discovered on the ground outside. The bathroom was located directly below Makani's bedroom, and the overgrown viburnum, which blocked the window's view, showed signs of having been trampled.

"The bush is right beside the water spigot. David's foot probably got tangled in the garden hose during one of his exits." The sergeant sniffed his ruddy nose. "It'd explain all the snapped branches."

A shiver rattled down Makani's spine. She knew *exactly* when David had snagged his foot. It happened the day after Haley's murder, while she'd been waiting for Ollie to call. She'd thought it was the neighbor's cat.

Makani imagined a hooded figure climbing into her grandmother's bathroom. Hiding in her shower. Peering through her private things.

And it was impossible not to *keep* imagining him as she closed her bathroom door and stepped into her own shower. Behind the clear vinyl curtain, she became Janet Leigh in *Psycho*. The shampoo stung her eyes, because she was too afraid to close them. Even with her eyes wide-open, she still saw the silhouette of a young man with a knife.

Ollie is right there. Right outside the door.

But Ollie had also been nearby when David had attacked her.

There's an entire squadron of cops downstairs.

But downstairs was so far away.

CHAPTER EIGHTEEN

"**WOULDN'T THAT TIME** be better spent looking for him?" Grandma Young cut someone off. "I know. I know about the search parties. I just don't understand why we can't *all* focus on capturing him first."

Makani and Ollie paused outside her door. It was a phone call— and not a pleasant one. Makani's heart swelled to hear Grandma Young sounding like herself, but they decided to wait in the hallway until the call ended. They didn't have to wait long.

"I can't *believe* you would ask that of her. It hasn't even been *one day*."

They heard a handset fall against a hard plastic receiver and realized she'd been using the hospital's telephone, which made sense. Her cell was still in their bag.

Makani knocked twice and peeked inside.

Grandma Young's energy and skin tone had improved over the night, though her posture remained exhausted. But when she shifted her gaze and saw them, she perked up. "I thought you were another nurse. Come here! Let me see you."

"How are you feeling? Who was that?" Makani kissed her cheek and then reached for the phone to place it correctly onto the receiver. It was hanging slightly off.

"Leave it. I did that on purpose. Already been too many calls this morning."

"Reporters," Makani said. They wouldn't hesitate to harass someone who'd been hospitalized.

"Oh, no. Well. Yes." She huffed. "But that was just someone from church."

It wasn't how those calls usually sounded. Makani frowned. "Who?"

"Doesn't matter." Grandma Young motioned for her to sit. "Show me your arm. Did I see it last night? I can hardly remember your visit."

Makani snuggled in on the side without all the wires and tubes. She'd changed into a clean pair of jeans, a long-sleeved shirt, and her surfer-floral hoodie. Ollie had resumed custody of his black hoodie. She'd been disappointed to return it.

"I'm fine, see? It was only a scratch." She lifted her sleeve to reveal the bottom of the bandage, expecting her grandmother to demand to see the rest. But the painkillers must have been pretty hardcore, because she accepted the partial reveal as the whole truth. The call seemed important, so Makani tried again. "What did they want?"

Grandma Young squirmed. Adjusted her position. "The town is planning some sort of memorial for the victims."

Makani glanced at Ollie, who'd taken a seat in the recliner. He gave her a small shake of his head, equally in the dark.

"It's happening this afternoon on Main Street," Grandma Young said, withholding eye contact. "The idea is that people are tired of being afraid, and fear didn't prevent the previous attacks, so we might as well go outside and support one another."

"But that sounds like a good thing," Makani said. "That sounds . . ."

"Brave," Ollie said.

"Yeah. Like those Parisians who went back to the cafés after the terrorist attacks."

Grandma Young's gaze snapped up. "It *is* brave. But if everyone put this much effort into the search, he'd be handcuffed by sundown. And *then* we could celebrate."

Handcuffed by sundown sounded very John Wayne, but Makani was more concerned by that last word. "Celebrate?"

"No, that's not what I meant. I just think the memorial can wait." Grandma Young was talking faster, agitated. Something else about this was bothering her.

"I don't know. I think it'd be nice to honor Haley and Matt and Rodrigo—"

"They want *you* to speak," she said. "The town. They want you to stand up in front of all those people and cameras and be their mascot."

Makani shriveled with revulsion. Now she understood.

"It'll happen over my dead body," Grandma Young said. "And I'm hard to kill."

Ollie burst into unexpected laughter. He covered his mouth with a hand, but Makani and her grandmother finally broke into smiles. He gestured to a cloth tote bag. "Hey," he said. "We brought a few things to cheer you up."

"Oh, yeah!" Makani slid off the bed, and they withdrew each item one-by-one like gifts. Purse, robe, pajamas, blanket, toiletries, phone, books, puzzle. All the comforts of Grandma Young's home. None of the carnage.

•   •   •

Makani's other home called around noon. Her mother's first inquiry was, "Are you okay?" It was an encouraging start, but the follow-up was, "I just can't believe it. There's always *something* with you, isn't there?"

Makani had always been a fleck of sand in the eyes of this person who was supposed to love her unconditionally. She was an irritation, a nuisance.

"Now, I'll have to fly to the mainland to babysit you while your grandmother—"

"Where were you yesterday, Mom? The police and the hospital tried calling you for hours. *I* tried calling you."

"Your father and I were in court. I called everyone back the moment I got home, which is more than he did, by the way." She didn't seem to be aware that *everyone* had not included her daughter. Nor was she interested in hearing her daughter's version of events as she launched directly into her travel plans. She would be in Osborne next week, probably. She had an important presentation at work—or maybe it was something related to the divorce proceedings, Makani's hearing had dimmed—that couldn't be missed.

"And now, look. Look what you're doing to me."

"I'm sorry, Mom—"

"I can't deal with you right now."

Silence. Makani stared at the blinking number on her phone. *Three minutes and fourteen seconds.* She'd almost been killed, and her mother had given her three minutes and fourteen seconds. And she'd turned it into *her* problem.

Of course it was about her. It was always about her.

But Makani felt unexpectedly devastated. The phone trembled in her hand. She hadn't realized that her mother could still hurt her like this.

Ollie stared at her, unable to hide the empathetic sorrow from his usually reserved expression. Something about that was painful, too.

"Have you eaten today?" Grandma Young asked.

The question surprised Makani. As she struggled to focus, she touched her arm. The wound was sensitive and sore. "I don't think I've eaten anything in the last twenty-four hours."

"Oliver, would you get my purse? There should be a twenty in my wallet. I'd like for you to go to the cafeteria and pick up a few things. Something that would be easy for Makani to digest—soup or bread. And whatever looks good to you."

"Sure, Mrs. Young. I'd be happy to." He found the twenty and gave a low wave of goodbye to Makani as he disappeared.

"She's my daughter. And I love her," Grandma Young said quietly. "But she's a raging narcissist who married an asshole."

Makani had never heard her grandmother say the word *ass*. Under any other circumstance, it would have been hysterical. Right now, it only stung like the truth.

"None of this is your fault," Grandma Young said.

"*I know*," Makani whispered. A lie.

"Do you?"

Makani nodded. Another lie.

Grandma Young patted the space beside her, and Makani sat. She patted closer. Makani scooted, and her grandmother cradled her with a tilted head. They sat like this for several minutes. The affection felt painful. Makani's whole existence was a mess of secrets and lies and pretending. Her grandmother was the only person in Osborne who knew why she was really here, yet she still loved her. Makani wanted to be comforted, but she didn't deserve it.

Her grandmother released a weary sigh. "You lied to me."

Makani stiffened. Terrified by her own transparency.

"You lied to me yesterday, and we'll have to deal with that. I'm not sure how yet. This is all . . . a lot to process. But I love you, and I want you and Ollie to be safe—"

Oh God. Wait. Was this about staying safe from murderers or safe sex? Makani knew it was wrong, but she hoped her grandmother was talking about murder.

"—in *all the ways possible* for you to be safe."

She wriggled out from her grandmother's embrace.

"We'll talk about it more soon," Grandma Young said. "When I'm not in the hospital, and your boyfriend isn't down the hall."

A tiny particle of hope shot through Makani's distress. It did seem like maybe Ollie was her boyfriend now. Or that he would be soon.

Her grandmother continued, "But I wanted to mention it, so that I can also say: I trust you. And I trust that you'll be honest with me from now on."

I trust you.

It rattled her. Those three words made Makani *want* to be more open and honest. They made her want to be the person that her grandmother believed she was.

Just then, a loud exclamation trumpeted down the hallway of the ICU. "You!"

Makani knew that voice. Her pulse quickened.

"You saved her!" Alex said.

"She was saving herself," Ollie said. "Her grandma and I only helped."

Makani could almost hear Alex's grin. "Hell yeah, she was saving herself."

"We're just glad that you're all okay," Darby said.

They burst into the room, energetic bundles of joy and relief, and threw their arms around Makani in an enthusiastic group hug. She hadn't realized how badly she'd needed them until this moment. Their embrace rejuvenated her spirits.

"How did you know we were here?" she asked.

"We heard that your grandma was hurt," Darby said, balancing a box of gas station doughnuts. "Where else would you be?"

Alex leveled a saucy look at Makani. "No help from you, though. Next time, answer your damn"—she glanced at Grandma Young—"dang phone."

"No next time," Darby said.

"Amen to that," Grandma Young said, and they bounded over to hug her, too.

Alex's hair was woven into a strange and complicated configuration, and a loose braid flew into the air when she spun back around to Makani. "We brought treats." She opened the lid to show off the sugary rings. "Maple for you, chocolate frosting for Ollie."

Makani was touched they'd remembered his preference. Perhaps it was only penance for accusing him of being a serial killer behind his back, but she was happy to grant them atonement. Ollie stood near the door. He was holding a tower of Styrofoam cartons from the cafeteria, but he smiled, not in the least upset to be upstaged.

"Mrs. Young, this one is for you." Alex pointed to a doughnut with orange frosting and black sprinkles. It was a Halloween doughnut.

"Because your house is always so seasonal," Darby explained.

Grandma Young glowed with pleasure, even though it would be a few weeks before she could eat solid food. Everyone was talking at once, lively and loudly, when a nurse that Makani didn't recognize popped his head around the door.

"We understand these are special circumstances," he said, "but I'm sorry. Only two visitors at a time are allowed in ICU rooms."

"Oh," Makani said as the chatter halted. It was clear that none of them had considered this.

"That's all right," Grandma Young said. "Why don't you go to the waiting room to catch up? I'm feeling a nap coming on, anyway."

She did look tired, so Makani kissed her cheek. "Ollie and I will be back in a bit."

Grandma Young thanked Darby and Alex for coming, and then Makani and Ollie followed them out. They were able to find a different waiting room from the main room the previous night. It was smaller, but the seating was more comfortable. Even better, it was empty of other people. Makani and Ollie took separate chairs beside each other, and Darby and Alex squeezed together into a love seat. They exclaimed over Makani's arm.

"It's not that bad, really," she said.

"Not that bad?" Alex was aghast. "A berserk teenage boy broke into your house and tried to stab you to death. Get some fucking perspective!"

Everyone froze as Alex realized that Makani probably already had a decent grasp on the situation. And then she lost it. Alex's laughter was crazed and contagious, the kind only borne from dark situations. Like giggles at a funeral, it infected them all. Out of the four of them, she seemed the closest to the edge. But perhaps Alex sensed Makani intuiting this fragility, because she grabbed a doughnut and waved it around. Feigning an air of composure. "Looks like we're real cops today. Think we can crack the case?"

"Hey," Darby said, licking glaze from his thumb as he took a doughnut for himself. "Stereotype. Brother of a cop right there."

Alex rolled her eyes, but Ollie gave Darby a smile.

"Speaking of . . ." Darby was hesitant. "What *are* they saying? The cops?"

With occasional interjections from Ollie, Makani filled them in on the last twenty-four hours. But she tripped up when she reached the part about him being naked.

"Hold up." Alex's gaze whipped to Ollie. "A minute ago in this story, you were covered by only a blanket. Did you run downstairs in a *blanket toga*?"

"Yes," Makani lied, as Ollie said, "Not exactly."

Alex cackled. "Ohmygod!"

An inevitable blush spread across Ollie's face.

"Please confirm, yes or no," she said. "You, Ollie Larsson, chased after the Osborne Slayer in your bare essentials." When he nodded the affirmative, Darby and Alex erupted with a fresh round of riotous laughter.

Sorry, Makani mouthed.

Ollie shrugged helplessly. *You tried.*

Makani understood where her friends' laughter was coming from, so she wasn't offended. It was the necessary moment of levity that would get them through the rest of the story. By the time she finished filling them in, their expressions had sobered.

"The part I can't get over," Darby said, "is *David.*"

Alex shook her head in equal disbelief.

"He seemed so normal and boring," Darby continued. "Like one of those guys who'd fade into the landscape to live the same life as his dad—"

"And his dad before him," she said.

Ollie stared at nothing. The shock of what had happened to them was circuitous; it kept coming back. "I guess you never really know what's going on inside someone else's head. His external life seemed dull, but his interior life . . . must be a lot more complex."

"It must be angry," Alex said.

He nodded. "Hurt."

Makani hadn't planned on telling them, not ever. Certainly not now. But as their words stirred inside her, they melded with her grandmother's trust, and that powerful undertow of resistance—as familiar as it was formidable—suddenly released its grasp. Her mother didn't care about her, but her friends did. She wanted them to know.

"He must have been planning this for months, maybe years," Darby said. "What cracked? What makes a person go from fantasizing to actually doing?" And as he turned to Makani in bewilderment, she knew his next question—the big one—before he even asked. "And why did he go after *you*?"

Makani took a moment before answering, but her voice was steady. "Because I think he might have learned something about my past."

Their silence was weighted with curiosity and pressure.

"My name," she said, "wasn't always Makani Young."

CHAPTER NINETEEN

ALEX'S EYES WERE saucers. "Ohmygod. You killed someone."

"What?" Makani was taken aback. "No. God, *no*. If I'd killed someone, how could I even be here? Wouldn't I be sitting in prison somewhere?"

Ollie and Darby stared at Alex in disbelief.

"Okay," she said shamelessly. "Overreaction."

Ollie turned his body toward Makani to encourage her. "Go on."

Makani Kanekalau startled awake with a terrified gasp as Gabrielle Cruz and Kayla Lum burst into her bedroom. They yanked her to the floor. Makani's skin smelled like body odor and day-old suntan lotion, and her hair was an untamed 'fro. She was wearing a tank top without a bra, and her pink pajama shorts were an old pair, see-through with age.

The girls pointed at her striped panties and laughed.

Gabrielle's teeth flashed like razors through the darkness—the last image Makani saw before she was blindfolded. "Tonight's the night, rookie," Gabrielle taunted. The blindfold was too tight, but Gabrielle was the captain, so Makani didn't dare complain.

Kayla hissed in her ear. "You're coming with us."

"I'm sorry," Alex interrupted. "These girls *kidnapped* you? Were they your friends?"

"Teammates," Makani said. "Sometimes friends, sometimes rivals. But they were seniors, and I was a junior. This was last October. My first year on varsity."

Darby seemed startled that she'd been an athlete. "Varsity *what*?"

The swim team's hazing rituals were notorious, and they'd been growing worse every year. Escalating. Now their turn, the senior girls of Kailua-Kona High School were hungry for revenge. The power of authority coursed through Gabrielle and Kayla, no doubt blinding them in its own way, as they tugged and shoved Makani down the hall.

Makani stiffened as her mother's harsh laughter cut through the narrow space. "Sorry again about the locked door, girls." A familiarity on the word *girls* indicated that she was on their side—and she wasn't surprised that they were here. "Glad I was still awake to hear your knock."

It was well known that parents were informed of the initiation ahead of time so that they could leave the front door unlocked for the older girls to get in. It was understood that the parents would play along, but that they'd also give their daughters the heads-up. That way, the rookies could already be dressed in their cutest pajamas with swimsuits underneath. That's what parents were *supposed* to do.

Makani tensed in hopeful anticipation of another

apology, this time for her. Or, at least, an excuse. But as she was pushed outside, all she heard was the *click*—and lock—of the door behind her.

"Umm. Your mom sucks?" Alex was both stating it and asking for confirmation.

Darby looked too sad to berate her.

Makani didn't want to see Ollie's reaction, so she kept going.

Gabrielle and Kayla prodded Makani outside and wrestled her into an open-air Jeep. Makani knew it was the captain's car. Gabrielle swerved wildly, purposefully, down the street as Makani fumbled for a seat belt. The wind blasted her as she jostled from one side of the Jeep to the other, frightening her with the sensation that she was about to fall out. At last, she managed to strap herself in.

"Where are we going?" She tried to sound like she was fine, down for anything. But fear clouded her voice.

The girls just turned up the radio, and Makani's neighborhood was left behind in a thundering wake of Beyoncé. The air was thick with humidity. The breeze was scented like salt water and sweet plumeria. Recognizing that she was being ignored, Makani lifted her blindfold for a peek. The dashboard clock said it was almost midnight. On the Queen Ka'ahumanu Highway, skinny palm trees were silhouetted by the night sky, the tallest vegetation amid the scrubland that characterized this side of the Big Island.

Only a few minutes later, Gabrielle cut the engine. The music vanished. Ocean waves boomed. "Time to deplane, rookie," she said, and Kayla laughed at the dumb joke. Kayla was always trying to impress the captain. They grabbed

Makani by the upper arms, one on each side, and steered her, barefoot, over a beach of volcanic rocks. Something punctured the ball of her right foot, and Makani hissed in pain.

Their grips tightened around her arms.

A crackling bonfire strengthened into a roar as Makani's feet touched sand. Peals of girlish laughter swirled and eddied. She knew they were aimed at her.

"Are we the last to arrive?" Kayla called out, reveling in the attention.

Catcalls and whistles rose above the laughter. The blindfold was ripped from Makani's eyes, and she squinted, holding up a hand against the sparks from the fire.

The whole team was there. The other rookies' blindfolds had already been removed. They were laughing at her, too.

Even Jasmine was laughing. She and the other three rookies were dressed in bikini tops and board shorts. Their hair was done—Jasmine's straight hair was pulled back into a neat ponytail—and some of them were even wearing makeup.

Mortified, Makani crossed her arms over her chest. She felt ugly and exposed. She'd swum with most of these girls since childhood. They'd seen her thousands of times in swimsuits, but it didn't matter that her ratty tank top and pajamas covered more skin; she was the only one wearing the wrong thing. The *private* thing.

A rush of anger washed through her humiliation. Clearly, Mrs. Oshiro, Jasmine's perfect mother, had warned her. Why hadn't Jasmine said something? She was her best friend. They texted each other first thing in the morning and last thing before bed. They'd texted less than two hours ago, and Jasmine hadn't given any indication of anything unusual. And she *knew* Makani's mom couldn't be relied on for things like this.

Gabrielle gestured at Makani's pajama shorts. "Might as well take those off."

Makani didn't move.

"The captain said strip!" Kayla screamed into her ear. "Strip!"

"Strip! Strip! Strip! Strip!" the other girls chanted.

The intimacy of her underwear made Makani want to cry. Shivering, she pulled down her pajama shorts and folded them neatly on the sand.

The captain snatched them up and waved them triumphantly like a flag. "Let the games begin!"

Cheering broke out as the girls split into five teams, with two veterans to every rookie. The rookies' veteran teammates were the same as their kidnappers. In block-lettered Sharpie, the captain wrote SLUT, NYMPHO, WHORE, and CUNT on the other rookies' foreheads. The marker pressed against her skin, and Makani was informed that she was BITCH. If she responded to any other name, she'd have to take a shot.

Four vodka bottles were produced, two in each of Kayla's hands, and she waved them like pom-poms. Kayla swam freestyle. She had insane endurance, and her muscles rippled in the bonfire's light. "What's your name, Bitch?" she yelled.

"Bitch!" Makani said.

"I said, what's your name, Bitch?"

"BITCH!"

"Okay," Gabrielle said. "Makani, your spot is between Hannah and Jasmine."

Makani took off.

"Wrong! Who's Makani?"

She couldn't believe that she'd already forgotten. Divers were precise. They performed well in the spotlight. Makani did not make mistakes. Everyone cracked up again as she downed the first repugnant shot, trying not to gag. She'd never liked vodka. It reminded her of nail-polish remover.

Gabrielle's best stroke was butterfly. The captain had the team's strongest arms, so when she clapped Makani's back, it stung. "Take your place, Makani."

Makani stood her ground. Swallowed her tears.

"Hey! The rookie bitch has learned her lesson," she said.

"Great job, Bitch." Kayla ruffled her curls. Few things grated Makani more than someone touching her hair. "Now get your ass in line."

Makani jogged to the area between Hannah (SLUT) and Jasmine (CUNT). It pleased her that Jasmine had gotten the meanest name.

"Are you okay?" Jasmine asked, placing a pitying hand on Makani's arm.

Two days ago, they'd gotten matching gel manicures of alternating silver and blue. School colors. Now Makani wanted to shove Jasmine to the ground and cram her mouth with dry sand until she choked. Makani fixed her with a livid glare. Jasmine seemed surprised by the intensity, but she removed her hand in silent surrender.

They were not a team tonight. She would *not* lose to Jasmine.

The games involved running and performing their usual dry-land calisthenics—lunges, jumping jacks, push-ups, and sit-ups—only they had to do twice as many reps and with two veterans yelling in their ears, forcing them to repeat pledges of team loyalty and tricking them into responding to their real names. It was the veterans' job to make their rookie finish last in as many rounds as possible.

Between each round, the rookies had to drink a shot of vodka. The last rookie to finish had to drink two. The veterans could drink as little or as much as they wanted, and they all took swigs before stalking toward their rookies with brown-paper grocery sacks.

The first round began. Makani ran the beach with grim determination. The veterans removed egg cartons from the mysterious sacks and hurled their missiles from a distance. The eggs were rotten and sulfurous. Some of the girls dry-heaved. As Jasmine's ponytail bobbed ahead of her, resentment scorched through Makani's veins.

It must be nice to have someone who gives enough of a shit about you to warn you. Must be nice to have been given the opportunity to prepare.

Kayla wasted her carton early, but the captain saved hers for the final lap, when Makani was panting and light-headed. Gabrielle jogged beside her, chucking her own dozen *hard.* With each hit, Makani felt an accompanying shot of adrenaline. She pushed ahead of Jasmine, and Jasmine finished in fifth. Last place.

Makani took a single shot, and Jasmine took two. The veterans also took shots. Gabrielle and Kayla drank more than the others, Makani's non-loss adding fuel to their competitive and exploitative inclinations.

As the rookies lunged, the veterans squirted them with baby oil and shaving cream. As they did jumping jacks, they flung mayonnaise and Spam. In a blur of screaming and vodka and exhaustion and confusion, Makani soon grew ill, but she kept her eyes on Jasmine. Forced herself to keep beating her.

"We've got a tough one." Gabrielle grinned. "But don't worry. We'll break you."

"Looks like she's out for your job, Captain," Kayla said.

Even though it was a joke, it was the first time that anyone had ever mentioned the possibility of captain. Divers never got to be captain because so much of their training was separate. But Makani *desperately* wanted to be captain next year. She was good at what she did. None of her teammates got more elevation from their takeoff, executed their twists so gracefully, entered the water with so little splash.

Jasmine stumbled into Makani and toppled her to the sand. A vodka bottle emptied the rest of its contents onto Makani's underwear.

"God, keep your failure to yourself!" Makani said.

"Sorry, sorry," Jasmine slurred. She'd never been able to hold her liquor.

The older girls were rolling with laughter. "I take it back," Kayla said to Gabrielle. "That's job security right there."

Makani's insides strummed with fury. She imagined seizing Jasmine's hair and yanking until the flesh ripped from her scalp. Thrusting her lacerated head into the salty waves. Holding her in place. Drowning her.

"Shit," Gabrielle said, brandishing a can of something. Makani couldn't tell what. "These don't have pull tabs. Did anyone remember to bring a can opener?"

None of the other veterans had, but a girl named Sarah kept a knife in her car. While she ran to fetch it, another bottle was passed around. The vodka burned as it slid down Makani's throat. She licked her lips.

Sarah's knife turned out to be large, something made for hunting or survival, and it easily pierced the cans. The smell released was repellent.

As the rookies did push-ups, chunks of meaty dog food were lobbed onto their backs. Crouching in front of Makani, Kayla pushed a wet handful directly onto her face and up her nostrils. Makani blew her nose and spit, retching. And then something thick was cascading down her head. An entire jar of honey oozed over her neck and through her hair. It would take days to wash out.

With each push-up, her body encrusted itself with more and more sand. "What's your problem, Bitch?" Kayla screeched. "Can't handle a few push-ups, Bitch?"

"Makani!" Gabrielle said.

"Wha—?" Makani turned her head, and her veterans high-fived.

Kayla lowered a bottle to Makani's lips. "Drink up, Bitch."

Another shot was forced down her throat. It mixed with the dog food and sickly sweet honey. She vomited. The veterans exclaimed with disgusted glee, but Makani couldn't escape the stench. The honey clung the puke to her chin. As the other rookies finished their reps, Gabrielle and Kayla whooped and danced. Two more shots. Makani threw up again, but she refused to go down alone. "Hey, Jasmine."

Her best friend was doubled over in sickness and exhaustion, but she glanced up at her name. The word CUNT was smudged but still legible. "Yeah?"

Makani pointed her finger. "Ha!"

It was a direct violation of best friendship. Jasmine's jaw unhinged, hurt and upset, while the other girls laughed at the deception. They made her drink.

As the final round began, Makani had no idea who was losing. Her eyes scrunched closed as she did the sit-ups—just trying to breathe, just trying to keep everything from coming up again. Someone straddled her legs.

"Look at me," the captain said.

Makani opened her eyes, and a bottle was thrust toward her face. She screamed as something splashed onto her eyeballs. The liquid burned like an instant inferno. She tried to wipe it away and then shrieked like she'd been wounded again. Her hands were still covered in sand and honey and gloppy food droppings. Blinded and in agony, she scrambled to her feet. "What is it? What did you to do me?"

Bedlam erupted as the other rookies cried out all around her. Screaming and yelling. Laughing and cackling. The intensity of the pain reminded Makani of being stung by a jellyfish. Someone said habanero Tabasco. Someone else grabbed her.

"Tilt your head back," the girl said.

Thinned filth streamed in every direction across Makani's face, but she could make out—she could *see*—a bottle of water. She crumpled to the sand. The girl ran off to help someone else. Makani moaned and gnashed her teeth. Through her tears, she saw another plastic water bottle near the bonfire, only a few feet away beside the empty cans and knife.

As Makani reached for the water, Jasmine swooped in and grabbed it. Her ponytail, thick with honey, smacked Makani across the eyes.

Orange sparks flew into the star-strewn sky. Rage, white-hot. With a deep guttural growl, Makani snatched up the knife. The blade flashed in the firelight. It was long and sharp and vicious. She grabbed the ponytail and sliced upward into the night.

CHAPTER TWENTY

"**THE TENSION RELEASED,** and her hair gave way."
In the waiting room, Makani could still see the limp ponytail in her
grimy hand. "It was this . . . instant, overwhelming shame. The realization that I'd done something terrible that could never be undone.

"Jasmine was so drunk"—her voice choked—"that she almost
drowned. A *swimmer*, and she almost drowned. And it was my fault."

Ollie's hand rested gently on Makani's back. He glanced at Darby
and Alex, but they weren't following what she'd said, either. "What
do you mean?"

"The other girls didn't see what had happened. Everything was so
chaotic." Makani paused, experiencing the trauma again. "Jasmine
freaked out, of course she freaked out, and ran toward the ocean. I
guess she wanted to rinse off—the Tabasco was still blistering our
eyes—and to get the hell away from me. She looked *afraid* of me. I
knew that I should go in after her, she was so out of it, but I didn't."

Makani had watched her best friend weave and stumble into the
ocean. And then she'd turned her head away in shame. It had been
too painful to watch the aftermath.

She'd figured Jasmine wouldn't even want her help, which was probably true. But Jasmine had *needed* her help. And Makani had curled up in the sand. Eyes burning, tears streaming. The knife in her right hand, the ponytail in her left.

"The captain was the one who finally noticed and dove in after her. She worked as a lifeguard on a resort, so she immediately started CPR. Jasmine wasn't breathing."

Makani shouldn't have been able to hear the wind shaking the palms or the waves lapping the shore, but the bonfire had burned to smoke and embers, and the other girls had trembled in quiet hysteria. Sirens cut through the silence. Compression and a defibrillator and some kind of alarm, another wail. Or maybe the banshee was only screaming in her head. Petrified, Makani didn't move throughout the whole ordeal.

"The paramedics arrived and got her breathing again," she said, wiping her cheeks with her fingers, "and she was okay—suddenly, she was okay—but then she was rushed away to the hospital. And by now, everyone had seen her hair . . . and they'd all seen me with the knife. The police put me in handcuffs."

They'd ushered her into the back of their car, behind the metal grate, and driven her to the station. She'd taken a Breathalyzer test, and then she'd been photographed, fingerprinted, and questioned. *"You're in a lot of trouble,"* an officer said. *"We could charge you with public intoxication, and you're looking at a third-degree assault."*

Makani's heart had plummeted into the dark sea.

Assault. She'd committed *assault.* On her *best friend.*

Even as she confessed the charge now, she couldn't look anyone in the eye. "The magistrate set the bail, and my parents arrived separately. They were already doing everything separately. But their anger . . . it *suffused* the entire station."

"I'm so sorry," Darby said. "This is all so awful."

"What about the parents who provided the alcohol?" Ollie asked. It was a question his brother might pose.

"They were charged a while later," Makani said. "That October was hell in slow motion. The school suspended me for thirty days, and I was kicked off the swim team. I'd *always* been a part of a team. And then I wasn't. The guy I'd been dating for over half a year, Jason— he was a diver, too—stopped returning my texts and unfollowed me on every platform. Our breakup was unstated but immediate."

Alex asked with atypical delicacy, "And Jasmine?"

Makani's expression gave the answer. Their friendship had died on the beach.

"Around school, her butchered hair couldn't be ignored," Makani said. "It looked so cruel. It *was* so cruel. Because I was a minor, my name wasn't reported in the media, but that didn't stop anyone from talking online. It didn't stop anyone from learning that I have a mug shot with the word *bitch* on my forehead or that the word *cunt* was still visible when Jasmine arrived at the hospital. The whole team was shamed, but people saw me as the ringleader."

"Even though you had a word on your head, too?" Ollie asked.

"They thought mine spoke the truth." Makani lifted her face to look at him squarely. "I was the one who picked up the knife."

Thousands of messages from classmates, neighbors, and strangers had focused their outrage on her. There were threats of scalping. Threats of rape. Threats of murder.

Shame on you, the internet said. *Why don't you just kill yourself already? #SwimSluts #KonaGate #CommitSuicideSquad*

Makani slept long hours and stirred aimlessly through her house. The barrage was endless. Immeasurable. Sometimes it hurt because everyone had the wrong idea about her, but usually it hurt because it felt like they had it right. She didn't know what to do or where to be or who to talk to. She kept wanting to call Jasmine—the one person who'd always understood—except she was the exact person Makani had failed.

"I wrote Jasmine this long apology letter. Like, I actually wrote it on paper and mailed it. She never responded, but I wouldn't have responded to me, either. Meanwhile, my parents hired an attorney who told me that I should never contact Jasmine again. And then I was asked to pay restitution."

When Makani saw that her friends didn't know what that meant, she explained, "I was asked to give her money for a professional haircut." She shook her head. "As if that were anything close to enough." Makani would have paid any amount they'd asked for. She would have cut off her own hair—she would have cut it off for the rest of her life.

"So, what happened?" Ollie's hand wasn't on her back anymore, but his body was close. "Do you still have an assault on your record?"

"No. About a month later, my district attorney dropped the charge, and I got my record expunged."

"You must have been so relieved," Darby said.

"Not really. I felt like I deserved it. And then the DA made the mistake of telling a reporter that I was sorry for what I'd done, but *one night of fun shouldn't ruin her life.* She literally used the phrase *kids will be kids.*'"

Everyone winced.

"Yep," she said. "Social media . . . did not like that."

The public wanted Makani to be punished. They became more furious, *more* incensed. The violent threats increased. The overreaction was catastrophic.

Ollie's countenance had taken on a perceptible weight, but it looked heavy with understanding—not judgment. At least, that's what Makani hoped she was seeing as he asked, "How'd you wind up here? When did your name change?"

"When my school suspension ended," Makani said, "my class-mates . . . the *looks* they gave me. The things they said. I didn't even make it to lunch. My dad picked me up from the nurse's office, and on the ride home, that's when he told me that he'd filed for divorce. And later that night, that's when my mom told me they were sending me here."

Ollie and Darby seemed dumbfounded. Alex swore.

"The DA was the one who suggested that I might have an eas-ier time adjusting if I changed my name to one that wasn't so easily traceable."

"Did you *want* to change it?" Ollie asked.

"I don't know." Makani had been so depressed that she'd just let it happen. And there *had* been some relief from having a new identity. Not much. But some.

Sharing her story now, however, had opened a valve of tremen-dous internal pressure. Her secret—this self-inflicted burden—had finally been released.

Darby set the doughnut box onto the floor, stood from the love seat, and pulled Makani into a determined bear hug. He wouldn't release her until she received it and returned it. "I'm sorry that you've lived alone with this for so long. I wish you would have told us."

"You're not afraid I'm a vicious sociopath? Someone who gets off on other people's pain?" Makani's jokes were only half jokes.

Darby pulled back, hands on her shoulders, to examine her. His nose and mouth screwed up in exaggerated concentration. "Nah."

"I don't know if you remember this," Ollie said, "but we've actu-ally met a vicious sociopath. And he wasn't anything like you."

"Besides," Alex said, "we already know that *pain* doesn't get you off. Ollie does."

Makani buried her face in Darby's shoulder, but it made them all laugh.

"Honestly?" Alex continued. "I think it's rad that you have a mug shot with the word *bitch* on your forehead. I'm gonna be you for Halloween this year."

Makani's body uprighted as her emotions crashed back down. "It's not funny. I ruined my best friend's life. I will *never* forgive myself—"

"David is ruining lives. By taking them. You did a shitty thing, and, yeah, she'll probably hate you for the rest of her life—"

"Alex," Darby warned.

"—but she still *has* a life."

"That's beside the point," Makani said. "My actions weren't harmless. I didn't just snap a wet towel or shoot my goggles at her."

Darby stepped in front of Alex to block her from Makani's view. "You're right. But I know what it's like to be angry—to think that everyone has it easier than you. Or that everyone is against you. And if you don't deal with those feelings, they don't go away on their own. They keep building and building until they *force* their way out."

Tears pricked Makani's eyes again as she stared at her bandaged arm.

"You aren't a bad person," Alex said. "You just had a bad night."

Darby guided Makani onto the love seat, squishing her in between him and Alex to confront the real issue. "So," he said, "you think David found out what you did."

Her head hung even lower. "Yes."

"You think he chose you—"

"Like Harry Potter," Alex stage-whispered.

"Oh. My. God," Darby said. "Can't you hold it in for, like, one second?"

She gave a nonchalant toss of a braid as he turned back to Makani. "You think David chose you as some sort of act of . . . antihero or vigilante justice?" he asked.

"There's nothing else it *could* be," Makani said. "I don't have any connection to the other victims. I think he found out something about all of us, and he's punishing—"

"No," Ollie said.

They looked at him in surprise. He sat, unmoved, across from them, and his voice was resolute. "You aren't being punished. You've *already* been punished. You were publicly shamed, and you've spent the last year shaming yourself. How would he even know? I didn't know, and I've Googled the hell out of you."

The love seat froze in astonishment.

Ollie's face skewed with regret. "Not anything *creepy*. Normal Googling." He paused. "But, like, a lot of it."

Darby's and Alex's eyes popped.

Queasiness and curiosity mixed inside Makani. "What did you find?"

"Not much." Ollie seemed pained, perhaps because he only had himself to blame for this conversation. "Small things, funny stuff you said. Pictures on their Instagrams." He motioned toward Darby and Alex.

Makani blinked.

Ollie was growing smaller. "Please say you've Googled me, too."

"We've *all* Googled you," Alex said.

Heat slipped up Makani's neck as she nodded.

"Thanks for leaving me hanging." Ollie exhaled, shoving his hands into his pockets. But then he sidled her with a grin. "So, what'd you find out about me?"

Makani snorted. "Even less. Though, I *did* already know that you used to wrestle in middle school. I saw a picture of you in one of those weird blue leotards."

"It's called a singlet."

"It's a leotard."

He laughed. "Now, you *have* to show me that swim team photo. You owe me."

But Makani's mind had already circled back to her worries. She chewed her lip. "You never found anything about my past?"

"No, I swear . . ." But then his head cocked.

She recoiled. "You did."

"Okay. I did do a search for 'Makani and Hawaii,' and I think, now, that I might have found something on Reddit." He didn't notice her shudder, but he spoke faster, betraying his concern. "How could I have known what I was looking at? I barely even remember the thread. I discarded it so quickly. It wasn't your name."

Her blood drained. There it was. Proof that her past was available for anyone to discover. It wouldn't be a huge step to notice the dates of the incident, search for her old name, and then find her in the swim team photos on the school's website.

Ollie was following her train of thought. "No. It's too unlikely."

"Too unlikely that a serial killer with an elaborate plan would have the patience to discover that I'm actually someone else?"

"You aren't *someone else*." This distinction seemed to bother him.

"But it's the only explanation that makes sense. I don't have a single connection to the other victims."

"That's not true," Alex said, jumping in. "He's clearly attacking one person from every clique. He's plucking out the shining stars for some macabre collection."

Makani glowered. "I'm not a member of a single club or team. I don't talk to anyone but you guys. And who says Rodrigo was a shining star?"

"*Me*," Alex said. "He was really freaking smart. Probably the smartest person in our whole class. Probably the whole school."

"So, what's my special talent? Having brown skin?"

Alex hesitated. "Well. You do stand out."

Makani stared at her for several long seconds. "Fuck," she said, looking away. She didn't know if she was angrier with Alex for pointing out something so stupidly obvious or for the idea that her skin color or being biracial or *whatever* might even be a *fraction* of David's motivation. Of course it could be.

Even smushed between Makani and the love seat's arm, Darby managed to tuck his thumbs under his suspenders. "Okay, let's pretend your theory is correct, and David was trying to punish you. What about the other victims? What did they do?"

"They were probably assholes, too," Makani said. "I mean, look at Matt."

Ollie frowned. "Some of his friends are worse."

"Yeah, but Matt was their leader. He set the example, and his friends followed."

"What about Rodrigo and Haley?" Alex asked.

"I don't know," Makani said. "But none of you knew what *I* did. Everyone has secrets." She couldn't help glancing at Ollie, but he was distracted, so he didn't notice.

"I don't know about Haley," he said. "But I do know something about Rodrigo."

Makani felt Alex's spine straighten beside her.

"It feels wrong to speak ill of the dead, but one of his friends gave the police a tip, which they checked out—and it was true. Rodrigo was a troll."

Darby frowned. "What kind? Like, a comments troll?"

"The kind who threatened women," Ollie said.

Makani's stomach dropped.

"Dozens of platforms," he continued. "Hundreds of aliases. Mainly against women in gaming. He stopped doing it a few months ago. The friend said Rodrigo realized it was wrong, but he wasn't sure what had happened to trigger his conscience."

Alex twitched sharply. This new information appeared to upset her more than Makani's confession.

"So . . . I'm right." Makani pressed her clenched fists against her forehead. Suddenly, everyone was taking her theory a lot more seriously.

Darby tugged on his suspenders. Their elasticity wouldn't last long under this much stress. "I don't know if you're *right*, exactly, but there is a strong pattern. And there *could* be something unknown about Haley."

"So, who else would David have on his list?" Ollie asked.

"But that's the thing," Makani said. "We don't know. Whatever they did, it's probably a secret."

"Unless . . ." He sagged with fatigue. "I mean, Zachary Loup. Right?"

The waiting room fell into a hush. This was the closest Makani had heard to Ollie admitting that he'd known the rumors about him and Zachary. He sighed. "Look, I know one of us was supposed to be the killer. And maybe I am a loner, but he's *definitely* an asshole. It's reasonable to assume that he'd be a target."

"Oh my God," Alex said. She didn't need to think about it.

"We have to warn him," Darby said. Instant agreement. "We can't take the chance."

Ollie called his brother. Chris sounded doubtful, but he promised to check in with Zachary. A minute later, a text arrived. It was the owner of Greeley's Foods: *Your shift has been canceled. Store closing early so employees can attend the memorial.*

"Shit!" Alex sprang from the love seat. "I'm supposed to be in the band room in five minutes."

Makani's fear reignited at the thought of anyone leaving her sight line. "What? Why? You can't go on campus!"

Alex tried to allay Makani's concern with a reassuring smile. It didn't work. "We're playing the memorial. They're just letting us in to pick up our uniforms."

"Don't worry," Darby said as he hustled Alex away, car keys already in hand. "I'll drop her off, and then we'll both be safe in the crowd."

When Makani and Ollie returned to Grandma Young's room, her bed was gone. The nurses informed them that she'd been wheeled away for a test. They sat on the floor and picked at the cold food that Ollie had brought earlier from the cafeteria. Now that they were alone, Makani wanted to talk more about her past—she wanted to be *comforted*—but Ollie was deep in contemplation about something else. The moment didn't seem right.

The vibration was faint, but they sat up like a shotgun blast.

"It's Chris," Ollie said, checking his phone.

Makani stood and walked to the mirror above the sink to give him the privacy of a few feet. Futzing with her shirt, she peeked at Ollie's reflection. His pale brows were pinched, which matched the frustrated tone of his conversation. The call was short.

"The police can't do much," he said. "They don't want to freak anyone out. But Chris did check in with Zachary, and he's safe. He's at home with his mom's boyfriend."

"So . . . that's it?"

Ollie's jawline was rigid. "Yep."

"I thought they might send a patrol car to watch over him or something."

"Maybe if they were a bigger department. Or if we had any shred of proof. But they're stretched thin, and now they have to work the memorial. Chris is already there."

Makani slumped. "I'll let Darby and Alex know."

Darby's response was immediate: *But we just saw him!*

Her breath caught. *z's at the memorial?*

Yeah we saw him walking toward main street. There are a TON of people here. I just dropped off Alex so I'll find him to make sure he understands how serious this is!

don't!!! what if david is stalking him?? we'll help you!! we'll be right there!

Ollie read the texts over her shoulder. "What about your grandma?"

Makani stopped, halfway to the door. She'd vowed to be more honest with her grandmother. What possible excuse could she give for leaving the hospital right now?

"We'll leave a message with the nurses," he said, decoding her troubled expression. "We'll say that we wanted to pay our respects, that we'll meet up with my brother, and that we'll be back as soon as it's over. None of that is a lie."

It wasn't a lie. But it didn't feel good.

CHAPTER
TWENTY-ONE

ZACHARY LOUP WAS stoned. He'd only come to the memorial because it was better than being at home, better than being alone with his mother's lecherous boyfriend. Zachary saw the hatred burning in Terry's eyes whenever Amber wasn't looking. What kind of man was jealous over his girlfriend's son? What kind of man felt *threatened* by that relationship? Zachary prayed that Amber had the sense not to marry Terry. Zachary's first stepfather had been bad enough. He was beating the shit out of some other family now.

Black satin ribbons were tied around every telephone pole on Main Street, and they fluttered in the crisp bite of the wind. The marching band was warming up in the grocery store parking lot. Brass instruments hummed and bass drums boomed. Cops were patrolling the two-lane street, which had been blocked off from traffic. The quaint thoroughfare was packed with county locals, vibrating with fury and injustice, as well as every news-media outlet that had raced to Nebraska to chronicle it.

The memorial was supposed to be a dignified remembrance of

the victims, but even Zachary could see that wasn't *exactly* what was happening. From the makeshift stage, a flatbed truck parked in front of the old bank, Principal Stanton shouted declarations to the masses: "This spring, the school fountain will be turned into a monument for the victims!"

Cheers.

"This weekend, our drama department will hold a fund-raiser for the victims' families!"

Cheers.

"And tomorrow night, our football team will take to the field in the playoffs!"

Losing-their-goddamn-minds cheers.

The principal was a balding man with a sturdy frame who wore his masculinity as if it were a badge of honor. Zachary detested him. Stanton was a son of a dick who punished Zachary for every fight, even the ones started by other students. Today, the principal sounded more defiant than respectful, and the spectators sounded more aggressive than supportive. The whole town was seething with outrage as their fear reached its boiling point.

Which came first, the outrage or the fear?

Ms. Clearwater, his favorite counselor, liked to give him Zen koans to keep his mind engaged. But koans were paradoxical riddles, which meant this wasn't actually a good example. Zachary knew from experience that fear always came first.

He drifted through the agitated flock. Every conversation was about David. A middle-aged woman spoke loudly to whoever was listening. "Did you see that picture where he was posing with that buck carcass?"

"Creepy smile," a guy with meth-mouth said. "Gave me the willies."

"His family goes to my church," a conspiratorial male voice said.

"The dad always seemed real shady. The mom's a prude, too. Never looks happy."

Zachary stopped wandering when he reached the fringes. He felt more comfortable on the outside of any crowd. Leaning against the brick storefront of Dream's Bridal, the outmoded boutique across from Greeley's Foods, he checked his messages to see if his friends were coming to watch the circus.

Damn. Drew and his brother were headed to an out-of-town wrestling match, and Brittani's mom had quarantined her until David was behind bars.

David Thurston Ware was born two days after Zachary. Zachary had been held back in eighth grade, so he was still only a junior, but they'd spent enough time together that he knew David wasn't what he seemed. Osborne was raring to cast ominous insights onto his character today, but just last night they'd been confused. *I can't believe it,* they'd said. *He seemed like such a normal teenage boy.*

Years ago, Zachary and David had lived next door to each other. Like most children who happen to be neighbors, that also made them friends. They watched cartoons, played Legos, went dirt biking. Zachary remembered David as a quiet kid prone to sudden outbursts. Unlike Zachary, who yelled at and threatened and terrorized the younger neighborhood boys, David held in his anger until he couldn't anymore. Until he snapped.

Admittedly, Zachary was no role model. But he still didn't think holding it in was healthy. He'd never forget the day when he'd borrowed David's new bike without asking, something he'd done a dozen times before, and David flew into the street and shoved him to the ground. The fall broke Zachary's arm, but that wasn't what had scared him.

It was the unbridled rage on David's face.

At the time, Zachary shook it off. Fair was fair. But deep down, it unsettled him that David had appeared from seemingly out of nowhere. He must have been hiding in the bushes. He'd been *waiting*.

But geography had been stronger than their friendship. When Zachary's mom remarried, his family moved into the trailer park, and things with David came to their natural end. The last time Zachary remembered talking to him was nearly two years ago, when they'd run into each other in the candy aisle of the drugstore. They'd debated the merits of chocolates versus gummies like they were kids again.

A new text vibrated in Zachary's hand: *BUSTED. ERIKA SAW U AT THE MEMORIAL!! GET UR ASS HOME RIGHT NOW!!!!!*

Not Drew, not Brittani.

Amber. *Mom.* Erika was Amber's coworker at Curlz & Cutz. She was only a few years older than him, and she was hot. Dark hair, sexy tattoo. Why had she ratted him out? Fuck that. Fuck them both. No way was he going home for some quality time with Terry. Amber picked the worst times to give a shit about him.

On the stage, Principal Stanton exited to make way for Pastor Greeley from Grace Lutheran, who introduced his son, Caleb. The Greeley family ran Osborne. The pastor's brother owned the grocery store and several of the buildings downtown. Their father founded the grocery store and had been mayor for a record-number of terms. They were the opposite of Zachary's family, and Zachary resented them for it.

Caleb was a senior, like David. Like Zachary was supposed to be. Caleb was round-eyed, square-faced, and as earnest as his khakis, but as he spoke about their classmates, it sounded like he hadn't really known them. He talked about Haley, Matt, and Rodrigo by using pull quotes that Zachary recognized from the news.

Zachary grew irritated. And then bored. His gaze roamed until it settled on a very pretty girl—a very pretty girl who was heading straight toward him.

Caleb Greeley hopped off the flatbed truck with as much dignity and respect for the dead as possible. He strolled to the edge of the crowd, and then, as his father raised his hands to address them, sprinted down the side alleys to the grocery store's parking lot.

Caleb played first trumpet. He didn't want to miss his second act.

After the sermon, his father would lead the crowd in a prayer, and then the band would march everybody up from Main Street to the memorial of flowers and cards in front of the high school. Everyone would be holding a candle. A cable-news program had donated them, though Caleb doubted the gesture was made out of goodwill. More likely, someone with a lot of money had recognized that it'd look better on television if the thousand crying marchers were also holding a thousand lit candles.

Caleb understood this, even if he didn't respect it. He was an overachiever, too. He'd been the youth leader for Grace Lutheran Church since he was fifteen and the trumpet section leader for the O.H.S. marching band since sixteen. Excelling in all his classes, he'd successfully campaigned to remove the word *evolution* from their textbooks, and he already had post–high school plans to do missionary work in Papua New Guinea. He would be the first Greeley to leave Nebraska in several generations.

His belongings were on the loading dock behind the store, where he'd left them. He hurried into the bibbed trousers and jacket—freshly dry-cleaned, that pungent uniform smell impossible to erase—and slid into the padded shoes. Slipped on the white gloves. Reaching for his hat, he realized it was missing its gold plume. Caleb grabbed his instrument and ran toward his section. "Alex! Have you seen my plume?"

Alex Shimerda's lip curled. "No one wants to see your plume, Caleb. Gross."

His face grew red with embarrassment. He hated jokes like that. They made him uncomfortable. "Has *anyone* seen my plume?"

The trumpeters who bothered to pay attention shrugged.

"Thanks for the help," Caleb muttered, jogging away.

"Ask the boosters," Alex called out.

But they hadn't seen it, either. A mother with a bobbed mom-hairdo scolded him. "It wasn't in your hat box? You'll have to pay to replace that, you know."

"I had it earlier. I must have left it in the store." Before the memorial, he'd been practicing his speech inside the employee break room.

"Better hurry," she said.

As he fumbled with the key to the back entrance, Alex dashed over to him. "We're lining up. It's just a stupid plume. Don't worry about it."

"Have you *seen* how many television crews are out there?"

Alex looked startled. And then her disgust returned. "Right. You wouldn't want to look bad on TV." She shook her head as she stalked away.

"I didn't mean it like that!" The key rattled inside the lock, but it wouldn't twist. *Dang it.* Caleb didn't care how *he* looked. He didn't want the band to look bad as a whole. It would be awful if they appeared sloppy—like they didn't care about the victims—because they all cared. They cared about their classmates a lot.

The key gave way, and Caleb burst through the door.

• • •

Zachary stared at the candle in his hand. It had a paper ring to catch the wax drippings, and it looked like the type that his church brought out when they all sang "Silent Night" on Christmas Eve. Amber only took him to church on Christmas Eve and Easter. He preferred the Christmas service. The world seemed more at peace.

Katie Kurtzman stood before him, talking about . . . something. She'd given him the candle for the walk. He tried to concentrate, but he was high, and she was pretty. Katie was tall and graceful with long hair that shimmered and changed colors in the light. Right now, caught by the rays of the sun, it looked like copper. Pretty copper.

She was different from the rest of the smart kids. Those other assholes acted like he was invisible, which was why he treated them like shit. Zachary *made* people look at him. But Katie was nice to everyone, and everyone liked her back. It's how she got to be student-council president. He'd tried to be rude to her once, and she'd called him on it. He respected that.

"Oh, no!" Katie dropped the cardboard box that held the candles. A man had spilled a blue slush on her arm.

Zachary sniffed the air for the signature Sonic drink flavor—Blue Coconut or Blue Raspberry. *Indeterminable.*

"Sorry!" The man was in his mid-twenties and wore tortoiseshell eyeglasses. "Oh my God. I'm so sorry."

Katie's cheeks flushed as she wiped the ice from her blouse. "It's okay."

The man tried to help her brush it off, but his touch made her wince, and he immediately backed off, looking even more chagrined.

Raspberry. For some reason, that was the wrong flavor. Zachary inhaled deeply and widened his chest. And he was already a big guy. "What the fuck, Glasses? Why don't you watch where you're going?"

"I—I was looking for my cousin in the band, and—"

"Really," Katie said. "It's okay."

"He should have to pay for your shirt," Zachary said.

The man went for his wallet, but Katie stopped him. "There's no need. These things happen." When Zachary puffed up again, she added, "I'm *fine*, Zach."

His father called him Zach. His real father. Zachary didn't let anyone else call him that, but with her coppery hair and leggy tallness . . . yes.

Zachary was tall and broad and fat. His ex-stepfather used to tease him about his weight. The bastard had known what he was doing—he'd known those jokes hurt boys as much as girls. Zachary had tried to deflect them, but the snide comments had landed anyway. He was perfectly aware that his thoughts were both corrupted and misguided, but tall girls made him feel like the right size. They made him feel like less of a freak.

His chest deflated. He let her *Zach* slide. The man with the glasses scurried away into the crowd.

Katie sighed. "I should go."

"Right. Gotta hand out the rest of those candles." But when Zachary peered into her cardboard box, it was empty.

She smiled. "You were my last stop. I just need to get home. My mom's leaving for work, and I have to watch my brother and sister."

"Do you need a ride?"

"Nah." She said it lightly, but she hugged the box against her chest. His question had made her uncomfortable. "I live nearby. I walked here."

"How old are your brother and sister?" Zachary had to keep the conversation going, if only to prove he wasn't that guy. He wasn't a threat.

"They're twins. Six. Do you have any siblings?"

"Nah," he said, echoing her earlier *nah*.

Katie smiled again, but this time it was tinged with something else. Sadness, perhaps. At least it wasn't pity. "Stay safe, okay? Find someone here to hang out with."

As she walked away, he changed his mind. It *had* been pity.

"Fuck you," he said. Louder than his normal voice.

Katie stopped. She looked over her shoulder and met his stare. "I don't think you mean that." And then she vanished in the crowd.

Maybe he'd been wrong about her.

Maybe he was just an asshole.

Zachary shoved the candle into his pocket. He leaned against the bridal shop and closed his eyes. His head swam. A drum began to beat, and his eyes popped back open, paranoid that he was about to see David—that David was about to attack Katie—when he caught a flash of camouflage in a window across the street.

"Oh, shit. Shit!" He glanced wildly around, but she was gone. He knew she was gone. He was really, really stoned. After all, he'd stolen Terry's good shit. He closed his eyes again. Opened them. Stared hard at the grocery store's dark windows.

Nothing. There was nothing there.

Caleb retraced his path to the dusty break room, but the plume wasn't there. The stupid feathery pipe cleaner wasn't *anywhere*. Had he missed it outside in his panic? Wherever it had fallen, it no longer mattered. The drum cadence had begun. The sharp *rap* of the snare reverberated off the thin walls of the empty store. The band was on the move.

As Caleb rushed into the back room, his face warmed with

premature humiliation. *Arriving late. Not properly dressed. Footage broadcast around the entire country, capturing my incompetence for all to see.*

Stop it, he forced himself. *This isn't about you.*

He hurried past the cardboard boxes and reached the exit.

And then, suddenly, it was exactly about him.

"Zachary! Zachary! Zachary!"

People were shouting his name, and an instant later—before he could figure out who or where or why—three figures bombarded him, buzzing with suppressed energy. His eyes widened before narrowing again, lazily. Suspiciously. Makani Young, Ollie Larsson, and . . . Darby. He just went by Darby now, he remembered. They were anxious and expecting something from him.

"What?" he said. Not politely.

"You shouldn't be here." Makani's face was partially concealed by the hood of her hoodie. "You shouldn't be standing by yourself."

He couldn't remember the new girl ever speaking to him before. When she'd transferred here last year, she'd seemed sullen and hurt, and her hips moved through the halls with a fuck-you energy that had intrigued him. He thought maybe she'd find her way to his group of friends, but she'd made Darby and Alex a trio instead.

Zachary pulled out his smokes and put a cigarette between his lips.

"Didn't you talk to my brother?" Ollie asked.

"Your brother, the cop?"

"He's the only brother I have."

Zachary lit the cigarette. He took a long drag. "No."

The three friends exchanged worried looks. "Chris said he spoke to you," Ollie said. "He told me he called your house."

"Maybe he called my house, but we sure as hell didn't talk. He probably talked to Terry."

Ollie frowned. "Who's Terry?"

"My mom's boyfriend." The shittiness of this person was implied in his tone. "What'd you do to your hair?"

"Dyed it," Ollie said with a straight face.

Ollie was good at that, at being expressionless. Zachary couldn't hide his emotions if his life depended on it. "I know *that*. Why?"

"Literally nothing could matter less right now," Makani said.

Ollie's mouth twitched unexpectedly with a smile. Something she'd said.

"You two," Zachary said, gesturing between them, "are fucking."

Makani flinched. Ollie's smile went cold.

Point, Zachary. And that's what you get for disturbing my solitude.

"You know," Darby said, "if you weren't maybe about to be killed, we'd walk away right now."

Zachary raised his eyebrows. "Fightin' words."

A few feet away stood a large family with several children. The dad glared at Zachary over his shoulder. They hadn't realized that the crowd had stopped talking to watch the band file down the street. But then an odd thing happened. The dad saw Makani and did a double take. He nudged his wife and whispered into her ear.

Zachary gave him the finger.

The dad turned away quickly. But then he glanced at them again, and Zachary had the craziest feeling that a murmur was traveling through the crowd.

Makani stepped closer. She was so focused on Zachary that it seemed like her eyes were avoiding someone else. That dad? "Listen," she said quietly, "we have reason to believe that you're David's next victim."

"Not likely," Zachary said. "Me and David go way back."

She looked surprised. Until she registered the smidge of doubt that he was unable to mask, and then her friends were pressing up against him, too, hissing about some lunatic theory that David was murdering everyone who'd been a bully.

Zachary stomped out his cigarette to push them away. "Well, if that's true, it won't be much longer until David kills himself. Problem's gonna sort itself out."

Makani grimaced—and he remembered. It explained why all these people were staring at them. It explained why the murmur was becoming a small furor.

"Oh, shit." Zachary finally lowered his voice. "You were the one attacked last night."

Her eyes widened with annoyance.

"So . . . wait. If your theory is correct, that makes *you* an asshole, too." He paused for a fiendish grin. "What'd you do, Young?"

"It doesn't matter." Makani rolled up her left sleeve. A bandage was wrapped around her arm, as high up as he could see. "All you need to know is that I earned this."

Her friends tried to protest, but she interrupted them. "We're worried for your safety. This Terry guy doesn't sound great, but can you trust him? When this is over, can you go home and stay with him?"

"No," Zachary said to the first question. He stared at her forearm, which she'd already covered back up. "But, yeah. I can stay with him."

"Good," she said.

Zachary didn't like the catch of fear in his chest. He side-eyed Ollie. Their classmates were always comparing them, lumping them together. "What about you? You've done some shit."

"Yeah," Ollie said. "But the only person I've ever hurt is myself."

"And your brother."

Ollie flinched. Not so stone-faced, after all. Makani glanced at him as if she were trying to figure something out.

Two points, Zachary.

"In the movies, it's always the kids who have sex and do drugs that are killed, right?" Zachary forced another grin. "I guess that means we're both gonna die."

"You aren't supposed to be here." It was the first coherent thought that Caleb could complete.

The hooded figure was blocking the exit. In one hand, he held a plume. In the other, a knife. "Where should I be?" David asked. His dull monotone matched his colorless appearance. The emptiness of humanity shook Caleb to the bones.

He took a trembling step backward. "In the fields. Or in somebody's barn."

David took a measured step forward. "I'm not."

"H-how did you get in here?"

"Why would I answer that?" David let go of the plume. "What if you escaped?"

The band started to play, but something about the music was strange and off-putting. They stopped bickering. Zachary frowned. "What *is* that? Why do I know that song?"

Darby looked stunned. "It's the graduation song. 'Pomp and Circumstance.'"

"Jesus," Makani said, as Ollie said, "Christ."

"I guess they didn't have a go-to funeral dirge in their repertoire," Darby said.

Zachary listened to the swell of rising pageantry. With each refrain, the march grew more disturbing. "You know, this is the only time this song will ever be played for them."

"This is so messed up," Darby said.

"This is gonna get old," Ollie said.

"This might be worse than if they hadn't played at all," Makani said.

The crowd progressed forward. It felt like everyone was staring at them, waiting to see if Makani would join in. She seemed resigned by her despair. Like she didn't have a choice anymore. Even though there was still an hour before dusk, the townspeople lit their candles. Zachary wasn't sure why they didn't wait until they reached the memorial. In the afternoon light, their flames looked weak and silly.

Makani, Ollie, and Darby removed candles from their pockets.

"Coming?" Darby asked.

Zachary pulled out his lighter and candle. "What the hell." He uncrumpled the candle's flimsy paper ring. He lit his wick first before touching it to Makani's.

It blackened. And then it sparked into flame.

Caleb tore out of the back room and into the store, knocking over glass jars, towers of canned goods, and racks of cheap clothing printed with the words LION PRIDE.

David dodged the mounting chaos with alarming ease. Caleb shot past the produce, battering down a carefully constructed pyramid of butternut squash, but David still reached him just before the entrance. David stabbed him in the back. Ripped the knife downward.

Caleb screamed, but no one could hear him over the sound of the band. He flattened against the cold floor. The drum line was poised in front of the doors—the last in line and the last to march away. Caleb pounded on the glass, stamping it with bloody fist prints.

David dragged him out of view.

"What are you gonna do?" Caleb was crying. *Haley's throat. Matt's brain. Rodrigo's ears.* "What are you gonna do to me?"

David straddled Caleb's body and stared down at him.

He didn't smile. He didn't scowl. He just finished his work while the people of Osborne marched to the school in their parade.

CHAPTER
TWENTY-TWO

MAKANI AND OLLIE walked back to Main Street. If the mood weren't so subdued, it might have even been called a stroll. The sun was setting, the candles had melted, and the memorial was over. Zachary had been escorted to his car, and Darby had been dropped off with Alex. They were meeting back up with Chris. Their brief time alone was dwindling to an end, and they were trying to make it last.

Makani didn't feel like Ollie was judging her, or even looking at her askance, but there was something new—faint but solid—wedged between them. They didn't hold hands. Their hands were tucked back into their pockets, unsure again.

As they turned onto Main Street, only a few short blocks away from Greeley's, where Ollie's and Chris's cars were both parked, she spoke out of last-ditch desperation. "Thanks for listening earlier. In the hospital. And for not judging me." She paused. "You *aren't* judging me, are you?"

Her directness loosened him up. He shook his head with a smile. "No."

The road had been reopened, and a tailgating stream of cars and trucks were heading home in both directions. Compelled to keep filling the space between her and Ollie, Makani kept talking. "It's just I never thought I could be that type of person. But I am."

Unexpectedly, her voice cracked like a mirror. Before the incident, she hadn't believed that she could be capable of cruelty. Now, she knew that she was.

Ollie stopped. His expression was serious. He waited to speak until she stopped, too. "Everybody has at least one moment they deeply regret, but that one moment . . . it doesn't define all of you."

"But it does. It ruined my life. And I deserved for it to be ruined."

"Makani. *Makani.*" Ollie repeated it, because she was walking away from him.

She halted. Kept her back to him.

"I'm not trying to absolve you from your sins," he said. "But the person I know? She's a good friend. And a good granddaughter."

Makani crossed her arms. Her uninjured arm pressed against her bandage, and she winced and uncrossed them. "I don't know. I'd like to think I'm a better person now, but for the rest of my life, I'll always have this question in my mind. I'll always have doubt. Something could trigger me, and I might snap or freak out again."

"Well, *I* know that our regrets change us, and that's how we grow—for either better or worse. And it seems to me, you're growing better."

Makani wasn't sure what to make of this.

"Hey." He gave her a small smile. "I'm still here, right?"

"Well, yeah, but—" She cut herself off.

The smile twisted into a knowing smirk. "Ah. But I'm a fuckup, too."

Makani looked away quickly. He shrugged like it didn't matter. But he wasn't looking at her, either. "I'm sorry," she said.

"It's fine." He started moving again. "It's not like this town can keep a secret."

She frowned. Stayed put. "I can't believe I'm saying this, but I disagree."

Ollie glanced back over his shoulder, a disbelieving eyebrow raised in her direction. But her expression made him falter.

"I mean, I've heard rumors," she said, "but not even real rumors. Like, *rumors* of rumors. And I have no idea what's true and what's not, so I assume most of it is not."

He grimaced. "Some of it's true."

"I wish you'd tell me."

There. Another confession. Now that she'd started, she couldn't stop.

Ollie's gaze fell to the sidewalk, and the hard exterior cracked, revealing some of the damage underneath. "I've *wanted* to say something, even more since you told us about what you've been through, but . . . I didn't want it to seem like I was comparing my situation to yours or like I thought mine was worse. Or even equal. But I don't mean to *not* talk about it. And I know everybody talks about me, anyway."

"I'd like to hear your version of the story," Makani said. "Whatever it is."

Ollie nodded, accepting her confidence. He gestured toward a neon sign behind them, at the opposite end of Main Street from Greeley's. "You know the Red Spot?"

She did. It was technically a greasy burger joint, but its regulars used it as a bar. And if you weren't a regular, you didn't go. The rumor was that you could buy anything there—as long as you were looking for illegal drugs or sex workers.

"After my parents died . . . it messed me up for a few years. When I turned sixteen and got my license, I started hanging out down there.

I should have driven somewhere better—somewhere out of town—but there was this girl who worked there. Dark hair, bleeding-heart tattoo. You know, those little pink flowers? Only these were actually dripping blood. I kinda had a thing for her."

Makani felt a sharp pang of jealousy.

"Everybody there knew who I was. They felt sorry for me, so most of them left me alone. I was like their depressed kid brother. It took weeks of relentless flirting, but I finally got her attention."

"How old was she?"

"Twenty-three."

Not as old as the rumors. But way too old for someone who was barely sixteen.

"I guess she pitied me, too." It seemed to hurt him to admit it. "We hung out at her trailer sometimes and got high."

"What happened?" Makani asked.

They started walking again. Dried leaves crunched under their shoes.

"Chris found out that we were sleeping together. He was *furious*. He wanted to arrest her, but . . . words were exchanged first." In his pause, Makani understood that Ollie's fight with his brother was still too raw to be spoken aloud. "It was just this whole big, stupid mess. He was still trying to figure out how to be a parent, and I was—I'm not sure what I was trying to figure out."

"Did he arrest her?"

"No," Ollie said.

"But I'm guessing you didn't see her anymore."

"He forbade me from seeing her, which wouldn't have worked, except it wasn't necessary. I think Erika was embarrassed." Ollie turned his face away from hers. "She didn't want anything to do with me after that."

Erika. The name pierced Makani's heart. "Does she still live here?"

"Yep. Comes into Greeley's a couple times a month. She's married now. Cuts hair. We don't speak," he added. There was something in his tone.

"You liked her a lot, didn't you?"

"I thought I loved her. I was an idiot, but that's what I thought."

The sadness expanded inside her, enough for the both of them.

"A few days later, I reached the genius and original conclusion that life was shit. I drank two forties and waded into the river. I was going to kill myself."

Makani sucked in her breath. She'd been severely depressed, but she'd never been suicidal. It was upsetting to learn that Ollie had stood so close to the edge.

"I stumbled and fell," he said, "and as I was flailing in the water, realizing that I *didn't* want to die, the manager of Sonic drove past. By some miracle, the guy saw me. He pulled over and dragged me out. The river was only a few feet deep—I was just scared and wasted." Ollie gave a regretful laugh. "It's probably the real reason I hate Sonic. Reminds me of my dumb-ass self."

An old pain distorted within Makani as she pictured Jasmine vanishing, also scared and wasted, into a different body of water. The situations were so different, yet eerily similar. She didn't have the strength to let her thoughts linger there. "Well, it makes *me* like Sonic more. I'm glad he saw you. I'm glad you're still here."

Ollie bit his lip ring. "I'm glad you're still here, too."

Recalling a rumor associated with the river, Makani blurted, "Were you naked?"

He glanced at her with surprise. "What? Do people say that?"

She nodded guiltily.

"No," he said. "In *that* particular brush with death, I had my clothes on."

It was so tragic and absurd that it made them both laugh. "I can't believe that happened," she said.

Ollie shook his head in amazement. "I know."

"You were *naked*."

"I *know*."

Her smile grew. And then faded. "What happened after the guy rescued you?"

"I wasn't arrested—thank you, nepotism—but I spent some time in a psychiatric unit. After that, Chris sent me to a therapist in Norfolk. But, by then, I wanted help. I stopped drinking and doing shit." He gave a loose shrug. "And that's it."

"Is that what Zachary meant when he said you'd hurt your brother?"

The lightness disappeared from his voice. "Yes."

Makani was relieved that nothing worse had happened. And Ollie hadn't even done anything truly awful; most of the disappointment was inside his own head. She could tell that, for Ollie, having worried his brother *was* the worst thing he could have done. Instead of pressing him, she backtracked. "When you said you got high . . ."

"Weed."

"You never did any harder drugs? Pills or opioids or anything?"

He shook his head.

"And you never sold them?"

Ollie sighed. "Cool. You heard that one, too." He shook his head again. "The only thing I've ever sold is produce."

"Did you sleep with anyone else?" *Please say no.*

"Only in my dreams," he said. "Only you."

It was cheesy—definitely a line—but Makani didn't mind right now. She smiled at him as they stood in front of Greeley's. "Hey, Ollie?" she asked softly.

"Yeah?"

"You know how you said that I'm a good granddaughter and friend?"

He smiled back. "Yeah."

"Do you think I could be a good girlfriend?"

Ollie's hands reached for hers through the dusk. Their fingertips touched, and the streetlights flickered on behind them. "I think you're *already* a good girlfriend."

They kissed while they waited for Chris. It felt absurd, kissing in public. Kissing after a memorial. Kissing when they'd been so close to being actual subjects of the memorial.

It also felt euphoric, rapturous, and profound.

Ollie's nose was cold, but his arms were warm as they slipped around her back. It was the thrill of summer, revived—making out beside the grocery store when they shouldn't be doing it. Except infinitely better, because the questions between them had been answered.

Their lips parted to catch their breath. Makani laughed, glancing aside. And that's when she noticed the blood.

Red handprints. Beaten fists. Dragged fingers. The fine lines of the skin that had touched the glass were shockingly clear and shockingly human.

Makani stiffened with fright.

Ollie followed her gaze, and they startled apart. They stared at the bottom left side of the store's automatic entry doors. The blood was on the inside.

Their limbs reached for each other again, clinging, as they

frantically checked their surroundings. Except for the cars, the parking lot was empty. The traffic had unclogged, and only a few people remained on foot. None of them were close by. None of them were Chris or any other officer. And none of them appeared to be David.

Makani's heart raced. Ollie cupped his hands to peer inside the dark store, while she kept her eyes on the street. "Is he in there?" she asked.

"I think somebody was dragged toward the checkout lanes. But I can't see them."

"Oh God." She ripped his phone from his pocket, bouncing anxiously on the balls of her feet. "I'm calling your brother."

"The whole place is ransacked."

"Shit! What's your password?"

"9999."

"What? Why would you do that? Somebody could guess that!"

"You didn't," he said. "Shit! Something just moved."

Makani lurched against the door. He pointed toward a shadowy area, a pile of . . . she couldn't tell what. "I think there's someone there," he said. "Someone on top of that."

It was impossible to tell. But there was definitely something that *might* be a person.

Chris's number rang emptily in her ear. The shadows shifted again, and Makani gasped. Before she realized what he was doing, Ollie unlocked the door. As a longtime and trusted employee, he had a key. "Someone's still alive!" he said.

The overhead sensor picked them up. The doors whooshed open. They rushed inside and then staggered backward, stunned by the true destruction. Overturned vegetables, boxes, cartons, bags, and cans were everywhere—an abundance of food, splattered like congealing fireworks across the linoleum.

Ollie yanked her aside so they wouldn't track through the blood, the streaks of a body hauled across the floor. They ran toward the shadows and then crashed into a halt. Makani clamped her hands over her mouth to mute her scream.

In front of the checkout registers was a permanent display of merchandise whose profits helped support the football team, something Makani had once found incredibly strange but she'd slowly grown used to. Now that she knew Osborne, it made sense. But tonight, it had been razed to the ground. And in the center of the debris of jumbled sweatshirts and flags and tchotchkes was Caleb Greeley.

The boy lay atop the heap like another item of garish memorabilia. His feet and knees were splayed outward. His face was on its side, and a swollen tongue protruded out from between his front teeth. The chest and stomach had been mutilated. Long incisions slashed through his blood-drenched band uniform, but, despite the clothing, the unnatural splaying of his limbs made him look more like one of those realistic sex dolls than a human being. It was his body's complete and utter lack of dignity.

But that still wasn't the worst part.

The worst part was the hands.

Caleb's fingers had been laced together, and then his hands had been severed. They rested over his heart in prayer position. Red gore and white bone.

But if Caleb was dead . . . someone else was the moving shadow.

Makani and Ollie backed into the cereal aisle, each placing a protective arm across the other person's chest. They pressed against the yellow Corn Pops and green Apple Jacks. Their hearts slammed against their rib cages.

The air was sharp. Acidic. It stung their nostrils and watered their eyes. Caleb must have been chased down the condiment aisle, one over. The vinegary fumes from the smashed jars of pickles and olives were ghastly. Makani covered her nose. She was still holding Ollie's phone, and Chris was shouting at them through the speaker.

The metallic thud of a push bar echoed throughout the building. Their hearts stopped.

And then a heavy door settled closed.

Makani whispered into the phone, *"David Ware just went out the back exit."*

CHAPTER
TWENTY-THREE

THE CAN OF tuna fish had been bothering her all week.

Katie Kurtzman had discovered it last Friday as she was moving a load of whites from the washing machine into the dryer. The flat can was eye level and sitting on the sill of the basement's only window. The long, narrow window was closed, but its latch didn't work. It was just big enough for a slender body to squeeze through.

The tuna had been cheap. A discount brand. The lid's edges were sharp and crude, as if the tin had been cut with a hand-cranked opener, not the electric one that they had in the kitchen. The can was empty, but it was still damp inside. That's how she'd noticed it.

That faint underpinning of *fish* underneath the cloud of bleach and detergent.

She'd asked the twins, but they claimed not to know anything about it. She didn't think they were lying. They were afraid of the basement, so they never played there. Her mother didn't know about it, either. She supposed that it had fallen down from one of the ceiling beams—a trash relic left behind from the previous homeowners. But that didn't make sense to Katie. The can was far from its stamped expiration date, and they'd been in this house for five years now. Plus, there was the dampness.

And the smell.

Katie knew she was being paranoid. She hadn't known any of the victims, not really. She'd never had any personal connections to them, and she'd only ever been friendly to David. Still, as she applied stain stick to her sleeve where the blue drink had spilled, she eyed the window ledge. She couldn't shake the feeling that someone had been here, sitting on top of the dryer, listening to her family upstairs. Eating tuna fish.

She undid the first few buttons of her blouse but then, thoroughly spooked, decided against it. She could wash the shirt tomorrow. Hurrying toward the planks that served as stairs, Katie glanced over her shoulder for one last look. She stopped.

A quart of latex paint sat on the floor beside her mother's old treadmill. She picked it up and placed it on the ledge against the window. And then she felt foolish. How could *that* protect her from an intruder? But she was scared enough to leave it. Perhaps it would be the magic charm that warded off the evil spirit.

Upstairs, Leigh and Clark were spread out on the living room carpet, reading comics. Leigh noticed her first. "What's for dinner?"

"What's for dinner?" Clark parroted.

Katie hurried past them toward their shared bathroom on the second floor. Her arm felt gross and sticky, and her cramps were getting bad again. "Mac and cheese."

"With hot dogs?" the twins asked.

"Only in Leigh's half," she said, and the twins cheered. Clark hated hot dogs. He also hated hamburgers and pizza. For a child, his eating habits were baffling.

As Katie bolted up the stairs, her mom thumped down them. She worked the twelve-hour night shift at the hospital. Three days on, four days off. She was currently on, without the option to take off any shifts to watch over her children. The staff was doing mandatory training in preparation—anticipation—of further attacks. "Do you have everything you need? What happened to your shirt?"

"I'm fine, we're fine," Katie said.

"Keep your phone in your hand. Don't open the door for *any-body*."

"I know, Mom."

"I love you!" she called out.

"Love you, too." Katie didn't look back as she said it. Her mom kissed the twins goodbye as Katie grabbed a clean T-shirt and pajama pants and locked herself in the bathroom. She removed her blouse to scrub her arm with a warm washcloth and *Sesame Street*–branded soap, and then she swallowed an Advil and peed.

Leaning over to grab a new tampon from under the sink, Katie startled. All the toiletries were in the wrong place. The tampons and extra rolls of toilet paper were out of reach and had been rearranged entirely with her makeup caddy, flat iron, and hair products in the back of the cabinet, and the twins' old bath toys in the front.

Katie's first thought was scary and irrational: *David.*

She'd heard a rumor at the memorial that he liked to mess with his victims before he killed them. That he moved their stuff around to make them think they were losing their minds. The man she'd over-heard swore that he'd gotten the information from a county deputy, though there hadn't been any mention of it in the news.

Her second thought was much more realistic: *Mom's been guilt-cleaning again.*

Katie usually cleaned, because her mother worked nights and took care of the twins during the day. Her off-days were for catch-ing up on sleep. But as Katie pushed the toys onto the bath mat and stretched for the tampon box, she noticed dust inside the cabinet. *Mom cleaned, but she couldn't even do it right.* Katie groaned.

Her mom claimed that Katie had obsessive-compulsive disorder. As a nurse who'd spent her early years working in psychiatric units, she was always diagnosing everyone.

Outwardly, Katie denied it. Inwardly, she knew it was true.

Katie worked long hours, too. School and the twins' bedtime routine, in addition to college applications, student-loan applications, extracurriculars, and volunteering at the hospital—all the while worrying that she *still* wasn't doing enough to get out of Osborne. Ritualistic cleaning and straightening and checking and organizing made her feel calmer in a world that was out of her control. Six years ago, everything had blown up when her dad stormed out only a few weeks after the twins were born.

Antisocial personality disorder, her mom had diagnosed.

Katie refused to go back to the way things had been.

As she moved everything back to its correct location, her eyes snagged on a fresh droplet of blood. It was on the alligator-shaped bath mat, near the toilet—and it was her own. Katie swore under her breath. She blotted it with a tissue and scoured it with cold water. There was a *thunk* downstairs. "Hey," she yelled. "What was that?"

"We don't know!" the twins said.

"What'd you guys do?"

"Nothing!"

Katie sighed. *Sure.* She changed into her pajamas and hustled toward them. Ninety minutes later, she tucked their warm, sleepy bodies into bed. She turned on their matching night-lights, closed their door, and sighed again. Time was hers, at last.

She headed back downstairs to work on an essay for the University of Southern California. All the universities she was applying for required a flight—or, at least, a lengthy car trip—to get there. She loved her family, but she'd love them more with distance.

Night had spread its bat-like wings. Katie turned on the porch lights and the overhead light in the kitchen, where her work was laid out across the table. As she reflected on a time or incident when she'd experienced failure (tonight's essay topic), it took all her willpower not to check the news. She wished that she could have walked to the school with everybody else. Even Zachary—*Zachary*, who smelled like stale cigarettes and unwashed clothing, who'd never given a crap about his grades and pretended not to give a crap about anyone—was in attendance.

Katie suspected that he actually cared about other people a lot, but he hadn't had enough people in his life who cared about him. Despite Zachary's abrasiveness, she had a soft spot for him. He was smart, and, if he applied himself, he could go on to do great things. It was frustrating to know that he probably wouldn't. Most likely, he'd drop out and get a job on the floor at Nance, the town's only manufacturer. It built machinery for food-processing plants. Or maybe he'd become a day laborer, detasseling corn and castrating piglets. Either way, it was unlikely that he would ever leave Osborne.

There was a creak on the basement stairs.

Katie's heart juddered as she whirled around in her seat. Beside her, the refrigerator hummed and the dishwasher sloshed. Above her, the twins' white-noise machine whirred. But below her, the basement remained silent. She picked up her phone—ears pricked—but set it down after another minute.

It's just the house.

She tried to refocus on the essay. She read her last sentence five times, but she couldn't shake . . . a feeling. Katie stared at the basement door.

Another creak.

She jumped up, the wooden chair legs scraping against the floor. Her pulse beat violently as she grabbed her phone and dialed 911.

Connecting, her phone said. *Connecting. Connecting.*

Heavy footsteps pounded up the stairs. Katie's senses exploded with terror as she threw herself against the door, which could only be locked from the other side. At the same instant, another body landed against it full force—just enough to open it.

They struggled. Open, shut, open. An arm and shoulder wedged through, and a knife slashed toward her body.

Katie pushed the door against the arm with all her strength. The arm flailed. There was another weighty thrust, and her side gave way. She fell, and her phone slipped from her grasp. It skidded across the floor as David Thurston Ware burst into the kitchen.

He was wearing jeans and a LION PRIDE sweatshirt. They were splattered with turquoise paint—the same color that her mother had meant to repaint the kitchen chairs last spring. The same color that Katie had propped against the basement window that evening. She took all this in, in an instant, as she scrambled to her feet.

He lunged for her. She ran toward the butcher block, reaching for the biggest knife as he stabbed her in the shoulder. When he yanked it out, she kicked him. David shoved her against the cabinets. His hands smeared her skin with red and turquoise. She was five foot ten, and so was he. Their weight was similar, and the same amount of adrenaline coursed through their bodies. But he was the one with the weapon.

Katie kneed him in the balls as David stabbed her in the upper right abdomen. They both buckled over. The knife pushed deeper into her liver.

She collapsed, frightened and crying. But oddly hushed.

David peered over her. His question was curious, though his voice was dead. "Why aren't you screaming?"

Because I don't want to wake up my brother and sister.

When she didn't answer out loud, he finished her off. He didn't have time to wait.

He checked her phone, which was still trying to connect to the police. David ended the call. The cops already knew he was in the area, and he was angry. He didn't like having to rush. He sawed through the rib cage—stomping on the knife to help crack the bones faster—and ripped out the heart. He slammed it on top of the glossy college brochures that had been stacked on the table for months.

Because Katie's *heart* had been *set* on college.

He was funny. Nobody seemed to get that.

Lights flashed outside the kitchen window. Red and blue, one street over. He tugged off the sweatshirt. It wasn't camouflage, but it had acted as camouflage. Nearly everyone on the street today had been wearing school colors. He threw it as he ran, and it landed on Katie—the Katie-husk—crumpled on the floor, no longer of use.

CHAPTER TWENTY-FOUR

MAKANI AND OLLIE had waited, terrified, in the cereal aisle until Officer Bev had escorted them out. Chris had tried to chase after David, but he'd already disappeared.

Makani and Ollie were interviewed and gave statements. Again. Now it was late, and they were back at the Larsson house, decompressing at the kitchen table and attempting to excise the horrendous image of Caleb's grotesque prayer from their minds. Chris was on the phone in the next room.

Ollie stared vacantly at the oven. "Maybe we should have chased him," he said. "Maybe we could have caught him."

Makani's knees were up in the chair. Her non-bandaged arm was wrapped around them, and her head was tucked down. She felt too broken to lift it.

"He killed *Caleb*," he said. "Not Zachary."

His words hung limply in the air between them. Out in the fields, the nighttime insects whirred and buzzed. The wind chimes on the front porch sang three notes.

"I don't think this is about bullying," he said.

She shook her head, but it was in agreement.

"So, what the hell *is* it about?"

It scared her to admit that she had no idea. She hadn't realized that she'd taken a measure of comfort in at least knowing *why* she'd been attacked. There'd been a *reason*. Not knowing David's motivation felt like everybody she knew was in danger again.

A shadow fell over them as Chris stepped back into the light of the room. His face was white with disbelief. "There's been another one."

The midnight sky wept in an unexpected drizzle. Chris moved his laptop, binders, metal ticketing notebooks, and food containers into the trunk of his car. Makani darted into the emptied passenger's seat, and Ollie slid into the back. In the rearview mirror, his face was printed with diamond-shaped shadows from the metal dividing grate.

They'd been at the house for less than thirty minutes. Chris had to return to work, so he was driving them to the hospital to stay with Grandma Young. He refused to leave them alone.

Makani felt so exhausted that she wanted to cry, but she didn't want to be left alone, either. As the endless rows of cornstalks rolled past her window—long corridors into murky blackness—she shivered with the unshakable feeling that David could be anywhere. Her lower legs pressed against the bulletproof vest resting on the floorboards.

Chris noticed her shivering and turned up the heat. The windshield wipers swiped at a slow and steady pace.

"She texted me this morning," Makani said, remembering.

He glanced at her sharply. "Katie contacted you? About what?"

"She said she was sorry to hear what had happened to me, and she was there if I wanted to talk." Another deadening inside Makani. "I didn't text her back."

"Did you talk to her often? Was she a close friend?"

"We weren't friends at all. We were friend*ly*. Sometimes we talked in class, but we never texted or hung out or anything."

Chris frowned. "So, why start texting you this morning?"

"That's just Katie being Katie." From the backseat, Ollie dismissed the notion of there being anything odd or sinister behind it. "She was nice to everyone."

"Who found her?" Makani asked. They already knew *how* she'd been found.

"Her mom." It seemed hard for Chris to say it. "Apparently, she works the late shift at the hospital, and Katie wasn't answering her phone, so she came home on her break to check in. Katie's younger brother and sister were still asleep upstairs."

Makani used to shave her arms for diving. Now, her arm hair stood on end as she remembered a laminated ID badge. *Kurtzman.* The kindhearted nurse who'd given her blueberry yogurt and watched over her was Katie's mother.

"She couldn't have known." Chris sounded shaken. Maybe he was picturing himself in her place. "I doubt that she actually expected to find something wrong."

The rain ticked staccato against the roof of the car. Perhaps sensing that his brother needed to think about something else, Ollie asked him to repeat his knowledge of David's whereabouts.

After attacking them yesterday at Makani's house, David had traveled upriver instead of down, which the police hadn't predicted. Under the cover of night, he'd crept back into town and hidden inside the back room at Greeley's, correctly guessing that everyone would be searching for him out in the countryside.

He'd been right under their noses the whole time.

At first, the police were flummoxed as to how he'd broken in, because none of the doors or windows had been damaged. But then Caleb's uncle, the owner, recalled having to cut a new key for Caleb a few months back. His uncle had found this odd, because Caleb wasn't usually forgetful or careless. The police speculated that David had stolen the key and entered the store as if he belonged there. It probably wasn't the first time that he'd broken in. And the key probably wasn't the only thing he'd stolen.

Several members of the marching band, including Alex, reported that Caleb had practiced his speech inside the store, and then when he returned from delivering it to the crowd, he'd claimed that his hat plume was missing. It seemed possible that David had stolen it while Caleb was practicing and then used it to lure him back.

"It's still not clear why he didn't kill Caleb *before* the memorial," Chris said, keeping his eyes on the two-lane road. "Maybe because people would have looked for Caleb sooner? And we also don't know—" But he cut himself off, with a glance in the rearview mirror at his brother.

"Know what?" Ollie asked.

Chris looked like he didn't want to answer. "We also don't know if David had more than one target inside the store."

Ollie's tense expression showed Makani that the thought had already crossed his mind.

"We *do* know that he stole a sweatshirt," Chris said, trying to hurry past it, "which he left behind at Katie's before jacking her 2011 Ford Fiesta. The sweatshirt was covered in blood and paint from her basement. We don't know what he's wearing now. We still haven't found his hoodie, and no one noticed him leave her neighborhood. Everyone was looking for someone on foot."

"So, he's leaving town." Makani wasn't sure if she believed it. And even if it were true, it wasn't what she wanted. She wanted to know *exactly* where David was. Until he was captured, she would never feel at ease again.

A pair of headlights loomed through the rain in the distance.

"What color was the car?" Ollie asked.

"Blue," Chris said quietly.

The headlights grew closer. Makani's heartbeat spiked, and Chris's grip tightened on the steering wheel. It was impossible to tell anything about the car, except that it was small. Everyone held their breath until the car passed.

Red. A Ford Focus.

They exhaled. A minute later, there was a new pair of headlights, and their lungs tightened again. And then released. Tightened. Released.

It was like that for the remainder of the drive.

Grandma Young was asleep, heavily sedated. Makani and Ollie tried to sleep, too, taking turns on the comfortable recliner, but their brains were wired. As the night droned on, they watched the cars in the parking lot below and stared at the flickering television screen. It wasn't a heavy storm, but it was enough to mess with the signal.

The TV was set on the lowest volume above mute. For hours, CNN cycled between an airstrike in Syria, a group of missing hikers in North Carolina, and the latest murders in Osborne.

Caleb Randolph Greeley Jr.

Katie Teresa Kurtzman.

Their full names were spoken aloud by strangers. The same atrocious clips of the same panicked citizens were replayed. The victims were turning into numbers, statistics that were being used to compare David with other notable serial killers. He'd obliterated two people within a three-hour gap *and* with a crowd nearby. It wasn't just Makani; the entire Midwest had the crawling sensation that he was standing right behind them.

But here, inside the hospital, it was even worse. Katie and her mom were the subject of every low-spoken conversation. It was impossible not to overhear the muffled crying coming from the nurses' station. The choked sobs. The noses blowing into tissues.

It was nearly daybreak before the talking heads had something to report. "Breaking news in the hunt for the Osborne Slayer," a woman's voice said.

Makani's and Ollie's bleary eyes sprang open as the Latina news anchor continued, "You're looking at footage from a truck stop near Boys Town, Nebraska, just outside of Omaha, at eleven o'clock last night. An unidentified driver called 911 after spotting a blue Ford Fiesta ditched on an embankment near the truck stop. When the police pulled the surveillance video, this is what they discovered."

Black-and-white footage showed a figure in a long coat walk up to a semi and speak to the driver through the window. Even though the outdated cameras made his movements jerky and pixelated, Makani could tell that the grainy figure was David. A nauseated chill washed over her. David climbed inside the truck, and it drove away.

"As you can see," the news anchor said, "the truck makes a right turn before traveling out of frame. It looks like the driver is headed *back* toward Osborne."

Makani glanced at Ollie. His face was a perfect reflection of her fear.

"At this time, the police have not revealed the driver's name, only that his tags were from Indiana. It is not yet known if he was aware of the hitchhiker's identity."

That was it. The news rehashed the story from the top. David kept climbing into the truck, and it kept making a right turn.

The killer kept going home.

CHAPTER TWENTY-FIVE

IT WAS THE eve of All Hallows' Eve. The rain had stopped, but the asphalt was still slick with water and oil. A lurid sunrise—worthy of Hawaii—illuminated the sky. It was such an obscene contrast to the overhanging dread that it felt like they were being mocked.

Makani and Ollie had slipped away from Grandma Young before she'd even known that they were there. Chris drove them back to the Larsson house. This time, Makani sat beside Ollie in the backseat. Their fingers were icicles as they grasped each other with all four hands. Despite the ideal opportunity to escape, David had chosen to come home. He'd tried to kill her and failed. What if he was returning to finish the job?

"The truck driver was stopped just past Norfolk at twelve forty-five a.m.," Chris said, filling in some of the blanks. "Must've been the only person in America who hadn't heard about the manhunt. He claimed that he only listens to Christian talk radio, and they've been yammering about the new Supreme Court justice all week. He told the deputy that David was quiet and polite. He also said it looked like he was wearing a woman's coat."

Despite seeing it in the surveillance footage, this last detail startled Makani.

"My guess," Chris said, "is that he's still wearing the same bloodstained jeans and hoodie, and he needed something to cover them up. The coat probably belongs to Katie's mom. The driver said he dropped him off in front of a farm near Troy."

Troy was only one town over. Alex lived on a ranch just outside it.

"David told him it was his parents' farm. We've already interviewed the farmers, but they were asleep. They didn't see or hear anything unusual. The other neighbors are being interviewed now, and there's a team searching the surrounding fields."

Makani and Ollie tightened their icy grips.

There was nothing else they could do.

The cold autumn air crackled throughout the countryside, electric with anticipation.

Makani and Ollie were bundled inside sleeping bags on Chris's hardwood floor. Heat whirred out from the registers. With the daylight, locked door, and armed police officer, Makani's body finally succumbed to rest. Her dreams began heavy and empty, but, over the course of the afternoon, they struggled into existence. *A sharp knife in one hand, a severed ponytail in the other. A hooded figure lurching out from behind a grandfather clock.* She would fight these nightmares for the rest of her life.

While the trio slept, strangers streamed in from out of town. Even more media, but also armchair detectives—online sleuths, some well-meaning and some not, jumping into ambitious action—as well as morbid gawkers, deceitful psychics, and drunk college kids, who thought it'd be a hoot to visit the famous corn maze. The displaced *Sweeney Todd* cast and crew had turned it into a *haunted* corn maze, and the Martin family would donate the weekend's profits to the victims' families.

"Knowing he's still out there just makes the maze a lot scarier," a student wearing a scarlet ball cap with a cream *N* said, speaking to a field reporter. His fraternity brothers whooped behind him on camera. "Plus, you know. Charity."

Even the National Guard rolled in. They were to stand watch over the football game so that the townspeople would feel brave enough to attend. There were no parking spaces left at the school. The tailgate party had started early. The playoffs didn't stop for tornado sirens, and they weren't about to stop for a serial killer.

And through it all, Makani, Ollie, and Chris slept.

Chris's phone rang when the sun was low on the horizon. Makani scrambled up to a sitting position against his bed, her bulging eyes on the door. It was still closed.

"Yeah," Chris said into the phone.

Ollie scootched out from his sleeping bag to hunker down with Makani. He was careful not to sit on the side of her injured arm.

"Shit." Chris sighed. "Okay, yeah. See you soon."

Makani burrowed into the shelter of Ollie's body as the phone thumped onto the bed above them. Chris released another sigh. "What is it?" Ollie asked.

"Nothing. Nothing new," Chris clarified. "Just . . . shouldn't have slept so late."

"You need to go in?"

"Yeah." His feet swung over the edge of the bed beside Ollie. "So, I've gotta head toward Troy, which is in the opposite direction of where you need to go. We'll take separate cars, but we'll leave at the same time. You guys are to drive *straight* to the hospital, okay? And you're to stay there until I tell you to leave."

Makani and Ollie nodded.

"I'm gonna check the house, just to be safe." Chris stood, picking up his gun from the nightstand. "I'll be right back. Wait here." In the doorway, he glanced back at them. "Do you have your phones?"

Their phones were already in their hands. They held them up.

Chris vanished down the hall. Ollie's under-eye circles were so dark that it looked like he'd been punched. Makani wished that she could touch his skin and heal it.

"You okay?" he asked.

"No. Are you?"

"No." But he smiled, which made her exhale a faint laugh.

Chris's bedroom was as disheveled as Ollie's. Bags from Sonic and the gas station were scattered everywhere, and heaps of clothing were piled in front of the closet. The clothes looked clean, though permanently unfolded. The only vestiges of his youth appeared to be the three dusty guitars hanging on the wall—one acoustic, two electric. Beneath them was an amp covered in coffee cups and mail.

The upstairs floorboards creaked as Chris moved from room to room. Makani's gaze snapped back to the door. "This is so messed up."

"The *most* messed up," Ollie said.

She held her breath as the footsteps continued toward the bathroom.

"I mean," he said, "I slept beside you all day and didn't think about sex once."

Her head remained locked, but her eyes swiveled toward him.

He grinned. "That was a lie."

The wooden stairs groaned as Chris crept down them. Makani shook her head, but she was smiling slightly. Their ears strained.

They waited.

Suddenly, a yell rang out, followed by a loud crash. Makani gasped and shrank as Ollie clung to her in horror. There was the indistinct sound of things settling to the floor.

"*Squidward!*" Chris said. "Fuck! You scared me."

Ollie pried his body off hers, embarrassed, though she sensed he'd been more scared for his brother than himself. She wondered if he was afraid every time Chris left for work. That must be tough.

A few seconds later, Chris returned. "Sorry about that." He seemed embarrassed, too. "We're good. We leave in fifteen minutes, okay?"

Fifteen. The number surprised Makani. Clearly, they weren't used to having a girl around. She hurried to wash her face and change clothes, and realized—as the brothers were both ready in under ten—that the number had actually been inflated for her sake.

Ollie handed her a steaming Pop-Tart as she slid into his car. She practically swallowed it whole. When they hit the highway, they parted from Chris.

"What the—?" Ollie said under his breath.

Makani looked up from checking her texts. The opposite lane of traffic was at a standstill. Dirty cars and trucks and RVs were backed up as far as she could see as a lone, redheaded employee with a flag waved them into the parking lot for the corn maze.

"Is it always this busy on a Friday night?" she asked.

"Never," Ollie said.

Vehicle after vehicle was packed with college-aged kids—voices hollering, music thumping, windows rolled down despite the frigid temperature. Makani stared at them with open displeasure, though not with disbelief. She'd lived through too much to feel disbelief. "People are sick. They think this is all a game."

On the other side of the maze, one of Ollie's neighbors was trying to turn out of their driveway. "That's gonna take a while," he said.

Makani texted her friends with an update and told them where she was going. It was important to know where everyone was right now. Darby was at home, and Alex was at school with the band. But as soon as Makani's message disappeared, her phone vibrated with a response from Alex: *I'm freaking out.*

Makani frowned as she texted: *???*

Too many people here. Too crowded. Can't breathe.

can your parents come back and pick you up?

They think it's safer in a crowd! I reminded them about Caleb and the memorial, but they weren't having it. I'm freaking out. I'm totally freaking out!!

Ollie watched her from the corner of his eye. "What's going on?"

"Alex. I think she's having panic attack."

He was a QUARTER MILE from my house last night. Now it feels like he's here. I can't do this. I SERIOUSLY CANNOT DO THIS!!!

"Does she need us to come get her?" Ollie asked as another text appeared from Alex: *Could you come get me?*

on our way, Makani said. Emoji heart.

Hurry, Alex said. Emoji scream.

The stadium was packed, and the wind carried the cheers and marching band and commotion all the way to downtown Osborne. As their car raced past Walnut Street, Makani looked toward her grandmother's house. It was just out of sight.

The bright lights of the football field pierced through the dusk. Alex was waiting for them at the front gate. The whole area was packed, but she stood alone.

Ollie unlocked the doors, rolled down his window, and waved to her. The aroma of cheap chocolate invaded the car. Tomorrow's trick-or-treating had been canceled, and word had spread to bring candy to the game. Costumed children dashed through the madness, collecting treats in their pillowcases and plastic orange pumpkins. Teenagers and adults had been banned from wearing costumes—in fear that David might hide among them—so they were decked out in scarlet and gold instead.

The home crowd was so huge that it had spilled onto the visitors' side. The cheerleaders were leading them in the "Lion Roar," a school-spirit chant, and a powerful stampede of feet pounded and rumbled against the metal bleachers.

Two members of the National Guard were visible just behind the main chain-link fence. They were dressed in fatigues and carrying assault rifles. They were supposed to make everyone feel protected, but Makani felt a nervous, unpleasant shudder.

Alex flew into the backseat with her trumpet. Her plume caught on the doorframe and knocked the hat sideways. "*Ow.*" She undid the chin strap and ripped off the hat. She glared at the plume. Or maybe she was scared of it.

"Are you okay?" Makani asked. It was a dumb question.

Alex slammed the door closed. "Go!"

"Won't you get in trouble for leaving?" Ollie asked.

"Fuck that," Alex said. "Fuck all this. I can't play a peppy fight song and pretend that you guys weren't almost murdered. I can't pretend that my crush and my section leader and three of my other classmates weren't *actually* murdered. And I can't pretend that the loser who did it isn't still out there!"

That was enough for Ollie. He pulled away from the curb. Makani unbuckled her seat belt and crawled over the console into the backseat, where Alex was fumbling to unzip her red uniform. Makani helped her with the hidden buttons, which Alex had forgotten about, and then out of the jacket. Alex shook it away on the verge of tears.

As Makani dug through her pockets for tissues, her phone rang. Darby had skipped straight past texting. "Is everything okay?" Makani asked.

"Put him on speakerphone," Alex said.

"I'm fine," Darby said. Makani pressed the button, and his voice filled the car. "I'm only calling because I'm driving."

"That's still unsafe," Ollie said. And then he winced for being the square.

Makani wondered if his reaction was triggered by too many car-crash stories from Chris. Or maybe any type of accident reminded him of his parents. She still wasn't wearing a seat belt, so she strapped in and motioned for Alex to do the same.

"I know, but I just got your texts," Darby said. "My signal was on the fritz from all these damn tourists. Is Alex with you?"

"I'm here!" Alex said. "Where are you?"

"I was coming to get you. I'm passing the Dollar General right now."

"We're almost to the hospital," Makani said. "Meet us in the parking lot?"

Darby's hatchback pulled up beside them less than five minutes later. Darby's and Alex's doors flew open, and they ran into each other's arms. They hugged for days.

Makani crawled back into the passenger's seat and rubbed her hands in front of the vents. Ollie turned up the temperature.

Darby and Alex popped into the vacated backseat. Darby was

dressed in an old-man tweed sport coat with actual elbow patches, and he was wearing a button-up and sweater underneath it for warmth. He snapped the suspenders of Alex's uniform. "Did you guys see this? She's trying to steal my look."

"Did you lock your car?" Ollie asked.

The question instantly brought the mood back down.

Darby assured him. "It's locked."

They fell into silence as they surveilled their surroundings. The parking lot was nearly empty. After several tense seconds Makani said, "We're running out of time."

No one challenged her. The apprehension in the car was suffocating.

"I can't just *sit* here," she said. *He might be looking for me.*

Alex agreed. "He's killing faster and faster, and since everyone's looking for him—everyone not at the football game," she added darkly, "he probably feels like he has to finish his stupid plan, whatever it is, *now*. Before he gets caught."

"I wish we knew who else he's been gaslighting," Makani said.

Ollie stared, unblinking, through the windshield. "Haley, Matt, Rodrigo, you, Caleb, Katie. What's the real connection?"

"Cliques?" Darby was hesitant. "None of you hung out together, but you all had a unique social group. Maybe David felt alone. Like he didn't belong to any group."

"Except he did," Alex said.

Darby shrugged. "I know, but . . . I *don't* know. It seems like there's something there. So far, he's singled out one person from every group."

"I still think he's targeting the most talented students," Alex said. "Or ambitious. Or maybe even just the people who stand out. Maybe you all make him feel inferior and invisible, and this is his way of becoming *more* visible."

When no one disagreed, Alex pressed on. "Who else seems exceptional? Who else is out there standing in front of crowds or making headlines or winning competitions?"

"*Shit,*" Ollie said quietly. His expression turned grave. "Do you remember the day when there was hardly anyone at school but us?"

He was still staring ahead, but Makani knew the question was for her. "You mean, Wednesday? Two days ago? The day we were attacked?"

This realization seemed to stun him. During periods of trauma, time could be funny like that. He tried to shake it off. "Right. But do you remember that bad joke I made? Stanton told us over the announcements that Rosemarie Holt had won a barrel race, and then *I* said that she should watch out."

Makani touched her lips in fear at the memory: *Clapping with the other students. So grateful for any small piece of good news.*

Darby shifted uneasily. "Rosemarie's been winning those events for a long time."

"Years," Ollie said.

"Oh God." Alex looked like she might throw up. "What do we do?"

Chris answered after the first ring. Ollie repeated their theory but was quickly cut off. His brow furrowed as he listened. "Yeah, we're fine," he said. "Yeah, okay—"

Ollie stared at his phone. "He hung up."

"What is it?" Makani asked. *What is it* now?

"They received a call from another trucker who picked up David. The guy just saw him on the news and recognized him. This new driver said he must have picked up David not long after the first driver dropped him off, and Chris said he knew the exact location. It was just stupid, random luck that neither driver knew who he was."

Makani's heart plunged. What were the chances?

"This guy claims to have dropped off David on the *other* side of Osborne. The police are headed there now. They think he's been snaking his way back to town through the fields. They think he might be headed to the stadium for a blitz attack."

Alex grabbed Makani's seat and shook it roughly. "I knew it!"

Makani fixed a hand over Alex's to stop her. "That doesn't sound like his MO."

"Are you kidding? What would shake up this town more than an attack during the first game of the playoffs?"

"What did Chris say about Rosemarie?" Darby asked.

Ollie frowned. "I think when Zachary wasn't a target, we lost any small sway we might have had."

"But someone needs to warn her!" Darby said.

Ollie was already scrolling through his contacts. He caught Makani's look and explained, "Neighbor. Her family lives on the other side of the corn maze."

Of course. Everyone was connected to everyone in Osborne. Makani tamped down her ill-timed jealousy as the call went straight to voicemail.

"Hey, it's Ollie Larsson. Call me as soon as you get this. It's an emergency. Everyone's okay, just . . . call me back."

Makani stared at him, her eyes wide and frightened. "What now?"

His voice hardened. "Seat belts, everyone." And then he turned the key in the ignition and pushed the pedal to the floor.

CHAPTER
TWENTY-SIX

MOONLIGHT GAVE A high-pitched whinny and pawed the fresh shavings.

"*Shh.*" Rosemarie Holt stroked the brush in calming sweeps down the horse's sorrel neck. "They're just a bunch of dumb rubberneckers. Nothing to be afraid of."

Lights strobed and music howled. Screams of rowdy laughter erupted from the cornstalks, carrying to the stable at the edge of the Holts' property. Normally, it was a minor annoyance to live beside the tourist attraction. Tonight, however, the land was teeming with drunken rednecks, frat guys, and sorority girls all out for a good scare. It was as if David Thurston Ware were a campfire urban legend and not an actual murderer-at-large.

In the next stall, Cash stomped his feet with nervous agitation. The maze had never had lights or music at night before. "I don't love it, either, buddy," she grumbled, feeling a fresh flush of anger at Emmet for leaving her with the chores.

When they were children, they'd each been given an American Quarter Horse. Emmet had chosen one with a black coat, so he'd named him after the Man in Black. This turned out to be prophetic as it reflected the way he treated Cash—like an accessory to look cooler. Rosemarie and their parents did most of the caretaking.

Rosemarie had always wanted a horse. When she was little, she'd never been interested in a book or movie unless it contained at least one. Moonlight had been named after her favorite fictional horse. Even though hers wasn't golden (she was a light brownish-red), nor did she have a white mane or tail (hers were flaxen), Rosemarie believed that she was just as loyal a friend as Alanna's Moonlight had been to the Lioness herself. Over the years, admittedly, Rosemarie had outgrown the name. But she still remembered why it had mattered. What it had meant to her.

"All right, girl." She touched the horse's rump as she walked around, so she'd know Rosemarie was there, and then tossed the brush into a plastic bucket of grooming tools. "Almost done. I'll get your hay."

Rosemarie took down the cross ties and picked up the bucket. She closed the sliding door behind her and left the bucket to grab the pitchfork, which was inside one of the empty stalls.

The stable smelled wonderfully familiar: wood shavings, sweet feed, and old leather, though it also held a pungent underpinning of ammonia. The urine scent was always stronger after mucking out the stalls, but it would fade within the hour. Her waterproof boots tread quietly over the rubber floor pavers.

Rosemarie and Moonlight were a good team. They started barrel racing when she was eight and competing when she was nine. The Sloane County Championship Rodeo used a traditional, three-barrel cloverleaf pattern. The event was timed, and if the racer knocked over a barrel, there was a five-second penalty. Some rodeos had hat fines, too, where they'd charge the racer twenty-five dollars if her hat fell off.

Moonlight rarely bumped a barrel. And Rosemarie never lost her hat.

Rosemarie wasn't without injury, though. A year ago, she'd broken her right arm when she slipped off while riding bareback. And only two months ago, her strap had broken when she was hanging upside down at a full-blown gallop while trick riding. It was the strangest thing. The strap wasn't even that old. She'd almost broken her neck.

The accident shook her up, but it didn't stop her. She was competitive, headstrong, and faster than the other racers. She was ready to go national.

As she strode into the dark stall, an earsplitting scream from next door startled her. Rosemarie waited.

Yep. Laughter.

Her jaw clenched as she imagined Emmet as one of the laughing imbeciles. *Hope you're having a good time,* she thought bitterly. He'd come home from UNL for the weekend. He was supposed to be *here*, helping her, but when he'd learned that some of his school friends had also driven into town, he'd ditched her to join them. Their parents were at the football game, supporting her cousin on the team.

Rosemarie reached for the pitchfork through the black shadow, but her hand only greeted air. Patting the rough, planked wall farther and farther into the stall, she finally fumbled against the handle in the far corner.

She grabbed it and turned back toward the light.

The bucket was gone.

A confused moment—a dreadful heartbeat—and then her nostrils filled with an unfamiliar and unwelcome odor. It was the unwashed scent of another human being.

• • •

The former cruiser tore out of Osborne, but as it hit the connecting highway, the car speeding ahead of them unexpectedly and drastically slowed down.

Makani glanced at the speedometer. It was five under the posted limit. "What the hell?" she yelled at the other car. "Go!"

Ollie's knuckles tightened on the steering wheel. "This happens all the time. People look in their rearview mirrors, and they think I'm a cop."

In the backseat, Darby tried to reach Rosemarie, but the cell towers were still overloaded. The calls either went straight to voicemail, or they wouldn't connect at all.

Ollie swerved into the oncoming lane and stepped on it. They raced past the car, and he zipped back into the right lane. With every mile, his adherence to safety regulations was going increasingly out the window.

Less than a minute later, it happened again. Makani and Alex moaned.

"All. The. Time," Ollie said, gritting his teeth and passing the second car.

Another speedometer check. Thirty over the limit. He caught Makani eyeing it. "No one's pulling me over tonight. They're all on the other side of town."

Makani liked that Ollie was a careful driver. She respected it. But she was grateful that he felt the urgency of their current situation.

She gave the road a grim smile. "I'm not complaining."

Rosemarie knew that scents could be comforting, but this was the first time she'd ever smelled a scent that was frightening. The stench of rancid body odor was close, and it was male.

And it didn't belong to her brother.

A slender figure stepped out in front of her stall. His gait was calm and measured. He was dressed in a strange coat, and he was holding the grooming bucket.

Rosemarie's knees began to quake.

David Thurston Ware set down the bucket. He didn't need it. He'd only brought it to show her that *he* was the one who'd moved it. He shrugged off the coat, which fell to the ground in a woolen puddle. He was wearing the hoodie that she'd heard about on the news. The camouflage was covered with splotchy brown stains that were darker than the fabric's pattern. Dried blood.

The reveal was both unnecessary and terrifying.

He removed his knife from a sheath on his belt. The blade glinted. Staring into the darkness of her stall, he kicked the plastic bucket, and the tools clanged together.

"They wouldn't have helped you much." He took a step forward. "But they would have been better than nothing."

Rosemarie tightened her grip on the pitchfork and lunged.

Traffic deadened into a complete stop. Hawaii was notorious for its impassable, two-lane roads, and it wasn't uncommon to get stuck behind a sightseer driving fifteen-under. Yet Makani had never felt road rage more intensely than she did right now.

"Her house is *right there*." Ollie gestured angrily at a plain one-story just before the corn maze. The house was set back some distance off the road.

Darby and Alex reached for their seat belts. "We'll make a run for it," Alex said.

"No!" Makani's rage turned into panic. "No splitting up. We stay together."

"I agree," Ollie said as the cruiser inched forward.

"But we can't just *sit* here," Alex said. "David could already be there!"

Darby attempted to soothe her. "Most likely, he's in town. It's probably okay."

Alex fumed. "Whose side are you on?"

Ollie craned his neck to see around the gridlock. A pickup passed, and then he sharply turned the wheel and accelerated into the oncoming lane.

A semi was coming straight toward them.

They screamed. The truck blew its horn. Ollie drove straight into the ditch beside the road and kept driving. The truck flew by, and the other drivers laid on their horns, shouting obscenities, as the cruiser hurtled down the length of the ditch, kicking up dust clouds into the night sky. The car bumped and rattled and thumped and shook.

"Oh my God, oh my God, oh my God," Makani and Darby said together as Alex shrieked, somewhere between pleasure and fear.

They hit the Holts' driveway, which was a dirt road. The car settled into a quieter grind, roughening as they picked up speed. Makani pointed at a small building away from the main house. Its lights were on. "There!" she said.

"Hold on," Ollie said, an instructional warning as he veered into the pasture.

Makani, Darby, and Alex screamed again.

"There was a fucking road up there!" Makani said.

"Sorry!" Ollie said as the car barreled through the grass toward the stable. "I got caught up in the moment!"

"What are we doing?" Darby yelled.

Alex shouted with the entire force of her lungs. "We'd better not be wrong about this!"

•   •   •

Rosemarie didn't grow up in rodeos for nothing. She was tough. A farm girl. And she wasn't about to be killed by a pathetic boy with a stupid knife.

David looked astonished by the pitchfork coming at him. He dodged, but he wasn't quick enough. The far tine gouged into his side. He cried out with shock and pain.

Startled that she'd made contact—that her weapon had slid through a living human being—she pulled it out. His body squelched as it released its hold.

He staggered backward.

"That's right!" Rosemarie said. She kept shouting at him, but she didn't know what she was saying. It didn't feel like any of this was actually happening.

David ran from the stable, clutching his bleeding left side.

The horses were upset. They neighed and kicked the walls as she raced through her options: She could wait for a signal and call the police. Or she could make sure that David wouldn't come back to kill her first.

Rosemarie gripped the pitchfork's handle so tightly that she felt bruises forming. She took a cautious step forward. Another. And another.

As she reached the stable door, a hand shot out and grabbed the pitchfork—right above her hand. She cried out as she struggled to regain control.

David pulled her toward the ground. For some reason, he'd set down his knife to seize the pitchfork, and now he was trying to pick it back up.

Like hell he would.

Rosemarie wrenched the pitchfork from his grasp. And that's when she became aware of a pair of headlights and a car thundering straight toward them.

They were both stunned, but David recovered first. He snatched up the knife and swiped. The blade sliced into the flesh of her right thigh. She whacked him on the back with the pitchfork. She saw him double over, and then there was a blinding white light.

And then she couldn't see anything.

CHAPTER
TWENTY-SEVEN

THE SPOTLIGHT FROM Ollie's cruiser sliced a blazing hole through the black landscape. Only a few feet in front of them, Rosemarie and David were hunched over. Their frames were locked together, knotted in a struggle.

"I changed my mind, I changed my mind," Alex said. "I wish we'd been wrong!"

Makani threw open her door and bolted through the icy air and muddy grass. The other three doors flung open behind her.

David twisted his body behind Rosemarie's, securing an arm around her neck. His knife aimed for her throat. It was coated with a liquid shadow of fresh blood.

Rosemarie's round face looked pinched and paralyzed. Makani saw the whites of her eyes like a spooked horse. Her long, straight hair leaned to one side as she held all her weight on a single leg. She clutched at the other.

Everything happened in an instant.

Alex screamed toward David. He turned in the direction of her caterwaul, angling Rosemarie toward her and leaving his back to

Makani. Makani jumped on him. Everyone toppled to the ground, and Rosemarie cried out. Arms and legs and torsos tangled, and other hands were prying them apart, but Makani couldn't tell whose hands were friendly and whose were *his*. Another cry shredded the night.

David wriggled out from the pile. His head turned back to them, and his eyes flashed as he recognized Makani. She was trapped, and he was right there.

But he was outnumbered. So he ran.

Rosemarie was curled up like a fallen leaf. Makani touched an unmoving shoulder, bracing for the worst. And then the girl looked up.

"Oh my God. Oh, thank God." Makani began to weep. "Are you okay?"

"Just this leg. It hurts to move." Rosemarie seemed a little dazed, but she gestured to the gash in her thigh. "How did you know—"

Darby dropped to his knees with a strangled sound. At first, Makani thought he'd been injured. But he was looking at Alex. Makani crawled forward.

No. Please. No.

It was starting to snow. Or maybe it had been snowing this whole time. Makani suddenly felt the cold wetness against her cheeks. She glanced up as David vanished into the maze. Plump flakes tumbled behind him through the car's spotlight and headlights.

Ollie stood frozen above them. Maybe he was back inside the cereal aisle at Greeley's, trying to decide whether to stay or give chase. The world felt locked in suspended animation. The only thing alive was the snow.

And then Darby released a gut-wrenching wail, and Makani knew. They all knew.

As Makani reached for Darby, Ollie shot toward the maze. Darby shuddered, hysterical, stretching to touch Alex but then pulling back his hand, afraid. The bumpy white vertebrae of her spine were exposed. Her neck had been slashed so deeply and so far across that she'd nearly been decapitated.

Makani's skin went clammy. Bile rose in her throat.

Rosemarie pulled herself toward them but then turned away in shock.

"Call the police," Makani said, clambering upright to face the enormous maze. The wind gusted, and the stalks swayed and rippled outward. Ollie dove into the current. So many people were in there. She couldn't leave him to face the massacre alone. The cops were on the other side of Osborne; it would take them too long to arrive.

Rosemarie made a noise of surprise, no doubt discovering the missed calls on her phone. "It's searching for a signal," she said with frustration.

Makani nodded at Rosemarie and Darby. "Stay together."

"No way." Darby scurried to his feet, wiping tears and snot onto his sleeve. "I'm coming with you."

Makani didn't protest. They ran, full throttle.

Snapped cornstalks revealed David and Ollie's entrance. The outer wall was at least a dozen stalks thick, and the brittle leaf blades scratched and tore Makani's skin. Snow that had landed on the plants flew back into the air. Strobes burst erratically. A sinister soundtrack blared. Screams chorused nearby, and Makani's chest seized, but the screams were followed by laughter. Just a couple of friends, stumbling across a costumed ghoul.

She exploded out from the stalks. Three guys shrieked, completely losing their shit. One of them was wearing a camouflage hoodie. Makani fell backward, but Darby caught her as he crashed through. The hoodie guy screamed again, but the other two were already cracking up. Thinking they were in on the haunted maze's joke.

Makani took a second look.

It was a David Ware *costume*. The guy was also holding a plastic knife. She held back her fury to warn them. "You have to get out of here. It's not safe!" She pointed toward the crushed cornstalks. "There are two girls out there who need your help!"

The hoodie guy grinned. "Ooooh."

"You don't understand," Darby said. "David is *inside* the maze. He just *slaughtered* my best friend."

"*Ooooh*," the trio said together, louder. They shook their hands with the universal sign for spooky.

Makani couldn't afford to give them any more time. "Which way did they go?"

Darby had the sense to look at the ground. Brace roots reached out from the soil like swollen fingers. Ears of fallen corn looked like blackened teeth and shrunken heads, their silks dangling like stringy hair. It was less muddy along the path—straw had been sprinkled over the whole thing—but it was muddy enough, and the indentations caused by two sets of running footprints were clear.

He pointed. "Here!"

The tracks led away from the point where Makani and Darby had entered the maze. "Go look! You'll see them," Makani shouted to the trio as she and Darby took off. As they rounded the corner, out of sight, Makani heard one of them ask, "Why weren't they dressed up like the others?"

They traced over the doubled footprints, turn after turn. Every time someone screamed, Makani jumped. A sharp right, and teenage boy covered in blood and wielding straight razor leaped out at them. Makani and Darby shrieked and recoiled. But he was in Victorian costume, and the razor wasn't real.

"So, you've found old Sweeney," the boy said in a rough accent, somewhere between cockney and Australian. "But will you discover his secret?"

Darby's brow rose with recognition. "Jonathan?"

"Ain't nobody here who goes by that name, mate. The name's Todd, Sweeney Todd, and—"

"*Jonathan.*" Makani didn't know who Jonathan was, other than clearly he was from the drama club. "Did you see them? Did you see Ollie or David?"

Immediately, Jonathan dropped the act. Even in the violent strobe light, even underneath his pancake makeup, she saw belief—and then horror—register on his face. "He's here? David Ware is *here*?"

"You have to warn them! You have to get everyone out of here!" Makani said.

"Go," Darby said. "Go!"

Jonathan skittered away as Makani and Darby raced back down the trail. "Get out of the maze," they shouted to everyone. "Get out of here, now! David is here!"

Nobody took them seriously. They either thought Makani and Darby were actors or that they were acting like obnoxious, insensitive teenagers.

It was snowing harder. Flakes swirled down and around them. Makani hunched as she ran so that she could still see the footprints through the white. Just as she feared they were chasing the wrong tracks, they busted through another wall. And there they were. Wrestling, like the days of middle school gone by.

David was on top, but Ollie had somehow managed to pin David's dominant wrist. The knife shook in David's hand, but he wasn't letting go.

Makani screamed again and rushed them. David made eye contact with her just as she kicked him in the forehead. His muscles loosened. The bodies shifted. David rolled over, and Ollie scrambled away through the straw. They were both coated in mud.

Makani planted herself between them. Darby shouted, another voice called out, and Makani was knocked to the ground. The wind sucked out from her lungs.

David was above her. His *knife* was above her.

She closed her eyes as it came down for her heart.

A wave of blood crashed against David's head and showered down onto her face. They gasped, and the pressure of his body released from her. Someone pulled her to her feet and held her securely, their arms wrapped around her waist and chest.

"I didn't know what to do!" a panicked voice said.

Makani wiped the blood from her eyes. A tall girl in rectangular glasses and Victorian dress was holding a bucket. *Brooke. Haley's best friend.* The blood trickled between Makani's lips, and she tasted something sweet. *Corn syrup.*

A heart was beating against her back. *Ollie.*

She squeezed his arms. He hugged her tighter.

Darby positioned himself between them and David. Brooke was backing against the far cornstalks as David wiped the fake blood from his face. He flicked it to the ground in disgust, sneering at Darby. "It was almost you."

"W-what?" Darby said.

"Before *she* moved here"—David pointed his knife at Makani— "I'd considered you."

Darby was already in tears. "I don't understand."

David had more emotion in his voice than usual. He sounded angry. "You want out, but your roots are too strong. She's the one who will leave."

"You don't want us to leave?" Darby said it like a plea. "We won't. We'll stay. We can help you. How can we help—"

David lashed forward, and Darby went down.

Makani screamed. Darby was on the ground, clutching the wound in his chest, which was gushing blood. Ollie pivoted to shield Makani—to place his body in front of hers—before releasing her to rush David. But David rushed Ollie first.

Ollie cried out near her ear. The blade sucked out. Squelched back in. Ollie's breath was hot on her neck. Back out. She was still screaming as Ollie crumpled limply to the earth.

Another chest wound. Gaping. Their hearts, or maybe their lungs.

Her screams turned into hyperventilating gasps. A group of tweens appeared from around the bend and shrieked. David spun to attack, but Brooke was right there, and she shoved them, hustling them back through the maze.

Makani trembled between the bodies of her last remaining friends. David stared at her, predator to prey. His face was long and homely, but his entire head was dripping red as the coagulating theater blood mixed with the real blood. He swished his knife and more blood flew off and through the air. Blood was everywhere.

The terror was finally spreading outward. If the corn were an ocean, the cries were its waves. Manic, frenzied people tore through the dry vegetation.

But Ollie and Darby had stopped twitching.

Ollie and Darby were dead.

"What . . . what the fuck?" Makani said it quietly, exhausted. She was crying. Her question was rhetorical and not one she expected David to answer. But he did.

"The *fuck* is," he said, "you were supposed to die two days ago, and I was supposed to have another week. But I pushed through. I made it work. And now we're here, and soon the cops will be here, and it's fitting that you'll be my last."

He stalked toward her. Backed her against an arrangement of hay bales and pumpkins and a life-size skeleton wearing a frilly Victorian corset.

"You'll be here forever," he said. "And I get to leave."

"To prison," she said.

"I was looking forward to turning myself in. But this gets me there, too."

He actually *wanted* to be caught. "So, it's about fame?" she asked. "You wanted a high body count so that you could be another Gacy? Another Dahmer?"

"Those assholes killed for sexual pleasure."

"And you're killing for the fun of it?"

"This isn't fun," David said as he lifted the knife above his head. "This is just something I have to do."

CHAPTER
TWENTY-EIGHT

MAKANI DUCKED AS the knife thunked into the pumpkin behind her head.

She ran for her life.

She fled down the path blazed by the terrified people before her—a straight line through the cornstalks. Her sneakers slapped against the churned mud as David crashed through thick stalks that hadn't yet toppled.

She burst out from the maze into a huge thoroughfare. It looked and smelled like an abandoned traveling carnival. Plastic soda bottles, hot dogs, funnel cakes, roasted corn on the cob—everything discarded and trampled in the rush to escape. Fried food blended into a manure stench as she raced past the live enclosures. Pygmy goats. A hunched zebra. Scraggly coyotes. The animals paced and howled.

Behind her, the footfalls grew louder. She glanced back just as David was close enough to swipe. She dodged and swerved, and then careened toward the vast corn pit. The parking lot was visible on the other side of it.

A split-second decision, and she hurdled herself over the edge. Corn sprayed over the rim like a pool. She hit the kernels hard. Stitches snapped in her injured arm, and her swimming muscles were weak from disuse, but her adrenaline was pumping. Makani stood, and the kernels were nearly pelvis deep. She slog-ran toward help.

Cars and trucks jammed the parking lot with everyone trying to exit at once. She yelled at them, waving her good arm, but their shouting and honking drowned her out.

She looked over her shoulder to find David hovering at the pit's edge. He was waiting to see what she would do, determining how he should respond. He climbed onto the rim and prepared to jump.

But he didn't see what Makani saw behind him.

David keeled forward, knocked into the pit by a blow to the head from an iron folk-art skeleton. He face-planted into the corn. His body didn't move.

Relief shocked Makani. "You aren't dead!"

"No," Darby said. "I'm not."

Mud and snow and blood spattered his tweed sport coat. He clutched the decorative skeleton by its spinal cord. He used it to gesture at David. "But is *he*?"

They bent toward the body. Afraid to get closer.

"I don't know," Makani said from the center of the pit. "I don't think so."

Darby hesitantly stepped forward and then rapidly backed away. "Screw this," he said, dropping the skeleton. "Meet you on the other side!" And he took off, sprinting around the perimeter.

Makani's mind shouted at her to run.

Her gut hissed that David was alive.

She saw her grandmother lying in the hospital. Heard Alex crying out into the night. Felt Ollie crumpling against her to the ground.

A hooded figure lurched out from behind a grandfather clock. A hooded figure lurched out, a hooded figure lurched out, a hooded figure lurched out—

"What are you doing?" Darby's voice sounded muted. "No!"

The parking lot was still packed with people, and the highway was clogged. Makani couldn't hear any sirens. If she ran, David could kill someone else.

David *would* kill someone else.

Makani waded toward his prostrate body. His hands were empty. Desperately, she foraged until she spotted it: a nub of black rubber poking out of the yellow corn.

She lunged for the handle. It slipped out as David rolled onto his back. His eyes were groggy and unfocused. She towered over him. Her hand was sweating. It was heavier than she'd expected, heavier than the knife in her memories.

David began to blink as his awareness returned. He gazed up at her. The blade flashed in the light of a distant strobe. It was long and sharp and vicious.

"You don't have it in you," he said.

"You don't know me," she said.

David didn't know her, but Makani knew herself. And neither of them was a monster. She was a human who had made a terrible mistake. He was a human who had planned his terrible actions.

You'll be here forever, he'd said. *And I get to leave.*

Standing above him, she realized it was about Osborne. Everyone on David's checklist had been destined to move away—whether it was because they were bound for greater things, or, like herself, they had never belonged there to begin with.

Growing up in a town like Osborne made it difficult to leave. It was easy to get tied down to family or the land or the community. Everybody depended on one another to survive. It took a person with extraordinary drive and ambition to break from the pattern.

Haley, Matt, Rodrigo, Caleb, Katie, and Rosemarie—they were ambitious. They rose above their peers. Makani *used* to be ambitious, but David didn't know that. He just viewed her as temporary.

It's why he'd chosen her over Darby, or even Ollie. They dreamed of other places, but to someone who didn't know them well, perhaps they seemed destined to become stuck here, too. Perhaps they seemed too passive. But it was impossible to know what was *inside* a person, or how they might change over time.

Years ago, Makani's mother had been ambitious enough to get out of Osborne, but as quickly as she'd left, she'd gotten tied down to a new place. She hadn't changed at all. Maybe that's why she resented Makani. When she looked at her, she saw the loss of her freedom, and she was too selfish to notice what she'd gained.

David had planned to turn himself in. He knew that he'd be sent to the Tecumseh State Correctional Institution, the same maximum-security prison Chris had visited a few days ago for work. Ollie had told her that it was only two and a half hours away.

For an instant—all this burned through her mind in an instant—Makani felt sad for David. His big, ambitious dream . . . it was so small.

Running away from home didn't change the fact that a person still had to live with themselves. Makani had learned this, though perhaps her mother never had. Change came from within, over a long period of time, and with a lot of help from people who loved you. Osborne wasn't David's problem. For Makani, Osborne had even been restorative. Being a psychopath was David's problem.

David was David's problem.

Maybe there had been more people on his list, or maybe she and Rosemarie were the only ones left. Maybe he had a bad childhood, maybe he was born this way, or maybe he just felt trapped. Whatever his plans, whatever his reasons—they didn't matter anymore. He'd made his decision. And now she had made hers.

As David dove at her legs to knock her down, Makani stabbed him in the middle of his back. The blade went in up to its hilt. His body collapsed into the corn.

She tugged out the knife and struggled toward Darby's voice.

Slowly, David crawled. A vile trail of blood slathered across the kernels behind him as Darby hefted her over the edge. Makani was shuddering in his arms, still grasping the knife, when she became aware of the crowd. They were circling the pit. Surrounding it. She didn't know if David was dying, but he wasn't getting away.

Osborne wouldn't let him.

He had underestimated them all. He had terrorized the community, but instead of tearing them apart, the townspeople had grown closer. As the sirens broke through the silent, snowy night, his body stopped crawling. And then it stopped moving altogether.

David Thurston Ware died knowing that he would never leave Osborne.

David Thurston Ware died knowing that he would be buried there forever.

CHAPTER
TWENTY-NINE

THE POLICE RUSHED toward them. When Chris saw Makani's wretched face, his body seemed to shatter. Officer Bev grabbed his arms to keep him from falling.

"Where is he?" Chris asked.

Makani could only point. He shook off Bev's grip and ran.

She approached Makani and Darby with caution. "May I take that?"

It took a few seconds for Makani to realize that Bev was asking about the knife. Bev removed an evidence bag from her jacket, and Makani dropped it in.

"Rosemarie," Makani said, remembering as the paramedics swarmed them.

"She's all right. Three college kids found her and stayed with her. One of them was wearing a David Ware costume," she added wryly. "The media's gonna love that."

At least it meant the kids had also stayed with Alex.

Darby lost control, sobbing, and Makani knew he was thinking about her, too. He'd been holding Makani, but now she held him as they were hurried into an ambulance. Bev stayed with them. Makani checked to see if her phone's signal was strong enough for a call. She needed to hear her grandmother's voice, or she'd lose her mind completely. The clock turned to midnight. It was officially Halloween.

Bev's shoulder radio fuzzed: "—alive! Do you copy? My brother is alive!"

All the atoms in the universe became motionless.

And then Darby whispered to Makani, *"Go."*

As the paramedics reached to close the doors, Makani burst back out of the ambulance. She tore through the fairgrounds and down the path of demolished cornstalks, officers and medics racing behind her.

Please, please, please.

Gasping and panting, she ran straight to him. He was still lying on the ground. Chris was holding his hand, and his police coat was bundled under his head as a pillow.

"Ollie," she said, falling to her knees beside him.

His eyes lit up when he saw her. Snow dusted his lashes. "Makani."

"I thought . . . I would have *never* left . . ."

He broke into a smile, but his voice was weak. "Darby?"

"He's okay. We're both okay. How are you?"

His smile widened. "Nothing your grandma's doctors can't fix."

Makani laughed, wiping the tears from her cheeks, and put on a brave smile of her own. She kissed his forehead. His skin was warmer than she'd expected. He tilted his head, and she moved to his lips. Softly, she kissed them.

A faint but reassuring pressure answered back.

Chris was still holding one of Ollie's hands. With his other hand, Ollie fumbled for hers. She grasped it, and the autumn moon shone brighter—rendering the night soft and cold and safe.

ACKNOWLEDGMENTS

I WANTED TO read this book, but my dear friend Kiersten White suggested that I should write it instead. This book exists because of her. She's also read it more times than anyone else. She's read *all* of my books more times than anyone else. She is a saint and a beautiful magic rainbow unicorn. Thank you, Kiersten. I love you.

Thank you to my fantastic agent, Kate Testerman, who made it happen, and to my brilliant editor, Julie Strauss-Gabel, who worked and worked and worked and worked to turn it into a fully functioning novel. I'm so grateful that they both took a chance on it.

Thank you to Lindsey Andrews, Lindsay Boggs, Anna Booth, Melissa Faulner, Rosanne Lauer, Bri Lockhart, Natalie Vielkind, and everyone else at the Penguin Young Reader's Group. Additional thanks and hugs to Sean Freeman, Eve Steben, and their team for creating such a gloriously eerie cover.

Writing this book required six years of research, critique partners, and in-depth discussions. Humble thanks to Leigh Bardugo, Luce Beagle, Lauren Biehl, Holly Black, Emily Brock, Cassandra Clare, Brandy Colbert, Alexandra Duncan, Shannon Fang, Leslie

Golden, Manning Krull, Myra McEntire, Marjorie Mesnis, Chris Prahler, Rainbow Rowell, Jon Skovron, Amy Spalding, Robin Wasserman, Jeff Zentner, Heidi Zweifel, and all the readers who answered my questions on Twitter and my surveys over email. And to David Levithan: I'm sorry. Ha! That happened before we became friends.

To the real Katie Kurtzman: Thank you for being more excited than *anyone*. Your enthusiasm gave me courage and strength.

So much love and endless thanks to my family: Mom, Dad, Kara, Chris, Beckham, JD, Fay, and Roger.

And thank you to Jarrod Perkins. My family-family. My partner in horror movies, life, and everything in between. Thank you for the laughter and for cleaning the mud off my boots in that cold Nebraskan cornfield. I love you the most of all.

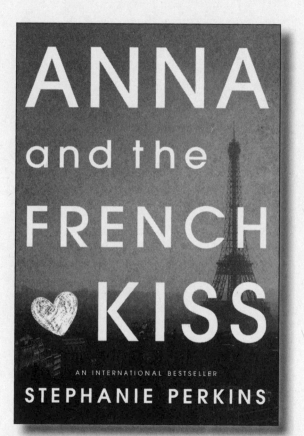

ANNA
and the
FRENCH
KISS

AN INTERNATIONAL BESTSELLER

STEPHANIE PERKINS

chapter one

Here is everything I know about France: *Madeline* and *Amélie* and *Moulin Rouge*. The Eiffel Tower and the Arc de Triomphe, although I have no idea what the function of either actually is. Napoleon, Marie Antoinette, and a lot of kings named Louis. I'm not sure what they did either, but I think it has something to do with the French Revolution, which has something to do with Bastille Day. The art museum is called the Louvre and it's shaped like a pyramid and the *Mona Lisa* lives there along with that statue of the woman missing her arms. And there are cafés or bistros or whatever they call them on every street corner. And mimes. The food is supposed to be good, and the people drink a lot of wine and smoke a lot of cigarettes.

I've heard they don't like Americans, and they don't like white sneakers.

A few months ago, my father enrolled me in boarding school. His air quotes practically crackled over the phone line as he declared living abroad to be a "good learning experience" and a "keepsake I'd treasure forever." Yeah. Keepsake. And I would've pointed out his misuse of the word had I not already been freaking out.

Since his announcement, I've tried yelling, begging, pleading, and crying, but nothing has convinced him otherwise. And now I have a new student visa and a passport, each declaring me: Anna Oliphant, citizen of the United States of America. And now I'm here with my parents—unpacking my belongings in a room smaller than my suitcase—the newest senior at the School of America in Paris.

It's not that I'm ungrateful. I mean, it's *Paris*. The City of Light! The most romantic city in the world! I'm not immune to that. It's just this whole international boarding school thing is a lot more about my father than it is about me. Ever since he sold out and started writing lame books that were turned into even lamer movies, he's been trying to impress his big-shot New York friends with how cultured and rich he is.

My father isn't cultured. But he is rich.

It wasn't always like this. When my parents were still married, we were strictly lower middle class. It was around the time of the divorce that all traces of decency vanished, and his dream of being the next great Southern writer was replaced by his desire to be the next *published* writer. So he started writing these novels set in Small Town Georgia about folks with Good American

Values who Fall in Love and then contract Life-Threatening Diseases and Die.

I'm serious.

And it totally depresses me, but the ladies eat it up. They love my father's books and they love his cable-knit sweaters and they love his bleachy smile and orangey tan. And they have turned him into a bestseller and a total dick.

Two of his books have been made into movies and three more are in production, which is where his real money comes from. Hollywood. And, somehow, this extra cash and pseudo-prestige have warped his brain into thinking that I should live in France. For a year. Alone. I don't understand why he couldn't send me to Australia or Ireland or anywhere else where English is the native language. The only French word I know is *oui*, which means "yes," and only recently did I learn it's spelled o-u-i and not w-e-e.

At least the people in my new school speak English. It was founded for pretentious Americans who don't like the company of their own children. I mean, really. Who sends their kid to boarding school? It's so Hogwarts. Only mine doesn't have cute boy wizards or magic candy or flying lessons.

Instead, I'm stuck with ninety-nine other students. There are twenty-five people in my *entire senior class,* as opposed to the six hundred I had back in Atlanta. And I'm studying the same things I studied at Clairemont High except now I'm registered in beginning French.

Oh, yeah. Beginning French. No doubt with the freshmen. I totally rock.

Mom says I need to lose the bitter factor, pronto, but she's not the one leaving behind her fabulous best friend, Bridgette. Or her fabulous job at the Royal Midtown 14 multiplex. Or Toph, the fabulous boy at the Royal Midtown 14 multiplex.

And I still can't believe she's separating me from my brother, Sean, who is only seven and way too young to be left home alone after school. Without me, he'll probably be kidnapped by that creepy guy down the road who has dirty Coca-Cola towels hanging in his windows. Or Seany will accidentally eat something containing Red Dye $#40$ and his throat will swell up and no one will be there to drive him to the hospital. He might even die. And I bet they wouldn't let me fly home for his funeral and I'd have to visit the cemetery alone next year and Dad will have picked out some god-awful granite cherub to go over his grave.

And I hope Dad doesn't expect me to fill out college applications to Russia or Romania now. My dream is to study film theory in California. I want to be our nation's greatest female film critic. Someday I'll be invited to every festival, and I'll have a major newspaper column and a cool television show and a ridiculously popular website. So far I only have the website, and it's not so popular. Yet.

I just need a little more time to work on it, that's all.

"Anna, it's time."

"What?" I glance up from folding my shirts into perfect squares.

Mom stares at me and twiddles the turtle charm on her necklace. My father, bedecked in a peach polo shirt and white boating shoes, is gazing out my dormitory window. It's late, but across the street a woman belts out something operatic.

My parents need to return to their hotel rooms. They both have early morning flights.

"Oh." I grip the shirt in my hands a little tighter.

Dad steps away from the window, and I'm alarmed to discover his eyes are wet. Something about the idea of my father—even if it is *my father*—on the brink of tears raises a lump in my throat.

"Well, kiddo. Guess you're all grown up now."

My body is frozen. He pulls my stiff limbs into a bear hug. His grip is frightening. "Take care of yourself. Study hard and make some friends. And watch out for pickpockets," he adds. "Sometimes they work in pairs."

I nod into his shoulder, and he releases me. And then he's gone.

My mother lingers behind. "You'll have a wonderful year here," she says. "I just know it." I bite my lip to keep it from quivering, and she sweeps me into her arms. I try to breathe. Inhale. Count to three. Exhale. Her skin smells like grapefruit body lotion. "I'll call you the moment I get home," she says.

Home. Atlanta isn't my home anymore.

"I love you, Anna."

I'm crying now. "I love you, too. Take care of Seany for me."

"Of course."

"And Captain Jack," I say. "Make sure Sean feeds him and changes his bedding and fills his water bottle. And make sure he doesn't give him too many treats because they make him fat and then he can't get out of his igloo. But make sure he gives him at least a few every day, because he still needs the vitamin C and he won't drink the water when I use those vitamin drops—"

She pulls back and tucks my bleached stripe behind my ear. "I love you," she says again.

And then my mother does something that, even after all of the paperwork and plane tickets and presentations, I don't see coming. Something that would've happened in a year anyway, once I left for college, but that no matter how many days or months or years I've yearned for it, I am still not prepared for when it actually happens.

My mother leaves. I am alone.

chapter two

I feel it coming, but I can't stop it.

PANIC.

They left me. My parents actually left me! IN FRANCE!

Meanwhile, Paris is oddly silent. Even the opera singer has packed it in for the night. I *cannot* lose it. The walls here are thinner than Band-Aids, so if I break down, my neighbors—my new classmates—will hear everything. I'm going to be sick. I'm going to vomit that weird eggplant tapenade I had for dinner, and everyone will hear, and no one will invite me to watch the mimes escape from their invisible boxes, or whatever it is people do here in their spare time.

I race to my pedestal sink to splash water on my face, but it explodes out and sprays my shirt instead. And now I'm crying harder, because I haven't unpacked my towels, and wet clothing reminds me of those stupid water rides Bridgette and Matt used to drag me on at Six Flags where the water is the wrong color and it smells like paint and it has a billion trillion bacterial microbes in it. Oh God. What if there are bacterial microbes in the water? Is French water even safe to drink?

Pathetic. I'm pathetic.

How many seventeen-year-olds would kill to leave home? My neighbors aren't experiencing any meltdowns. No crying coming from behind *their* bedroom walls. I grab a shirt off the bed to blot myself dry, when the solution strikes. *My pillow.* I collapse face-first into the sound barrier and sob and sob and sob.

Someone is knocking on my door.

No. Surely that's not my door.

There it is again!

"Hello?" a girl calls from the hallway. "Hello? Are you okay?"

No, I'm not okay. GO AWAY. But she calls again, and I'm obligated to crawl off my bed and answer the door. A blonde with long, tight curls waits on the other side. She's tall and big, but not overweight-big. Volleyball player big. A diamondlike nose ring sparkles in the hall light. "Are you all right?" Her voice is gentle. "I'm Meredith; I live next door. Were those your parents who just left?"

My puffy eyes signal the affirmative.

"I cried the first night, too." She tilts her head, thinks for a moment, and then nods. "Come on. *Chocolat chaud.*"

"A chocolate show?" Why would I want to see a chocolate show? My mother has abandoned me and I'm terrified to leave my room and—

"No." She smiles. "*Chaud*. Hot. Hot chocolate, I can make some in my room."

Oh.

Despite myself, I follow. Meredith stops me with her hand like a crossing guard. She's wearing rings on all five fingers. "Don't forget your key. The doors automatically lock behind you."

"I know." And I tug the necklace out from underneath my shirt to prove it. I slipped my key onto it during this weekend's required Life Skills Seminars for new students, when they told us how easy it is to get locked out.

We enter her room. I gasp. It's the same impossible size as mine, seven by ten feet, with the same mini-desk, mini-dresser, mini-bed, mini-fridge, mini-sink, and mini-shower. (No mini-toilet, those are shared down the hall.) But . . . unlike my own sterile cage, every inch of wall and ceiling is covered with posters and pictures and shiny wrapping paper and brightly colored flyers written in French.

"How long have you *been* here?" I ask.

Meredith hands me a tissue and I blow my nose, a terrible honk like an angry goose, but she doesn't flinch or make a face. "I arrived yesterday. This is my fourth year here, so I didn't have to go to the seminars. I flew in alone, so I've just been hanging out, waiting for my friends to show up." She looks around with her hands on her hips, admiring her handiwork. I spot a pile of magazines, scissors, and tape on her floor and realize it's a work in progress. "Not bad, eh? White walls don't do it for me."

I circle her room, examining everything. I quickly discover that most of the faces are the same five people: John, Paul, George, Ringo, and some soccer guy I don't recognize.

"The Beatles are all I listen to. My friends tease me, but—"

"Who's this?" I point to Soccer Guy. He's wearing red and white, and he's all dark eyebrows and dark hair. Quite good-looking, actually.

"Cesc Fàbregas. God, he's the most incredible passer. Plays for Arsenal. The English football club? No?"

I shake my head. I don't keep up with sports, but maybe I should. "Nice legs, though."

"I know, right? You could hammer nails with those thighs."

While Meredith brews *chocolat chaud* on her hot plate, I learn she's also a senior, and that she only plays soccer during the summer because our school doesn't have a program, but that she used to rank All-State in Massachusetts. That's where she's from, Boston. And she reminds me I should call it "football" here, which—when I think about it—really does make more sense. And she doesn't seem to mind when I badger her with questions or paw through her things.

Her room is amazing. In addition to the paraphernalia taped to her walls, she has a dozen china teacups filled with plastic glitter rings, and silver rings with amber stones, and glass rings with pressed flowers. It already looks as if she's lived here for years.

I try on a ring with a rubber dinosaur attached. The T-rex flashes red and yellow and blue lights when I squeeze him. "I wish I could have a room like this." I love it, but I'm too much of a neat freak to have something like it for myself. I need clean walls and a clean desktop and everything put away in its right place at all times.

Meredith looks pleased with the compliment.

"Are these your friends?" I place the dinosaur back into its teacup and point to a picture tucked in her mirror. It's gray and shadowy and printed on thick, glossy paper. Clearly the product of a school photography class. Four people stand before a giant hollow cube, and the abundance of stylish black clothing and deliberately mussed hair reveals Meredith belongs to the resident art clique. For some reason, I'm surprised. I know her room is artsy, and she has all of those rings on her fingers and in her nose, but the rest is clean-cut—lilac sweater, pressed jeans, soft voice. Then there's the soccer thing, but she's not a tomboy either.

She breaks into a wide smile, and her nose ring winks. "Yeah. Ellie took that at La Défense. That's Josh and St. Clair and me and Rashmi. You'll meet them tomorrow at breakfast. Well, everyone but Ellie. She graduated last year."

The pit of my stomach begins to unclench. Was that an invitation to sit with her?

"But I'm sure you'll meet her soon enough, because she's dating St. Clair. She's at Parsons Paris now for photography."

I've never heard of it, but I nod as if I've considered going there myself someday.

"She's *really* talented." The edge in her voice suggests otherwise, but I don't push it. "Josh and Rashmi are dating, too," she adds.

Ah. Meredith must be single.

Unfortunately, I can relate. Back home I'd dated my friend Matt for five months. He was tall-ish and funny-ish and had decent-ish hair. It was one of those "since no one better is around, do you wanna make out?" situations. All we'd ever done was kiss, and it wasn't even that great. Too much spit. I always had to wipe off my chin.

We broke up when I learned about France, but it wasn't a big deal. I didn't cry or send him weepy emails or key his mom's station wagon. Now he's going out with Cherrie Milliken, who is in chorus and has shiny shampoo-commercial hair. It doesn't even bother me.

Not really.

Besides, the breakup freed me to lust after Toph, multiplex coworker babe extraordinaire. Not that I didn't lust after him when I was with Matt, but still. It did make me feel guilty. And things were starting to happen with Toph—they really were— when summer ended. But Matt's the only guy I've ever gone out with, and he barely counts. I once told him I'd dated this guy named Stuart Thistleback at summer camp. Stuart Thistleback had auburn hair and played the stand-up bass, and we were totally in love, but he lived in Chattanooga and we didn't have our driver's licenses yet.

Matt knew I made it up, but he was too nice to say so.

I'm about to ask Meredith what classes she's taking, when her phone chirps the first few bars of "Strawberry Fields Forever." She rolls her eyes and answers. "Mom, it's midnight here. Six-hour time difference, remember?"

I glance at her alarm clock, shaped like a yellow submarine, and I'm surprised to find she's right. I set my long-empty mug of *chocolat chaud* on her dresser. "I should get going," I whisper. "Sorry I stayed so long."

"Hold on a sec." Meredith covers the mouthpiece. "It was nice meeting you. See you at breakfast?"

"Yeah. See ya." I try to say this casually, but I'm so thrilled that I skip from her room and promptly slam into a wall.

Whoops. Not a wall. A boy.

"Oof." He staggers backward.

"Sorry! I'm so sorry, I didn't know you were there."

He shakes his head, a little dazed. The first thing I notice is his hair—it's the first thing I notice about everyone. It's dark brown and messy and somehow both long and short at the same time. I think of the Beatles, since I've just seen them in Meredith's room. It's artist hair. Musician hair. I-pretend-I-don't-care-but-I-really-do hair.

Beautiful hair.

"It's okay, I didn't see you either. Are you all right, then?"

Oh my. He's English.

"Er. Does Mer live here?"

Seriously, I don't know any American girl who can resist an English accent.

The boy clears his throat. "Meredith Chevalier? Tall girl? Big, curly hair?" Then he looks at me like I'm crazy or half deaf,

like my Nanna Oliphant. Nanna just smiles and shakes her head whenever I ask, "What kind of salad dressing would you like?" or "Where did you put Granddad's false teeth?"

"I'm sorry." He takes the smallest step away from me. "You were going to bed."

"Yes! Meredith lives there. I've just spent two hours with her." I announce this proudly like my brother, Seany, whenever he finds something disgusting in the yard. "I'm Anna! I'm new here!" *Oh God. What. Is with. The scary enthusiasm?* My cheeks catch fire, and it's all so humiliating.

The beautiful boy gives an amused grin. His teeth are lovely—straight on top and crooked on the bottom, with a touch of overbite. I'm a sucker for smiles like this, due to my own lack of orthodontia. I have a gap between my front teeth the size of a raisin.

"Étienne," he says. "I live one floor up."

"I live here." I point dumbly at my room while my mind whirs: French name, English accent, American school. Anna confused.

He raps twice on Meredith's door. "Well. I'll see you around then, Anna."

Eh-t-yen says my name like this: *Ah-na.*

My heart *thump thump thumps* in my chest.

Meredith opens her door. "St. Clair!" she shrieks. She's still on the phone. They laugh and hug and talk over each other. "Come in! How was your flight? When'd you get here? Have you seen Josh? Mom, I've gotta go."

Meredith's phone and door snap shut simultaneously.

I fumble with the key on my necklace. Two girls in matching pink bathrobes strut behind me, giggling and gossiping. A crowd of guys across the hall snicker and catcall. Meredith and her friend laugh through the thin walls. My heart sinks, and my stomach tightens back up.

I'm still the new girl. I'm still alone.

FALL IN LOVE WITH THESE INTERNATIONAL BESTSELLERS BY STEPHANIE PERKINS

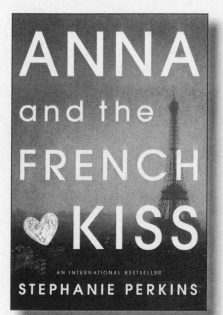

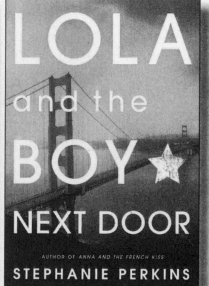

ISLA and the HAPPILY EVER AFTER

STEPHANIE PERKINS